WHAT PEOPLE ARE SAYING ABOUT DAVID PUTNAM:

About *THE VANQUISHED*

"The most real cop book I've read in ages. Good old authentic storytelling from someone who s been there and done that."
— Marc Cameron
New York Times best-selling author

About *THE SQUANDERED*

"…so well crafted, readers will zip right through this poignant crime thriller."
– Publisher's Weekly

About *THE REPLACEMENTS*

"Putnam steadily ratchets up the tension, while memorable supporting characters, like the courageous Marie, help engage reader interest."
– Publisher's Weekly

About *THE DISPOSABLES*

"[Putnam] wields his archetypes with skill and a sincerity born of long experience in law enforcement."
– Publisher's Weekly

DEDICATION

To my lovely wife
Little Sweet Mary

FIRE
AT WILL

DAVID PUTNAM

Copyright © 2017 by David Putnam

Putnam Press, an imprint of:
Parker Hayden Media
5740 N. Carefree Circle, Suite 120-1
Colorado Springs, CO 80917

This is a work of fiction. Names, characters, places and incidents are either the products of the author's imagination or are used fictitiously. Any resemblance to actual persons (living or dead), events or locations is entirely coincidental.

All rights reserved. No part of this book may be reproduced in any form or by any electronic or mechanical means, including information storage and retrieval systems, without permission in writing from the publisher, except by a reviewer, who may quote brief passages in a review.

ISBN eBook: 978-1-941528-41-9
ISBN Print: 978-1-941528-42-6

Cover design: LB Hayden

Dead Body © znm666/DepositPhotos
Sun Sets Behind Joshua Tree and Desert Scene © kvddesign
    /DepositPhotos
Barrel © malamuki0/DepositPhotos

1

DEBRA ANN HAD been dead two years by the time I returned to Joshua Tree station.

I'd been transferred to the big sandy, the Mojave Desert, where even a camel could die of thirst. A town of about seven thousand souls, the population constantly declining because the Tree itself was its own kind of hell.

Dorothy Lamont ignored the bell that chimed when I opened the door and went right on typing. Wolford's secretary was as old as the desert, her leather face framed by thinning black hair that came out of a box. Reading glasses hung from a chain around her neck, though I'd never seen them sitting on her face. She was all right, I guess. If you don't mind a woman with the disposition of a Mojave Green rattler.

"Here to see Captain Wolford," I said to get things rolling.

"You'll have to wait."

I rested my elbows on the pony wall and watched her scribble something on a faded yellow pad. "Got nothing but time," I told her.

She smirked as she moved her skeletal hands away from the pad and over to the phone. That's when I saw what she'd written: *Bad Bill arrives several days late.*

The *Bad Bill* moniker had been built from the bastardization of my initials. William Alan Donnelly was the name on my driver's license but most folks called me Will. Will, never Bill. At least not since I graduated from the Sheriff's academy almost three decades ago.

Back then, as a fresh-faced, bright-eyed recruit barely old enough to drink, it didn't matter so much what others called me, so long as they called me. Hell, I even liked the nickname a little back then. But no more. Somewhere along the way, I'd garnered deep lines along my cheeks and forehead, and my blue-sky enthusiasm had been replaced with full-dark cynicism. Now I wanted nothing more than to be left alone to do my job.

Dorothy faked a reach for the phone and looked up at me. "You know, your meet-and-greet with the captain was scheduled for last Friday."

"Cut me some slack, Dot. It was a hundred-mile trip and day—"

"Day shift started at seven," she said, turning back to her computer. "It's now eight-fifteen."

I just wanted to get in, unpack my gear, and get out, but Dot got off on watching others suffer, especially yours truly. We'd worked a kidnap case together a couple years back. Girl by the name of Peggy Kellogg had been taken by some recidivist pederast called Abel Jenks. Jenks had abducted the girl, no question. Still, we never found her, never landed enough evidence to prove Jenks took her. The case was a black eye I felt in my heart, even now, two years out. Jenks continued to travel along the dirt shoulders of Landers, a shabby sub-district of Joshua Tree station. Still out there, doing God knows what to God knows whom, and it killed me.

"Come on, Dot. Is the captain in?"

"He gets here at nine. But what you need to do is check with the front desk, have them call in Sergeant DeWitt from the field. You'll be riding with him until further notice."

"Nah," I said, lifting my equipment bag off the dusty floor, "I think I'll wait for the captain in his office."

"You most certainly will not."

I ignored her, went through Wolford's open door and sat down in one of the two chairs in front of his desk. Toots took the other.

Dot appeared in the doorway, her glasses swinging from the chain around her neck.

"You'll get out of this office this instant," she said.

"Or what, Dot?"

Dot had no answer to that. She vanished from the doorway as I settled in, crossing my right leg over my left.

Toots turned to me and said, "That wasn't too bright, Bub. She's the captain's secretary. You get on her bad side and she can make your life a living hell."

A living hell, I thought.

Here I was, banished to the fire-breathing desert, taking advice from a woman in a diaphanous red dress and shiny black pumps.

A woman who called herself Toots.

A woman no one but me could see.

A woman who'd been dead two years.

"A living hell?" I said to Toots. "Honey, I'm sitting in the middle of the Mojave Desert, having a conversation with a woman who I watched die. If Joshua Tree ain't my own living hell, then I don't want to know what is."

"Snap out of it," Toots said. "If you can just keep your head down for a little while – lay low – you can work your way out of this mess and get back to Specialized I.N.V."

Toots was the only person – living *or* dead – who called it that. Spelled out the I.N.V., like it was some sort of hit television series on CBS or NBC.

I didn't say anything. Toots was right. She was always right. That's why I'd made her my second wife. Toots – who everyone else knew as Debra Ann – was the love of my life. Even in death. Hell, especially in death.

When Debra Ann died two years ago, I couldn't let go. She died a horrible death, a death no man should have to witness. But I witnessed it.

So it didn't come as much of a surprise when Toots started showing up around the house. Early on, her visits were brief, always occurring at the tail end of a Jack Daniels binge. The department shrink told me that it wasn't *too* abnormal. Said it was all right as long as I didn't let it last too long and saw this alcohol-fueled hallucination for what it was – a way of coping with my grief.

Sure, I saw it for what it was. I had loved Debra Ann more than life itself and was having an impossible time letting her go.

So Debra Ann – Toots to me now – kept coming around. Wearing that same red dress and those shiny black pumps. Showing off that spectacular ass. And every time she showed I experienced that familiar pang of desire. When she left I suffered that same rapid heartbeat and shortness of breath. Suffered it until the moment she deigned to appear to me again.

Nowadays she followed me everywhere. Sometimes, if she had

something particularly important to say, she even followed me to the john.

Sure, I heard the whispers; people talking, joking, saying things like, *He sees dead people*. But it didn't bother me. I wasn't crazy. Just scared to death. Afraid that if I had to give up Toots I'd have to give up my sanity. Maybe take a self-imposed dirt nap.

Still, I did my best not to talk to her when others were around. I didn't care what people thought, but I didn't want to end up in the psych ward either. But then, you can't always be sure that you're alone. Not these days, in the era of instant media. You never know when there's a tiny camera pointing at you. These days I had to be extra vigilant if I didn't want to end up jabbering with myself on Facebook or YouTube. That happened once, and I had one hell of a time explaining.

I glanced at Toots. Reached over and rested my hand on hers. I knew it wasn't really there. Knew I was just rubbing the arm of a chair. But it felt good. So good that I leaned over and started whispering in her ear. Telling her how much I still loved her.

And that's precisely when Captain Wolford walked in.

2

"AS I LIVE and breathe," Wolford said as he stepped into his office, "if it ain't Bad Bill Donnelly."

Toots shot him a look, which Wolford couldn't see, of course. She didn't like Wolford much to begin with. And she sure as hell didn't need him rubbing in her face that he was still living and breathing.

"Morning, Captain," I said, standing, my hand outstretched.

"Bill, when we're alone, you can call Wolf."

We're not alone, I thought, as Toots crossed her arms in disgust.

"Sure, Wolf," I said. "But the name's Will."

"Will? Not Bill?"

"Never Bill."

Wolf took his sweet time rounding his desk. He was a good four inches shorter than my six feet, yet thirty pounds heavier, his head sitting like a square block on broad shoulders, no neck in sight. Back in the day, when we all had nicknames, folks called Wolford *No-neck*.

Wolford exposed his true colors to me back when he and I were rookies together. One night we'd both been working the West End, in different patrol cars, when a *shots fired* call went out. We arrived at the scene simultaneously. Exited our vehicles, service revolvers drawn.

We were still two blocks from the subject residence when a suspect emerged, highlighted by the pale yellow bulb illuminating the front porch.

Bastard had a double-barreled shotgun in his hands.

Wolford and I both froze. When I could move again I slowly made my approach, hoping the gunman couldn't make us out in the shadows.

When I was about thirty feet away still in the street, the man abruptly raised the shotgun to his shoulder. I tensed, while Wolford turned heel and fled in the opposite direction, right down the middle of the street.

I dove for the asphalt, hoping the concrete curb would afford enough cover.

The gunman fired, explosions from both barrels igniting the night.

Smoke obscured the suspect in the naked yellow porch light, but I could hear him attempting to reload.

With six in my revolver, I got up and sprinted right at him.

He raised the shotgun and pulled the trigger.

I flinched but nothing happened.

A click but no kick.

Panicked, he turned and reentered the house.

I crossed the yard, leapt onto the porch as he turned to slam the door. I kicked it a split second before it latched. The edge caught the shooter in the face, mashing his nose. He went down unconscious.

I handcuffed him. Stood over him, breathing hard, looking around the room. The house might have belonged to the man's grandmother: pristine old furniture, area rugs, coffee and end tables, antimacassars on the divan. The stereo played a vinyl record, an old 78, Flight of the Valkyries. Next to a wooden rocking chair sat a case of shotgun rounds; double-ought buck. On top of the case was an empty fifth of Old Granddad.

The suspect, face down on the area rug, bleeding from the nose, was Nelson Rowlins, a Vietnam vet.

Outside, empty green shotgun shell casings littered the

grass around the porch like the husks of a deadly fruit. Apparently, Nelson had been shooting for a while before we arrived on scene.

A few minutes later, Wolford finally returned from the darkness, his eyes wild, gun out, just as code-three backup arrived.

Wolford escorted Nelson out to his cop car. And took credit for the arrest.

I didn't care, but Wolford knew I would always know.

And he'd always resent the hell out of me for it.

IN WOLFORD'S OFFICE, I sat back down, dreading the inevitable game of cat and mouse that was about to follow. Wolford would want to know why I'd been transferred. But I was under strict orders by Internal Affairs not to discuss it with anyone. Not even Wolford, my new captain here in Joshua Tree.

Sure, Wolford wasn't supposed to know anything about the investigation they'd been running on me – but he did. Most all command staff in the department had heard of my fuck-up, my lapse in judgment. My foray into the criminal world.

So it was tough not to spill my guts. After all, despite that shotgun incident three decades ago, Wolford was still a brother law officer. That's just how it was on the street.

Wolford lifted his polished black cowboy boot and set it on the desk with a clunk.

"So," he said, "you finally caught the midnight train out to my neck of the woods."

"Yes, sir, it was time for a change. That assignment can burn you out quick."

He chuckled, eyelids fluttering. "Don't give me the party line, Bill. And don't delude yourself. Any sergeant in this county would give his left nut to work Specialized Investigations. You had the slot, how many years?" He leaned forward and opened the file on his desk. "Ten years."

Toots said, "He's got your personnel file on his desk. How did he get that?" I loved her voice, the way she spoke out the side of her crooked little mouth. "And don't let him talk to you like that. Slap that smug look off his face. You had that job ten years because you were good. No, because you were great at it. Tell him that, Bub. Stand up for yourself. Go ahead and tell him."

Difficult as it was, I did my best to ignore her. She'd always had a higher opinion of me than anyone else.

Wolford said, "No one in this department holds an assignment more than five years."

I knew that. Hell, everyone knew that.

Wolford said, "With few exceptions, the Sheriff's policy is to let everyone get the cross-training and experience..." He brought up his hands and made air quotes. "...to build a well-rounded department."

I tensed up. Here it was.

He said, "You must have done something really heinous to get bounced this far out into no-man's land." His lips turned up in a Cheshire grin. "What did you do?"

Toots leaned over. "Ask the fat ass how come he's been assigned out here for the last eight years. Huh? Go on, ask him. They buried him out here and forgot about him, because of that sexual harassment beef. He knows it and now he's trying the old misery-loves-company thing on you." She shuddered. "I can't even imagine what that poor clerk went through, having his fat ass on top of her like that, humping and grunting away."

Toots liked to embellish. She didn't know exactly how the sexual harassment beef went down. But she did have a lot of information. Too much information.

Where the hell did she get it all?

I said, "As you know, Captain, it's an ongoing investigation and I'm not at liberty to say at the moment. When it's all over I'll be glad to have this conversation with you."

He brought his leg down off the desk and stared at me. "Okay, then, off the record, *mano y mano*, just tell me – did you do it?"

Toots jumped out of her chair and faced me, fists clenched. "You believe this guy? Don't tell him a damn thing. If you do he'll be on the phone to headquarters the minute you leave the room. He's trying to make Deputy Chief on the back of your misfortune."

I whispered, "Sit down."

Like Toots, I was surprised Wolford was being so blatant. He had to be operating under orders from headquarters, which meant they wanted my head more than I'd thought.

Wolford leaned forward over the desk a little more. I realized that in my confusion I'd spoken to Toots; told her to sit down. Not loud, but loud enough.

"What the hell did you just say?" He smiled. "Who are you talking to, Bill?"

He'd heard the rumors like everyone else. Getting run out of the department on a psycho was just as bad and served the same purpose, and No-neck knew it. He could smell his promotion to deputy chief. Finally, his ticket out of the Morongo basin.

Toots marched around the desk, sat on the right corner a few inches from him. She raised her finger, pointed it right in his face. "You better come down off your high horse, mister. Instead of going after him you should turn him loose on the crooks you got out here. He's the best man you've got. He'll do a good job for you. Make you look like a star."

At times like these she was impossible to ignore.

I said, "What I meant was, I'm good for any assignment you have for me out here."

"So, you're not going to tell me?"

"With all due respect, sir, I'm in enough trouble as it is."

Wolford sighed. "I understand. But I reserve the right to ask you again. I think once we get reacquainted you'll be more forthcoming." He lifted his large frame out of his seat. "I'm going to put you with a patrol sergeant for now. You've been away from patrol a long time and things have changed. I bet you've never even seen an MDT before, have you?"

He was referring to the Mobile Dispatch Terminal which was in all patrol cars. He was the one who'd been out of touch in the Mongo too long. All the detective cars where I worked—well, where I used to work—had MDT's.

I said, "I admit, I'm a little rusty."

"Fine, we'll give it a couple of weeks and see where we are." He pulled his pants a bit higher on his waist then came around the desk, his hand extended. "Good to have you aboard, Bill."

I shook.

He said, "Get with Dewitt. He'll be your mentor sergeant. He'll get you set up with a locker and show you around."

"Thank you, sir."

Toots got right up in Wolford's face and saluted. "We'll do our best, sir. You can count on us."

I smiled.

He didn't.

I guessed he'd caught me smiling at Toots again.

"Ah, Bill, I, ah, know you're under a lot of stress with all that's going on. You know my door's always open. Especially for you. If you, ah…have the need to see the shrink, you'll come and tell me, right?"

"I'm fine, Captain, really."

Toots took a step back. "Relax, fatso, he's not going to go all 'Texas Tower' on you, if that's what you're worried about. Although if he did, you'd be the first one he'd take off the roster." She turned to me. "Right, Bub? You tell him. Go on and tell him."

I sighed, long and loud. Toots might be good for my soul, I thought, not for the first time. But she was already proving to be pure hell on my career.

At least the few days I had left of it.

3

PHIL DEWITT lumbered into the squad room. Toots was sitting, legs crossed, on the table next to my gear. Eating an Almond Joy from an open box resting next to her.

DeWitt stepped up to my chair, a huge smile on his simple face. "Good to have you with us, sir."

"Will Donnelly," I said, giving his hand a good hard shake.

"Yeah, I know. Well, by reputation at least."

Toots popped the last piece of chocolate into her mouth, crumpled the white and blue wrapper, and flicked it onto the table.

"See, Bub?" she said. "Everyone's heard of you. Why don't you tell him a good war story? Tell him about how you tracked down that weaselly little bastard Trask. The cop-killer. Tell him that one – he'll eat it up with a spoon."

Before I could say another word, DeWitt's eyes cut away to the crumpled wrapper sitting on the table. His forehead wrinkled as he stepped back and said, "Hey, let's not get off to a bad start here."

I sat there, puzzled and silent.

"Here it comes," Toots said. "What he means is, he doesn't really want to be riding with a department pariah. It's bad for his career and he's about to tell you as much."

DeWitt said, "Hold on, what am I thinking? I'm sorry. You were probably going to put the money in the box *after* you finished off the candy bar, right?"

I glanced at the open box of Almond Joy, saw an index card with black scrawls, standing on its side. Read:

Support Joshua Tree Little League

For each bar, donate $2

I shook my head and sighed in Toots' general direction. Pulled a five from my shirt pocket and tossed it on top of the box.

DeWitt went for his wallet, said, "I'll get your change."

I said, "Don't worry about it. Let the kids play ball."

DeWitt thanked me and moved to the door.

Soon as the door closed I ran my tongue side to side over my top row of teeth.

I'd be damned if I didn't taste chocolate and almonds.

Maybe even a little coconut.

THE SUN HUNG high in the cloudless, cornflower sky as DeWitt and I headed east on Highway 62, toward Twenty-nine Palms. As the desert flashed by – Joshua Trees, jumping cholla, sage and salt cedar – I was reminded of the last time I'd worked here, the relentless frustration I experienced during the Abel Jenks investigation.

Looking straight ahead, watching Marine vehicles painted in desert camouflage crawling in the opposite direction, I said, "Is Abel Jenks still living in Landers?"

DeWitt turned toward me, taking his eyes off the road. "How do you know about Jenks?"

I glanced at him, told him to watch where the hell he was going.

"Oh, that's right," he said, "that was your investigation. Abel Jenks, no, he moved. Wormed his way in with some lonely old widow in Yucca Valley."

He rattled off the address on Val Verde in Yucca Valley.

"Does the widow know about him?" I said.

DeWitt nodded. "The deputies made sure of it."

"And she continues to let Jenks stay with her?"

"During the day at least. At night she sends him down to the garage to sleep."

"The garage?"

"She had the garage renovated into a large bedroom. Sends him out there soon as dark hits, then dead-bolts the house doors."

"Why's that you think?"

DeWitt shrugged. "She's afraid Jenks is gonna do something to her in her sleep. Can you blame her?"

No, I can't. But then, what the hell's she doing letting that monster stay with her in the first place?

"You know," I said, "I'd love to swing by there when we get the chance. Remind Jenks that we still have love for him."

"Can do."

The image of Peggy Kellogg, long ago seared into my brain, came calling again now. Suddenly, my breathing quickened, sweat formed at my hairline. My heart began to pound in my chest.

"You all right?" DeWitt said.

"Yeah, sure, I'm fine."

But I was a hell of a long way from fine. I twisted my neck, scanned the back seat through the black metal screen. Felt a pang of relief when I saw her, sitting in the rear behind DeWitt, still – always – in that stunning red dress, legs crossed, head titled back, smiling that crooked smile of hers while smoking a cigarette.

Toots said, "Take it easy, cowboy. Mommy's not gonna leave daddy." She blew a stream of smoke in my face and winked at me. "Least not today."

"Smell that?" DeWitt said, wriggling his nose like a beaver about to sneeze.

Nothing but that foul-smelling cigarette. Christ, when the hell did she pick up that nasty habit?

"Probably that guy in the Mustang in front of us," he said.

"What's that?"

"The driver must be smoking a cigarette. Out here, where

the air's completely fresh, you can smell tobacco smoke a mile way. That whacky tobacky, too."

I kept my mouth shut, my eyes glued to the tail end of that blue Mustang. Imagined myself locked up in some garage – maybe Abel Jenks' – sucking on that Mustang's tailpipe.

Only after putting a couple of slugs in ol' Jenks, of course.

DeWitt said, "I know I hardly know you, Will, but I'd like to let you in on a little theory of mine."

"Oh, yeah?"

"This desert, Will, it brings on the fear. Attracts the madness."

Toots shouted from the back, "What the hell's he talking about?"

"What the hell you talking about?" I said.

"All this sand and heat makes it kind of like a swirling vortex," he said, "some folks can really lose their grip. People out here, they're living on the edge, Will. The edge of sanity."

"Is that right," I said.

"Oh, yeah. Folks out here are on the fringe, Will. Square pegs, every last one of them."

The Mustang moved into the left lane, accelerated to pass a large U-Haul, then vanished into the dust.

"It keeps things interesting though," DeWitt said. "From call to call, you never know what's coming next."

"That's your theory?"

"Nah, what I mean is... Oh, hell, I'll wait on telling you my theory until you've been out here long enough to genuinely appreciate it."

"You do that," I said.

DeWitt pointed his nose toward the roof, took in several deep breaths.

"That's weird," he said.

"What's weird?"

"That Mustang's long gone but I still smell the damn cigarette smoke that was blowing it out of it."

"Maybe you've just been out here in the desert too long, Phil. Maybe you've lost *your* grip." I leaned back in my seat and smiled. "You're living on the edge, man. Maybe you're one of those folks on the fringe and don't even know it."

DeWitt thought about it a few moments and frowned. "Sure as hell hope not," he said.

Then he surreptitiously took a few more sniffs of the air.

4

WELL, I'LL BE DAMNED.

After the grueling two-hour drive home from Joshua Tree, my eyelids felt like sandbags and it was all I could do to keep them open. Until, that is, I saw Joan's Mercury Cougar sitting in front of my house.

Toots, who'd been out cold next to me in the passenger seat, came wide awake, too.

"What the hell's your ex-wife doing here?" she said.

I didn't say anything. Following my ten-hour shift and four hours round-trip, I didn't trust myself to open my mouth in front of Toots. Not that she left me much of an opening.

"Doesn't the bitch have a life?" Toots cried. "You know what, I'd bet that tooth doctor of hers finally sat up in bed this morning, looked over at her, and said, 'Joan, you're one lazy, grade-A whore. Get your skinny ass out of my bed and don't come back.'"

"Come on, Toots," I tried.

"And now she's over here on hands and knees groveling to get you back." Toots ripped off her seatbelt and started opening the door while the Taurus was still rolling. "Well, I'll show her—"

"Toots, wait," I said, pressing the brake. "I can assure you, that's *not* what this is about." I raised my left hand and pointed to my white-gold wedding band. "Besides, you know better than anyone I'm still happily married."

Her face softened in the light spilling in from the lamppost. Smiling, she reached up to touch my face.

"No *death do us part* for us, huh, Bub?"

"Never."

My desire to feel her gentle hand on my cheek was, at that moment, like a hunger I'd never felt before. I'd have given anything just to have her – to have *Debra Ann* – in my arms for the rest of the night.

As I pulled into the driveway, Joan stepped out of her off-white Lexus SUV. I put the Taurus in park, unlatched my seatbelt, and opened the door. Stood and stretched in the driveway, while Joan approached.

My ex was dressed to the nines, as usual, in sheer apricot and eggshell-colored silks, with low heels, an expensive handbag, and enough jewelry to feed a small village in Africa for a year.

Toots stared at her, then back at the Lexus, and chirped, "That outfit come with the car?"

Joan's silver-blonde hair was pulled back in a tight ponytail. But that was all that was tight on her these days. Surprisingly, her and her periodontist had never caught the plastic fever that spread throughout most of Southern California. Or if she had gone in for the Botox, she'd had one hell of a shitty doctor.

"Hi, kid," I said.

To which she icily responded, "We need to talk."

IN THE KITCHEN, I took three tall glasses down from the high cabinet and placed them on the granite counter. I poured tea from the pickle jar I stored in the refrigerator then carried two of the glasses back into the living room.

Toots followed with the third. "Let's keep this real," she

said from behind me. "Remember, she took Bosco."

Our little Jack Russell terrier had been dead several years now, and for a moment, I wondered why I never saw *him* running around.

Joan sat on the divan, legs crossed, her left foot bouncing nervously. When I handed her a glass, she immediately set it down on the coffee table. She wanted to get right down to business.

But I wasn't quite ready.

"Stuffy in here, isn't it?" I said, moving toward the window. "Hot day." I opened the first then went on to the second, mumbling about how nice the breeze was this evening.

"You know why I'm here, Will, don't you?"

"I sure do, Joan," I said, looking for another window to open. Alas, I was fresh out.

I slowly walked over to the divan and sat. I knew what she wanted and tried to head her off at the pass. "But I've been ordered not to talk about it."

Joan's expression changed; she smiled. "Will, it's *me* here. Not some rat who is going to run to the department."

Spoken like a cop's wife, I noted. Not some Molar Queen.

Joan said, "They came to me, you know. Asked if I knew anything about any money. Whether you asked me to keep anything for you. Like a safe or a safety deposit box. They said if I didn't cooperate they'd come back with a warrant."

She placed a hand on my knee, eliciting a shriek from Toots.

"No touching, Bub. You tell her no hands, or I swear, she's gonna pull back nothing but a stump."

"You never wanted anything more than you earned," Joan said. "What happened? Did you need money?"

I leaned back and closed my eyes, wishing I could sleep for a month.

"They got me on something solid, Joan," I finally said.

Felt good to tell someone. Someone real, someone who wasn't a mirage.

"A few months back we were going after this mid-level

dope dealer," I told her. "A guy named Velasquez who was into this higher-up named Belisarius. Belisarius had duct-taped two victims together in the back of a camper shell, shot them in their heads and then lit the truck on fire.

"We knew Belisarius was involved but didn't have any evidence. I thought we'd go for someone on the periphery, get a solid case on Velasquez, and flip him against this murderer Belisarius. It was a long shot but it was all we had, and HQ really wanted a clearance on this one. The media was completely roasting us.

"Anyway, we got a search warrant based on the word of this street-level guy who pointed out Velasquez' house during a drive-by. This street guy was scared to death because of who was involved. Mike Crosley did the drive-by with the street-level guy. You know Mike. Later, after it was all over, Crosley told me the street guy sat reclined in the car seat and pointed over the car's window ledge as they drove by.

"Well, we served the warrant and hit the house hard. The containment team broke out windows of the house as a diversion for the entry team. I went with the entry team."

"At your age?" she said.

I ignored her, said, "This woman stood in the middle of her living room screaming like hell. 'You've got the wrong house.' Over and over again. 'You've got the wrong house.'"

I shook my head from side to side. "You know, they do that sometimes. Even the guilty ones. *Especially* the guilty ones. '*You've got the wrong house.*' Or '*You've got the wrong guy.*' You're in there on a valid warrant, you can't pay it any mind."

Joan nodded; she understood these things happen. Cops have to do their job.

"The woman who lived in the wrong house was hysterical," I said quietly. "I felt bad for her. So I went next door — by then we'd found and secured the *right* house and arrested Velasquez — and I took some of the money we'd seized from him. Dope money. I only took several hundred dollars from a little over thirty-six thousand, enough to fix the damage we'd done. I gave it to the woman for the broken-down front door and all the windows."

"Oh, Will."

"Yeah, I know. It seemed like the right thing to do at the time. It was Velasquez' fault, I figured. If he hadn't been selling coke we wouldn't have broken the windows. He owed her, not the Department. That's the way I looked at it."

Joan thought about it. "But you didn't keep the money for yourself. That *has* to count for something, doesn't it? Get yourself a good attorney. This doesn't sound all that bad."

Toots jumped in, said, "Oh, that's not the bad part."

Joan sat quiet for a moment then said, "But that doesn't make sense. Why were they asking me about safety deposit boxes and home safes?"

Toots said, "Hey, Bub, this bimbo can be pretty astute."

I opened my eyes and sat forward. Said to Joan, "Hey kid, I'm really exhausted. You mind if we continue this another time?"

5

DeWitt read off the assigned patrol areas and their corresponding patrol cars, then introduced me. I acknowledged the nine deputies in the briefing room with a slight nod of the head and received nine awkward smiles in return. I only recognized a deputy named John Randle. I knew him from two years prior during the Peggy Kellogg search. Randle loved animals, particularly horses. He's supervised the mounted posse during the search. He had five acres in Yucca Valley and took in unwanted and abused horses. He paid for their feed by selling bails of hay and delivering them himself on his off time. He sat next to a brown haired dispatcher, introduced as Sarah Lang who obviously had eyes for him. Dispatcher periodically came out and rode along with the deputies in order to become familiar with the area they dispatched deputies to. The dispatchers also wanted to put a name to a face, in this case with Sarah it was something more.

Toots sat in the chair next to me and listened intently as DeWitt went on to read off the briefing, the events of note from prior shifts.

While DeWitt spoke, I glanced around the room at the deputies, all of them male except for one. All but two looked too young to be carrying guns and working the street. Both of the exceptions were ex-Marines who put in their twenty then came here to begin a second career. Those two – Mannerly and

Somers – appeared as though they could handle any call that came in, especially ones that turned violent. They were gruff, hard-looking men sporting salt-and-pepper flattops. With eyes that could probably penetrate brick walls.

The Twenty-nine Palms Marine base remained a major influence in the area. Whether you were running into ex-Marines at the local diner or watching a convoy rolling west on Highway 62 toward Camp Pendleton for maneuvers, the military was a constant presence.

DeWitt cleared his throat, making it known that it was time to pay attention. "Most importantly," he said, "is the continuation of illegal dumping. This is the fifth time in the past six months. Until we find out who's doing this, the county has to foot the bill for the clean-ups, and the taxpayers are none too happy about it."

According to DeWitt, 50-gallon drums of some sort of yellowish toxic chemical were being dumped unlawfully, and the department didn't have a single suspect.

"The exact nature of the substance is yet to be determined," DeWitt said, "but whatever it is, it's leaking from the barrels into the earth. Which, in each case, requires costly excavation."

I'd seen pictures of the clean-up in the paper. Several men and women wearing spacesuits transporting the toxic dirt to some deep salt mine in Nevada, where it would evidently be stored for eternity. For a price.

"We find out which company's dumping this stuff, federal statutes call for high fines and prison time. They may think they're saving a ton of money now by avoiding the high costs that come with removing these chemicals legally. But they clearly didn't place Joshua Tree station into the equation. The county wants this company identified, and identified quickly."

❖

A FEW MINUTES after the briefing, DeWitt and I stepped outside and moved slowly toward our patrol car. Constructed of brick and steel, Joshua Tree station sat on the south side of Highway 62 on a slope overlooking the desert valley. When the population outgrew the station, the county annexed two portable buildings in the rear. One housed the station detectives; the other, which we'd just exited, was used as the briefing room and Watch Commander Office.

Our first stop was Denny's, the only restaurant in Joshua Tree that served a decent breakfast. DeWitt pulled into the lot and parked right up front. Toots, who'd been riding in back behind the black screen, was first out of the car. When I opened the door I found her standing a few feet away, her hands on her hips, her eyes glued to a male figure standing next to the entrance. He was an odd sight, a middle-aged man with thick, puffy black hair, mutton-chops, and a beer belly that made him appear eight months pregnant. He was dressed in an Elvis ensemble, a gold lame suit, complete with matching cape.

And they say I'm weird.

As we reached the door, DeWitt stopped and said, "Hey, Elvis, let me see your driver's license."

Elvis complied, reaching inside his suit and fishing out a gold wallet. He opened the wallet and pulled out his ID. Without so much as glancing at it, DeWitt handed it over to me.

The license read: *Elvis Aaron Presley*, and showed a date of birth of April 26, 1971.

I felt a pang, thinking of my mother. She'd been an avid fan of the King. Cried on and off for a week when we died even though she'd never met the man. That was August 16, 1977, a date that was seared into my brain, as vivid as any birthday or anniversary I celebrated to this day.

DeWitt took back the license and handed it to the impersonator. "I told you, Elvis, no loitering at Denny's."

In a familiar, sonorous southern drawl, the oddball said, "You got it, sergeant, sir. Elvis has left the building."

Toots said, "Dude, Elvis left the building a long time ago."

DeWitt held the door open for me. "If you're wondering about the driver's license," he said, "he legally changed his name. Denny's doesn't mind him hanging around. It's good for the tourist trade. The folks who come from all over the world to visit Joshua Tree National Park get a real kick out of it. Captain Wolford's the one with a bee up his bonnet. He wants all the Elvises run off."

"Elvises plural?" I said.

DeWitt shrugged. "Should I have said *Elvii?*" He walked past the *Please wait to be seated* sign and motioned for me to follow. "There are two other Elvises who work the night shift," he continued, "holding up the front of this place, waiting for photo ops, begging for tips. It's like an unofficial Elvis Mecca. Part of that vortex thing."

We took a booth in a closed alcove. Toots slid around so she'd be sandwiched between the two of us. She rested her forearms on the table.

When the waitress arrived two minutes later, I ordered a Belgian waffle and coffee.

Toots said, "I'll have the eggs Benedict."

I opened my mouth to give the waitress Toots's order then caught myself.

Just as I did, the voice of the dispatcher from Eagle Center came on the air.

"Seven Paul One, Seven Paul Two, 374b, illegal dumpers, there now, at the dead end of Jack Daw Lane, cross of Filbert. Per your captain, handle code three."

DeWitt and I quickly slid out of the booth on opposite sides.

"Terrific," DeWitt said, keying the lapel mic hooked on his shoulder. Seven Sam Three copy. We're responding."

"What's the big deal?" Toots said, trying to keep up with us as we made for the exit.

"Captain's violating department policy by having units respond to a misdemeanor, code three. Lights and sirens aren't authorized for misdemeanors."

DeWitt had reached the door and was looking back at me.

"You know, you're a weird duck talking to yourself like that," he said.

6

DEWITT JUMPED IN the car and started it up. Punched the accelerator but didn't use the lights or sirens. We drove in silence as the speedometer climbed to one hundred then hovered there. Hot wind whistled through the open windows.

"How far?" I said.

"It's a ways, maybe twenty-five, thirty miles."

After ten minutes he braked hard and the back of the car fish-tailed, on the razor edge of spinning out. He turned down a narrow dirt road and stepped on the gas to regain some of the momentum we'd lost in the spin.

In the rear, Toots was tossed from side to side. Behind us, the spinning tires kicked up a rooster tail of dust that obscured all else but was probably visible from the highway.

In the side mirror I could barely make out a white, full-sized tractor-trailer rig pulling out from the desert and heading west.

Dewitt made two more turns onto dirt roads with no street signs. He was either driving by memory or instinct, or using landmarks known only to him.

Dewitt suddenly snatched the mic. "Seven Sam Three's going ninety-seven."

We sped through the middle of the desert, with nothing around but sage and Joshua trees and cholla. Finally, DeWitt slowed, the car dipping down into an arroyo I hadn't seen.

At the bottom of the arroyo sat a patrol car, its overhead lights still turning. No one else was around. Dewitt struck the steering wheel with his palm. "Son of a bitch."

All three of us got out at the same time. Off to the right, about fifty yards away, the arroyo flattened out and turned into a wash area with sand and boulders. There sat a stack of orange fifty-gallon drums. One had fallen onto its side. On the ground next to them lay two bodies. One wore a Sheriff's uniform. The other was Sarah Lang, the dispatcher who'd been riding with Randle.

Dewitt keyed his lapel mic. "I have an officer down. Expedite fire and the Hazmat team."

I took two steps, intent on going down the arroyo to render first aid. But DeWitt caught me by the scruff of the neck and yanked.

"You can't go down there. Can't you see? You'll end up just like them. That damn Randle knew better than to get too close. Damn him, he was showing off. Probably wanted to get some evidence as to who's doing the dumping and didn't think it through. Wanted to be the big hero."

I looked at DeWitt and then back at the downed deputy. "We can't just stand here."

"There's nothing else we can do. We should move up-wind and set up a perimeter and a command post."

Toots rang in quietly. "He's right, Bub. You go down there, your Johnson's going to shrivel, turn green, and fall off. And you and I both know how much you love Mr. Johnson."

DeWitt had a hold of my arm. I shrugged it off. "All right, all right." I took a couple a steps away from him and watched for movement from Randle or Sarah Lang. I'd never felt so helpless.

Well, that wasn't entirely true. *One other time.* Chasing Debra Ann. But I didn't intend to let this one end the same way.

I narrowed my eyes and saw Sarah raise a trembling hand that promptly fell back onto her chest.

I ran, this time with a two-step lead. I poured it on. Dewitt gave chase for ten yards, until we both got a whiff of the orange barrels: pungent and sweet with a chorine finish that lit the sinuses on fire. Dewitt stopped and turned back. Yelled, "You're an asshole, Donnelly."

I took in a huge lung full of air, held my breath, and kept going.

Toots kept pace, breathing normally. I motioned for her to go back but she ignored me.

With ten yards to go my lungs started to burn from the lack of oxygen. I wasn't going to make it, not on that single lungful of air.

Sirens suddenly pierced the poisoned desert air.

As I closed, still running full out, I could see the ground was wet from the leak in the area around Randle. This was real bad. I made it there and stopped, for a moment absolutely stunned. Randle lay on his back staring up at the blue sky, a milky film formed over his eyes.

This was now a homicide – voluntary manslaughter.

Had I still been in Specialized Investigations, my team would have been called out to this scene.

Randle must have walked up to the barrels and was overcome by the fumes. He fell, the right side of his head landing in the leaking waste. His hair and skin bubbled and oozed as the substance slowly absorbed him. Sarah Lang, who'd made the mistake of following him, lay in uncontaminated dirt. Her mouth was open, her tongue protruding, swollen and purple.

Toots said, "Snap out of it, Bub. We've got to shag ass out of here. There's no helping these two, not now. Let's move. *Move.*"

My eyes bulged. I knew a person couldn't hold his breath till he died; he'd pass out first. If I passed out I'd only add to the pile and in all likelihood never wake up. I bent over, the pressure in my brain worsening. I picked up Sarah Lang's petite form, turned and ran.

After only twenty giant steps, I couldn't hold my breath any longer and pushed it out, giving me another couple of seconds, my feet heavy now, trudging in the sand.

I inhaled. Had to, or risk total collapse. Air rushed into my lungs. The blue sky turned a tinted green, then red. In the grip of dizziness I swayed but then added a burst of speed. I wasn't going to make it back to the cars, but I needed to get as far away as possible, back to some clean air.

When my legs became too heavy to move I stopped. Up ahead DeWitt waved, his voice battling as though underwater. "Coooome ooon, yooou can maaaake it."

The world twirled under my feet. I'd entered a semi-conscious dream state. Nothing around me was real. In an instant, black clouds rose and it started to rain. Torrential rain. Water sluiced underfoot, making it difficult to stand. Sarah Lang opened her eyes, mumbled, "You can put me down now. I can walk from here."

She'd become as heavy as a tank. So I carefully set her down on her own two feet.

This wasn't real. A wave of water washed down the arroyo and swept us both away. My mouth filled with water. I choked and couldn't breathe. I struggled to grab on to Sarah, but it was too late. She'd disappeared into a swirling vortex.

Toots? Where was my Toots?

I tumbled over and over. Came up, choked and sputtered, "Dewitt, hurry, hurry. Get the rope. Get that dumb-assed fast-water rope."

He couldn't hear me. I'd traveled too far down the arroyo. I went under again, the water churning all around with uprooted Joshua trees and sage, the world turning dark as pitch.

Up ahead the water rushed toward Highway 62. We were miles from 62, yet here it was. The semi and trailer were still stuck in the sand, the live wire arcing in the desert, snapping and flashing like blue lightning. I was headed right for it. I tried to swim away, but there wasn't any control in the turbulent brown water. The current took me right at it. The wire touched my skin. I saw a flash of yellow light that quickly turned bright white and finally snapped into perfect blackness.

7

I WOKE STILL in the dream, lying in the sand next to the big rig. The dark clouds remained but it had stopped raining. The torrential water had ebbed. Toots knelt by my side holding my hand. It took a second to recognize her; she wasn't wearing her red diaphanous dress and black heels. She wore trim black slacks and a cream silk blouse: the clothes she'd worn the last time I saw her, clothes that had burned off of her right in front of my eyes. This was the first time Toots had changed clothes in two years.

"Debra Ann?"

"I'm right here, Will."

"Debra Ann," I croaked again. "What happened?"

"You were shocked."

Then I realized I actually *felt* her hand in mine. Warm and soft. I started to cry.

"Debra Ann, I can feel you."

"I know, but not for much longer. You're going back."

"I don't want to go back. I want to stay here with you."

"I know."

I said, "I...I tried to save you. I ran as fast as I could. But the car...it was just going too fast. I'm sorry..." I choked back a sob. This was something I had always wanted to tell her, how hard I had tried. She had to know. She had seen me running the day she died, knew I was trying. That day I'd been close enough to see the stark panic and fear in her eyes. Close. But not close enough. It hurt so badly that I couldn't help her when she needed me most.

She leaned over and kissed my lips. Warmth spread through my entire body, from my lips all the way down to my toes.

She pulled back and said, "I'm sorry, Will, you're going to be shocked one more time."

Electricity shot through my body. My back arched and fell back to the gurney. Through a dense blur I saw that I was in a hospital—an emergency room, doctors and nurses all around caught up in frenetic activity. I was naked.

"You okay, Bub?"

Toots was back. Still Debra Ann, but not. The *after* Debra Ann. She still loved me and I her, but she was angry that I had not saved her from an agonizing death. This Debra Ann – Toots – had a smart mouth and used my own cynical cop jargon. She sometimes said things my subconscious held back from me.

The doctor said, "Okay, we got him back. Let's stabilize him and move him to ICU."

HOURS, DAYS, MAYBE even weeks later, I woke in a sanitary hospital room, the hall partitioned off with a glass wall. My eyes were gummed shut, residue blurred my vision, and I had to blink furiously to clear them. Toots sat in the chair at my side, her hand in mine, only now I couldn't feel it.

I remembered the dream, the delirium when I had felt Debra Ann's warm, soft hand. Felt like moments ago. I wanted that sensation back so badly it brought tears to my eyes.

"Oh, Bub, you're back, you're *back*. You scared the hell out of me."

She hugged me. I didn't feel it but was glad she was there anyway.

But suddenly she pulled back and slugged me, her delicate

fist passing right through my abdomen.

"You're a grade A asswipe," she said. "That's what you are for playing the hero like that." Tears filled her lovely eyes. "Don't you ever do that again. You know we almost lost you? They had to shock your heart *twice*. They were one thin hair away from declaring you dead. I know; I saw it in that doctor's eyes. He almost gave up on you."

"How long have I been out?"

A gruff male voice from the corner startled me. "Three days."

I cocked my head at an uncomfortable angle to see. It was Jim Novak, the Sheriff.

"How long have you been sitting there?" I said. "I hope it wasn't three days."

Novak stood and walked over. He wore denim pants over black cowboy boots, a tan blazer over a white shirt, and a black bolo tie. He held his black cowboy hat in his hands.

"No, the doc called. Said you were restless and he thought you'd be coming out of it anytime."

"What's with this room?" I said. "Looks like I might be quarantined, but you wouldn't be standing here if I was."

He glanced at the door. "I ordered the room, put a guard on the door, and restricted visitation."

I nodded. "You didn't want me talking in my delirium."

"Yes, that's right."

I said, "I know why you're here. I wasn't at the station long enough to find anything out. I only met with Wolford once. If I went at him too fast he'd know something was up."

Most folks thought my transfer to Joshua Tree station was a *midnight transfer* pending the on-going internal affairs investigation into what I had done. That's what Novak wanted everyone to believe. I'd been the perfect shill. Everyone had heard about my theft and knew it was true. My time at the department was limited to a few days. Who better to put undercover? No one would suspect a thing.

Originally, guilt had driven me to confess, which started this whole mess rolling. Three weeks ago I had walked into

Novak's office and told him I had done it. I'd stolen the three hundred thousand dollars. My team had hit a house in Hawaiian Gardens, a little city in the suburb of the greater Los Angeles area. We'd found an empty house, no furniture. Mats and bedding littered the floor, rifles were propped at every window and door. A safe house. Someone had called ahead, a last-minute phone call. In the living room hall closet we found boot boxes that went from floor to ceiling full of twenties, fifties, and hundred-dollar bills.

Four million dollars.

In the kitchen were eleven trash bags filled with ones, fives, and tens – too much of a hassle for the *narcoticos* to count, and even a bigger hassle to launder. Their intention had been to throw it out with the trash when they left.

At a weak moment, on the anniversary of Debra Ann's death, I took the trash, the three hundred thousand.

Novak suspended me pending termination and, of course, criminal prosecution. What else could he do? Two weeks later he called me back in and offered me a deal: investigate an internal corruption conspiracy by going undercover. And of course give the money back and there would be no criminal prosecution. I'd still lose my job, but keep my pension and not go to prison. I told him I would do the investigation but I couldn't give the money back. I had donated it to MADD, Mothers Against Drunk Drivers, the reason why I had taken it in the first place.

Now in the hospital room Novak looked down at the hat in his hands as he turned it around and around. "I thought I needed to come here and tell you in person."

Toots said, "Here it comes. He's going to throw you to the curb. And after all you've just gone through. He's a real piece of work. What a tool."

"No, wait," I said. "It's not too late. I'll be up and around in no time. I can still do this."

I didn't want to go to prison, sure. But even more, I didn't want to let Novak down. I had worked for him when he was a lieutenant and again when he was a captain. I liked him, and I respected him. He was in a terrible bind, and I didn't want to let him down.

He still didn't look at me. Just shook his head. "You don't understand."

"What? Tell me."

"It's your heart," he said. "The doctor's going to tell you all this." He looked me in the eyes now. "I'm sorry, Will. I can't be more sorry than I am. What you did out there was heroic, and I owe you for it. You exemplify what this department stands for. I wish I could give you the medal of valor, but under the circumstances…well, you understand."

"How's Sara Lang?"

Novak smiled. "Looks like she's going to make it. Thanks to you."

A warm tingling feeling flowed through my entire body. Must have been the drugs they had me on. My breath became short. I gasped like a fish out of water.

"There's nothing wrong with my heart."

Toots said, "I overheard the doc talking to this chump here. He said the combination of the chemical contamination and the defibrillation—twice—that it weakened your heart. You can't have any excitement, none whatsoever. Never, not ever. Including me and you and Mr. Johnson. They're going to ask you to sign up, get on a list for a heart transplant." Toots' voice caught in her throat on the last part. She'd been trying to be a trooper and lost it right at the last.

Novak said, "I'll let the doctor explain. But the way it stands now, you'll never get past risk management. They won't clear you to go back to work. You'll get a full medical retirement. That's the best I could do."

A medical retirement I'd receive while in prison, with prison medical care. They don't hand out heart transplants in prison. He was telling me that he had no choice. No choice but to hand me a death sentence.

The news hit me hard. I didn't believe him. There was nothing wrong with my heart. I felt fine. The machine next to the bed, wired to my chest, started beeping. My breath came hard and fast.

A nurse ran in. "Mr. Donnelly, you need to calm down. Please relax. Breathe slower. I know you're feeling panic right now, but you need to breathe slower." She turned up the oxygen. That's when I noticed the plastic hose attached to my nose. I immediately started feeling better. I could breathe.

Everything Novak had told me was true.

After a couple of minutes the sweat on my forehead started to dry and I felt more in control.

The nurse said to Novak, "You're going to have to leave now. How did you get in here in the first place? Out. *Out.*"

He said, "I'm sorry, I just need a minute more and then I'll go."

"You'll go right *now.*"

I said, "It's okay, I understand my situation now and I can control my emotions. Please let him stay for one minute more."

"I cannot and will not." She turned to him. "If you don't leave right now I'll call security."

Novak didn't move. The nurse stomped out.

I said, "I know what you're going to ask and you needn't. I won't say anything to anyone about the investigation into the two Sheriff's captains."

"I know you won't." He came over and shook my hand. "I just wish it could have worked out."

Wasn't his fault, I thought. I'd made my own bed.

Now I had to lie in it.

8

TWO DAYS LATER I drove out to Joshua Tree station. Toots sat in the passenger seat, her arms across her chest, angry that I would "*risk my life*" like this. I had checked myself out of the hospital AMA – *against medical advice*. I felt better. My heart situation had improved; well, somewhat, anyway. I still had to constantly focus on maintaining a steady emotional state or my heart would race and my breath would shorten. The doctors were less than optimistic that my heart would heal on its own.

I didn't have a medical clearance but thought I could bamboozle Wolford into believing I had. I couldn't tell Novak my plan, of course. He'd nix it for sure. Had to, because of the liability he'd face.

Out in the parking lot I sat in my car with my eyes closed, concentrating, focusing on the task at hand. All I had to do was walk into the station and speak with Wolford, get him to take me into his confidence. No problem, I thought. I could do it.

A knock at my window startled me. When I jumped, so did my heart, right into my throat, from a hundred beats a minute to a thousand, in half a second. Just in case, I reached for the nitro bottle with my pills. I took a deep, easy breath and let it out before opening my eyes.

At first I didn't recognize him, though he wore the tan and green sheriff's uniform. When my eyes adjusted, I realized it was Mannerly. One of the deputies who'd retired from the

Marine Corps and made law enforcement his second career.

Dark green aviator sunglasses covered Mannerly's eyes. His leathery face broke into an uncharacteristic smile.

I rolled down the window. He stuck his hand into the car.

"Sir, I just wanted to thank you for what you did out there. It took a lot of balls."

Toots said, "He's not Major Dad, he's more like Major Beefcake."

I took his hand. His skin was hot and too rough, with an abnormal strength.

My fluttering heart caused sweat to break out on my forehead. All I could muster was a weak, "Thanks."

He didn't let go. His glasses reflected the sun. "Sir, you need anything from anyone in this station, all you need to do is ask. Understand?"

I nodded. "Thank you."

"That was really a great thing what you did out there."

I said nothing.

His expression didn't change. "You didn't by chance see anything out there, I mean, that would give us some idea who these douche bags are who dumped those barrels and killed one of our own?"

I'd thought about it constantly over the last two days and could not vividly remember anything about what happened out in that arroyo with Deputy Randle and Dispatcher Sara Lang.

Toots said, "On second thought his ears stick out too much to qualify him for the beefcake category. He looks more like a jug head. Mess with him, Bub. Tell him you found a wallet out there, something like that. Of all things, asking if you saw something. How many people have asked you that? Doesn't he think you would've said something to someone by now if you *had* seen something?"

Toots could run off at the mouth at times, though Mannerly did look a bit full of himself.

I said, "Yeah, I did, matter of fact, when we made that first turn off the highway onto the dirt roads. I saw a white truck coming off one of those side roads and onto Highway

FIRE AT WILL

62."

I remembered it right then and wondered why my mind had hidden it away from me.

Mannerly let go of my hand and took a step back. "You did? You get a plate or see anything about it that stood out, like writing or markings on the side?"

Toots slapped her thigh. "You hooked him, Bub. Now throw him up on shore and let him flap and gasp."

I hadn't hooked him at all. It was the truth. Or had my memory merely manufactured it? Was it wishful thinking?

I said, "Yes, I did see the truck and I guess I didn't tell anyone because I wanted to take the guy down myself."

This part wasn't all true, but somehow I wanted it to be, that I did know something that would help.

Mannerly's confusion was comical, the way he stood there with his mouth moving without words. He said, "Did DeWitt see it?"

Mannerly had heard about my delusional ramblings, the talking out loud to no one at all. He was fishing for confirmation from a reliable source.

I suddenly felt dizzy and had to get inside, cool off in the air conditioning. Something at the back of my brain niggled at me. I couldn't bring it forward. I opened the door, pondering whether I had seen something on the side of the truck and it was buried in my subconscious. I said, "No, DeWitt was too busy driving like a crazy man. You've seen him drive, I'm sure. No, I got a pretty good lead and I'll let you know when the hammer's about to come down. The whole station will be in on this one."

He took another step back, lifted his sunglasses to check my eyes, to see if I had a hold of his leg and was yanking real hard. After a moment he nodded. "You do that. Be sure and do that, let me know. I definitely want a piece of this action."

He turned on a precise military heel and walked away. I got the feeling he wasn't comfortable in any social environment, that maybe his previous job of professional warrior suited him better.

❖

IN THE STATION all the deputies I passed wore black bands around their Sheriff's badge in memory of John Randle. Set up in the hall just inside the door, on a big easel was a blown up color photo of John in uniform with his posse epaulette sitting on his horse Beau. Deputies I passed in the hall stopped, shook my hand and patted me on the back, some with tear-filled eyes. I looked for Mannerly to straighten him out before word got around and I'd have to explain myself to too many people, embarrass myself for not being able to remember more in a timely manner.

Dorothy Lamont looked up from her computer. Her face broke into surprise, then into a smile that was out of character, and it transformed her face into a different woman, someone who actually cared. "Why, Sergeant Donnelly, how in the world are you doing? Are you sure you're well enough to come back to work? You look a little pale. You should take a few more days. You've earned it."

Toots said, "Yeah, right. She thought you were down for the count and she never thought she'd see you again. It's written all over her sour puss."

I ignored her. "Is the captain in?"

His door stood open, and I had seen his car parked out back in his slot.

"Sure, go right in."

Today Wolford wore his Sheriff's uniform with the gold captain bars on his collar instead of a suit. Even though it was custom tailored, he still looked more like a masquerading football dressed in a uniform. He hurried around his desk, his hand extended. "Bad Bill, good to see you."

I took his hand, moist and wet, like a dead fish.

He pumped it up and down. "Are you sure you're supposed to be back to work so soon? I was told...I mean, I thought you'd be laid up a while longer."

He had a good pipeline for internal information.

Toots said, "The turd knows all about your medical

condition. That violates that medical information act. What's it called, HIPA? He never thought he'd see you again. You can read it all over his stupid mug. *Bad Bill.* What the hell, tell him that's not your name. What a horse's ass." Like before, she sat down in one of the two chairs in front of his desk. "Come on, take a load off, Bub. Sit down. You're sweating and you're white as a sheet."

She was right. I sat down next to her and immediately felt better. The long drive out to the desert had just about used up all my energy for the day. I just wanted to lie down and curl up somewhere cool. I hoped my endurance would gradually return. I didn't believe the docs about my heart and the need for a transplant. I'd be better in a few weeks. I'd never been sick my entire life, and I found it hard to believe my body would give up on me after one incident.

Wolford stood next to the chair, too close. "Man, that was some show you put on out there. You should hear how DeWitt tells it. You ran right into the muck, grabbed that little dispatcher, and ran back." His expression suddenly turned grim. Too bad about Randle. He was a good man. He was on the list for detective, you know."

Toots said, "Detective? He was better suited for a dogcatcher. He was a fool for walking up on those barrels in the first place. Poor Sara Lang didn't know any better and followed him right along."

"Toots, don't talk that way."

Wolford took a step back. "Huh? What'd you say, Bill? You just call me Toots?"

Dizziness clouded my thoughts. I'd made a mistake talking to Toots out loud and in front of Wolford. I waved my hand in the air. "Nothing," I said. "Never mind. I'm ready to go back to work."

He went around his desk and sat down. "It doesn't look like you should be out of bed, let alone out driving a cop car around. You have a back-to-work order from the doctor?"

"Hey, fatso," Toots said. "If he says he's ready to go back to work he's ready to go back to work." She had given me hell the entire two-hour drive from Montclair to the station saying the same thing; that I should be in bed. Now she'd changed her tune because she didn't like Wolford telling us what to do.

I tried to dodge the question. "Did you find out anything about where the barrels came from? If and when you do, I want to be in on the take-down."

"Bad Bill, always wanting to be first through the door." He stared at me for a long, uncomfortable moment. He got up went to the door and said to Dorothy, "I'm not to be disturbed." He slowly closed the door, then came back around his desk and sat down.

He took up that stare again. Said, "Can we be honest here? I mean, like one old-time street cop to another?"

I nodded. My heart fluttered. This was it; he was going to take me into his confidence.

Toots said, "Street cop, huh? This piece of work's got a yellow streak a mile wide down his back. What a bunch of trash trying that Mano y Hermano crap on you."

Wolford said, "Word on the street is that you're going to take a big fall."

I waited, staring, not breaking eye contact. "What does it matter now?" I said. "I'm being thrown to the dogs."

Wolford sat back, smiling. "Exactly my point. What they're doing to you is wrong on so many levels. Have you given any thought to what you're going to do afterward?"

"After what?"

He waved his hand, his eyelids fluttering. "This ain't about nothing." He slipped into street jargon as if it linked us closer as two street cops. He said, "With your record, you'll maybe get six months in the can, and that's county time, easy time, and three years probation at best. What's really going to kick your ass, though – and think about this – you're going to have to pay back that three hundred thousand plus fines."

"Bub, how the hell does he know about that? Sure, everyone knows about the theft, but no one should know the amount except Internal Affairs. Bub, you think the second captain that Novak is looking for is in Internal Affairs?"

Still looking at Wolford, I waved her off. "Cut it out." Then I said to Wolford, "How exactly do you know about my problem?"

"I know a lot about your problem, and personally I think it stinks, stinks to high heaven."

Real imaginative, this guy. He likes to talk in clichés.

"Mary Rymes been talking out of school to you about my case?"

Rymes was the captain of IA. I'd known her a long time. We'd worked the jail together. And dated more than a little. I'd been more serious than she wanted to be. For that short time we had together there was a spark, something red hot and difficult to control. She finally broke it off, saying I scared her and that she needed to focus on getting her career started before she settled down. After we separated I realized I liked her even more than I thought. I loved her. When I went out to the valley to work patrol, she went up to the high desert. Our paths hadn't crossed in better than fifteen years. But I followed her career in the department bulletins.

Her nickname was Ordinary Mary, mostly because she didn't stand out in a crowd or open her mouth to comment on anything unless you got to know her. Mouse-brown hair cut short, average build, nothing special, with a spray of freckles across her nose and under her eyes. She'd always kept to herself and maintained benign neutrality on department politics. I'd always thought she held back a latent intelligence, which was probably true if she'd made it to commander of IA, one of the most trusted positions in the department.

Wolford shook his head. "What does it matter now, huh? It's over. The fat lady already sang."

Toots said, "Ordinary Mary, huh? I never liked that wench. Hey, she would be in the perfect position to stop any investigations before…"

I said to Wolford, "I'll get by."

Wolford said, "The worst of it, and I don't think you've thought this out, is the IRS is going to crawl up your ass on that 300K. Any chickenshit little ex-felon job you can land, the

IRS is going to take half until you pay them back. With interest and penalties, that's going to be a big *never*, pal. You'll never catch up with that monkey on your back."

I hadn't thought of that, and the sad part was he was right.

Wolford let it sink in. He was making a strong case. I was there to elicit information from him and he was doing a good job convincing me I should come over to his side. He leaned forward, his eyes going a little wider. "Just tell me one thing. Did you do it?"

"Why do you need to know? I really don't understand, why exactly do you need to know?"

"I have a proposition for you but I have to know if the greatest street cop who ever lived, the infamous Will Donnelly, really took a bite from the poison apple."

"How can you help me?"

"Yes or no?"

I hesitated. "Okay, I succumbed at a weak moment, made a poor decision. Now how can you help me?"

He smiled wide this time, gloating.

Toots said, "He's a real dipshit. I hate it that you have to bend over and kiss this guy's shoes like this. You know he's got a little penis. That's why he treats people like this. I'm sure Freud has an explanation for it, the little penis thing."

Wolford said, "Not now, not here. Meet me tonight at nine at The Tick Tock. And there's no way I'm going to let you work, not in your condition."

I started to protest but Wolford cut me off.

"Go home and get some rest. And meet me at the Tick Tock. Trust me. You won't regret it."

9

Toots and I didn't make it to the Morongo grade before I had to pull over in Yucca Valley. The windows were down to help keep me awake. The panic started with an odor that wafted in, that same odor from the orange-colored barrels, sweet and pungent with that strange chemical finish.

Impossible.

For no discernible reason, my heart went crazy, thumping out of control. My entire body turned sweaty, my hands shook, and the bright afternoon became unbearably brighter. I was going to faint.

I zipped into the closest parking lot, Xavier's fast food Mexican restaurant. I missed part of the driveway, thumping over the curb. Foot on the brake, I fumbled with the nitro bottle, got one pill out, dropped a bunch. Stuffed the pill under my tongue, laid back, and let the air conditioner wash over me. Someone turned it on high.

"Thanks, Toots. Thanks."

She put the car in park.

I fell into a deep slumber. Oddly, though, I knew I was asleep. Disembodied, I hovered over myself within the car's small confines. Down below, Toots had curled up next to me and she, too, slept soundly. Everything was vivid and alive. Finally, I swept down and stood outside my tired old Ford Taurus.

Cars came and went from Xavier's drive-thru. Folks pulled up, got out, and walked in, some of them talking, some just going in to refuel themselves.

A warm hand touched my arm, and I turned.

"*Debra Ann.*"

"Hi, sweetie. You need to sit down. You're about to drop dead. You know that, don't you?"

The look in her eyes was sincere and filled with adoring love.

"Debra Ann."

She said, "I mean it, for real. Dead. You're in that place halfway between the here and the there. I want you to sit down and take a load off."

She wore the cream silk blouse and black slacks, the diamond tennis bracelet, and white bead necklace, that she'd worn the day she burned to death right in front of me, the day of our anniversary. We'd been going out to a special dinner. I'd had another ring in my pocket. Planned to ask her to marry me, again, to reaffirm our vows. She knew me so well she'd figured something was afoot. I'd seen it in her smile that morning, over toast and scrambled eggs.

But I was late that night, tied up in an investigation, on a hunt for a kidnapped little girl. I could think of nothing else except that poor little girl. What was she experiencing? I was the one tasked with helping her, the leader of the men working to find her. Had I been doing everything I could to find her?

I shouldn't have been late, not for our anniversary, not that night. If I'd been on time Debra Ann would not have had to go through that horrible ordeal which resulted in her death.

In front of Xavier's, I took her in my arms and kissed her mouth, hungry for her. Her mouth was wet and hot and real. I couldn't believe it. Couldn't believe this was happening. I couldn't get enough of her. She responded with the same ravenous desire. My heart ran a hundred miles an hour, but this time it was strong. I realized the comparison. My husk in the car, sitting next to Toots, *his* heart was weak and on the verge of total collapse; not this one.

FIRE AT WILL

We broke the clench. I pulled away, short of breath, and looked at her. "It's you. It's really you. My beautiful Debra Ann." I hugged her, maybe a little too hard. I couldn't believe she was physically there.

"Take it easy, Will. I have to breathe too." She laughed, put a gentle hand on my shoulder and pushed gently away.

I tried to pull her back in for another kiss. I wanted more of her, *needed* more. I needed all of her.

"Wait," she said. "There's time enough for that. Look." She pointed to the street.

A large four-door Buick glided in on soft suspension, pulled right up to the handicap-parking slot by Xavier's front door, and parked cockeyed as if the driver owned the world. The woman in the passenger seat had a large mop of unruly gray hair, thick shoulders, and behemoth breasts easily visible under the bulky triple-XL pale blue tee shirt.

The skinny male driver got out and walked next to her. Something about him sparked a memory that I couldn't quite summon fully.

The old woman playfully slapped the thin man's shoulder. "You should've come around and opened the door for me. Be a gentleman around a lady."

He hesitated at the door to the restaurant, hand ready to open it. He turned slightly, and I got a better view of him.

I *did* know him, but couldn't put a name to that long, thin face. His sunken eyes sat atop half-moons of dark, puffy flesh.

He said, "I would've opened the door for *a lady*." He opened it and jetted in, dodging the old woman's foot as she tried to kick him.

She followed him in. "Abel, you're not a nice man, and just for that I'm not going to buy you lunch."

Debra Ann took my hand. "Come on."

We walked together to Xavier's. "What? Where're we going? Can we just sit down and talk? I really need to talk with you."

"No. For now, let's go in here."

"Debra, honey, please. I need to talk to you...I need to

talk to you about what happened that day."

"Hush, not right now. I want to show you something." She pulled the door open.

I said, "It's nice and cool in here." I looked down, found that I was buck naked. "Oh, man." This *was* a dream. Of course it was. Depression sauntered in. What a fool I was, thinking this was real.

The people on line to order their food, and the ones milling about waiting to pick up their orders all turned toward the open door. Debra Ann leaned up and whispered in my ear. "Be careful. They can't see you, but they can hear you. They saw the door open and heard what you said."

"Am I a ghost?" I said it out loud, not yet fully comprehending the situation.

A woman screamed. Everyone took one or two steps back, their eyes wide, trying to see who'd said it. I saw how public hysteria could catch like wildfire as fear rippled through the crowd.

Debra Ann took my arm, still leaning up and whispering. "Sssh, I told you, they can hear you. Come on." We headed across the room to the door on the opposite side of the small restaurant, the side with the drive thru where all the scared patrons were now pushing and shoving their way out. Debra Ann said, "From now on, you should go out the door that's already open so it doesn't scare people so much."

"From now on?" I whispered.

We'd caught up to the throng trying to exit. Too terrified to scream, the people grunted and groaned. The thin man from earlier shoved on the old woman, trying to get out ahead of everyone else.

That's when I recognized him. That's why Debra Ann wanted us to go in.

"Abel Jenks," I whispered.

Abel heard it and yelped like a little girl. I remembered the case file, the picture of little Peggy Kellogg, the pain and pure anguish on her young mother's and father's faces. My hand snaked out and grabbed Abel by the throat, choking off the scream that tried to slip out when he felt my hand. I shoved him and he stumbled backward, his arms wind-milling as he tried to regain his balance.

Everyone made it out except the old woman who stood in the open door watching Abel do his lonely dance. The old woman wrung her hands. "Abel, Abel, shug. Come now, quit your messing around. Get out here. You're scaring me, shug. Come on now."

I shoved him up against the glass wall. Some of the people outside stood watching Abel's back mashed up against the glass. His body rose slightly, his feet dangling. In my anger I'd lifted him off the ground. Nothing wrong with my heart now. I had the same strength I had when I was thirty.

Then my vision sparked and snapped. For an instant, I flashed to the torrid brown rainwater washing me down the arroyo, the arroyo where I'd been contaminated with the dumped chemicals, the wire arcing in the distance, coming right at me.

I returned to Xavier's.

Debra Ann put her warm hand on my arm. "Will, you're not strong here like you think. You still have a weak heart, and if you push it too hard you're going to die. It's the nitro, the pill you took, that's giving you this false sense of eternity."

I quit looking into Abel's piggish eyes and shifted to hers, cool and calming. My voice croaked with fear. "Debra Ann, honey, will I see you…I mean, where you are? I mean, if I die, will I be with you…"

She said, "I don't know. Not likely, though, to be honest. You're not really seeing me now. You only think you do, just like with her out in the car, Toots." Debra Ann smiled. "I like it that you call her Toots."

10

A SHERIFF'S CAR rolled up, code-three, lights and siren. I let Abel down to his feet. He kept going, fainting dead away, his face purple and bloated. I'd almost throttled him too long, almost given him the justice he deserved.

Debra Ann guided me outside and over to the Taurus. Nobody was in the car. I thought I'd see me and Toots, but the car was empty. My clothes lay deflated on the front seat as if my human husk had been whisked away all at once.

I said, "What's this?"

She didn't answer and pulled me aside, out of the way of Dewitt who ran, stopped at the Taurus, and leaned over the hood, his gun drawn. Debra Ann put her finger to her lips.

I nodded and followed her deeper into the parking lot, out of earshot, as the scene played out like a television crime drama.

She said, "Okay, here's the deal. What I'm going to tell you, you already know. You figured it out in your subconscious and your consciousness is hiding it from you. I told you a little fib. You're not in the halfway place like I said. I said it because I thought it might scare you too much to know the truth."

"I'm listening."

Her eyes were a lovely aqua, though her driver's license read hazel.

"Will, physically, you're in a very delicate state." Tears

filled her eyes.

A lump rose in my throat. I said, "You're not really standing here talking to me. I understand that." It hurt like hell to say it. "I don't want you to be sad. I don't have enough time with you as it is. All I want is to see that great smile of yours. Your smile lights up my world. Lights up my screwed-up world."

She nodded and pasted on a smile.

I said, "That's better."

Another Sheriff's car pulled up. Mannerly jumped out, racked a shotgun, and held it over the outside spotlight as a brace. A cigarette hung from the corner of his mouth, bobbing up and down as he keyed the mic to the PA with his free and spoke. "You, in Xavier's, come out with your hands in plain sight."

The door opened a little. The widow, who was with Jenks, stuck her head out. "It's okay. Whatever it was, it's gone now. We're okay in here."

"Lady, tell everyone inside to come out now."

She nodded and disappeared. A moment later the employees, in greasy-food-soiled aprons, came out in single file at a pace just short of a run.

Debra Ann continued in my ear, "You know this already. *You* made up that thing about being in the middle place and had me tell it to you. It was something easier to believe than the truth. You *know* the truth."

"What's going on, sweetie? What's happening here?"

"Will, you're invisible."

"Get outta here. There's no way."

"No, it's true. And keep your voice down."

"I'm dreaming. I'm asleep in the front seat of the car and I'm dreaming all of this."

"No. Think about it; think about it very carefully. No one was in the car when we walked by, because you're standing out here. And Toots isn't real to begin with. You do know that much for sure."

Having come to, Abel Jenks bolted out of Xavier's,

running fast. "Help, help me! Someone's trying to kill me."

Mannerly held his position, aiming the shotgun at him. "Stop! Stop, right there!"

I saw the way Dewitt's mind put it together. Instantly Dewitt looked at Mannerly, then back at Jenks, and saw what I saw, that Mannerly intended to take this opportunity to rid this world of Abel Jenks. He'd call it self-defense, justifiable under the circumstances. One less kidnapping, murdering pervert.

Dewitt yelled, "No, hold it. Hold it!" He left his position, ran into the line of fire, and tackled Jenks, taking him down hard to the asphalt before Mannerly could pull the trigger.

Jenks wasn't having a good day. Screw him.

I looked back at Debra Ann. "Invisible? How?"

"You don't know for sure, but this is how you put it together and I think you're right. That chemical contamination did something to your genetic structure. It somehow altered your physical make-up."

"Okay then, how about Sara Lang? Is she invisible? I might just buy it if she were invisible, too."

"Will, honey, Sara Lang was DOA."

TEARS STUNG MY eyes. I shook my head no.

Debra said, "You *knew* that, Will. You knew Sara was dead."

"Novak told me Sara made it," I cried. "He told me, and he wouldn't lie, not to me." I pounded my chest with my fist. My heart fluttered.

"Honey, take it easy. That's not a wise thing to do in your condition." She took my fist and held it, gently opened the fingers, and massaged my hand until I relaxed. I dearly loved the way she felt, her warm skin on mine. My face was wet with tears.

She said, "Don't blame Novak. He couldn't tell you, not while you were in that condition. He was told you'd never walk out of the hospital. They told him your DNA was irreparably damaged and your immune system would start to break down. They told him you only had days to live. That's where you got the information. They were in your room talking when you were in the coma."

I put my other hand up to stifle a sob. "So, you mean that…that you're really not here and that I probably won't see you if…I mean, *when*, I go?"

She said nothing.

"Deb, you know…that day when…you know our anniversary—"

"Sssh, don't say it. I know. You tried your best. I know that."

Even though I knew she was merely a mirror of my subconscious, I took some solace from her words. "Can you ever forgive me?"

She shook her head no, and put her other warm hand up on my cheek. "No, darling, because there's nothing to forgive you for."

I choked on the lump in my throat. "How much longer do I have to be with you?"

"Not long. When your heart rate moderates you'll turn visible again."

I nodded. "That's some kind of chemical they're dumping out in the desert. Does the manufacturer know it makes people invisible?"

"No, it's not like that. It's not just the chemical. The way you pieced it together was it's not just the particular quantity of the chemical you absorbed, it's also combined with—"

I finished it for her. "The electroshock. When I was on the table in the ER, the electroshock to restart my heart. Twice. The chemical and shocking—the combined effect caused some kind of reaction."

She nodded. "See, you know. All you have to do is relax your brain and let it bubble to the surface."

Off to the right, fifteen feet away, Jenks was on his feet, his face bloated red with rage, piggish eyes bulging, his finger right up in Dewitt's face. "I'm going to sue you. I'm going to own the Sheriff's Department. When I'm done, this county's going to be called Jenks County. You understand, Sergeant Dewitt? I'm going to own your house and your kids' houses and your kids' kids' houses. You can't treat me like that. I'm the victim here. The victim."

The second time he said it, spittle flew from his rabid mouth.

I wanted to spend every second I could with Debra Ann, but Jenks had lit my fire. I walked over with Debra Ann close on my heels.

She whispered, "Don't do this, Will. People aren't ready for the invisible man, and you're sure as hell going to let them know about him if you don't stop right now."

I pulled up short. She was right, of course. I couldn't sucker punch Jenks like I intended. I thought about it for a second. I wasn't going to let Dewitt take a tumble for saving Mannerly. Mannerly's brand of curbside justice would have been ruled a good shoot. Legally good, but morally wrong and civilly punitive, and the County would have to pay off.

Jenks waved his arms and screamed, trying to get witnesses to gather around as he backed away from Dewitt. Jenks was enjoying this.

I moved in close and whispered loudly enough so only he could hear. "Shut your mouth, you little pinhead."

He jumped back. "Who's that? Who said that?"

"This is Will Donnelly, the guy who chased you two years ago, remember? I'm dead now. I'm here with little Peggy Kellogg. Say something to him, Peggy. Go on, tell him. What, you don't want to? Okay, I'll tell him. We're going to haunt you for the rest of the sad excuse you call a life."

His head jerked from side to side, trying to make out who was saying it, his eyes wide in terror. All around people in the parking lot watched. Some caught it on their cell phone video recorders that would forever memorialize it on You Tube and act as physical evidence of his insanity.

"*Will Donnelly?*" He squeaked. "*You're* Will Don-nelly?"

I'd never used my nickname before but made an exception this time. I said, "Yeah, but you can call me Bad Bill."

"Bad Bill? *Bad Bill?*"

Mannerly came around from his door, shotgun still in hand. He walked toward Jenks, his aviator sunglasses reflecting the afternoon sun.

Jenks paid him no mind.

Dewitt said, "Mannerly what're you doing?"

"Sarge, this little douche bag's 5150."

He was referring to the Welfare and Institution's code for someone who is a danger to himself or others, and who can be taken into protective custody for his own safety.

Mannerly let the shotgun dangle at his side as if it weighed nothing at all, and in one long, fluid motion pulled his Taser from his leg holster.

I stepped away from Jenks. Fifty thousand volts, in my condition, would finish off my heart for sure.

Mannerly fired the Taser. In a microsecond, the little darts attached to copper wires shot out and embedded in Jenks.

Jenks went stiff, jerked, and convulsed. He fell forward, his face making a mushy splat on the pavement.

I smiled. It felt good to smile. I hadn't really smiled, not like that, in the last two years. My heart rate started to slow. And suddenly I smelled the heavenly aroma of cooking food coming from the vent at the top of Xavier's. I hurried to my car, surreptitiously eased the passenger door open, and slipped in. I dressed as quickly as I could, given the close confines, and finished as Toots appeared in the driver's seat smiling, her hands on the wheel.

She'd never smiled before either, not like that. I liked it. It warmed my heart.

She said, "Where are we going?"

"Scoot over," I said. "Hallucinations can't drive."

11

I WOKE TO a blinking green light across the room and the smell of cigarette smoke, which must have been a remnant from the dream. The green light emanated from the clock.

9:15

I didn't know what had awakened me. I lay there thinking about what had happened in the desert at Xavier's—what Debra Ann had said about my situation.

My situation?

On the way home in the car I couldn't even look *my situation* in the eye, afraid to peer into the rearview to see if I was still there. Fatigue made the drive one of the most difficult in my life. I had to do something about my energy level.

We got home at noon, barely, and I laid down on top of the covers for a brief nap.

Darkness crowded into the room. Something niggled at my brain, something I was supposed to do, something important. I turned to the other side of the bed and found Toots laying there, her chin cupped in her hand, elbow propping her head.

"Have a good sleep, Bub?"

"I do feel somewhat refreshed."

"Refreshed enough to...you know?" She lay back on the pillow. "Come on over here, big boy." Her tone mimicked a sexy, buxom, white blond woman from old movies, Mae West.

In the two years Toots had been around...well, we'd never had relations, and I found it odd that she'd ask at this particular juncture. She was Debra Ann in her physicality, in her facial features, and especially in her eyes. But in every other attribute she was Toots: her demeanor, her language, and most important, her inner person. I liked Toots. I needed Toots. Really, when it came right down to it, I had to have Toots at my side, but she wasn't Debra Ann. Debra Ann was my wife, not Toots.

Still, I didn't want to hurt her feelings. "Not right now, okay?"

The smile disappeared, replaced with a pout. She turned onto her side, facing away. "What's the matter, I'm not good enough for you now? What, now that you kissed that sleaze bag, Debby Ann, I'm not exciting enough for you?"

"Don't speak that way. Jealousy doesn't become you." I got up from the bed too fast and stood still for a minute to let the dizziness dissipate, a state you simply cannot get used to. Toots got up on the other side of the bed. Her voice turned soft, mimicking Debra Ann's. "Bub, did I ever tell you, you were my first orgasm?"

I froze, shocked. This sexual tack was new. Toots had never broached this topic before. *Does everything Toots say apply to Debra Ann?* Had I been Debra Ann's first—

How ludicrous.

Anger rose in me, though I wasn't sure of its origin. I blurted, "You're a hallucination."

For a fleeting moment, I thought now was the time to push Toots away, that I had finally slipped too close to that tenuous edge of insanity.

Invisibility, of all things. No chance, no way. That had been an illusion, a dream.

"Please, Bub, please? I need you." She slipped the spaghetti string strap of the red diaphanous dress off her shoulder. The dress drooped, exposing her large breast, and pink areola. An unbidden groan slipped past my lips. It had been a long time.

Toots giggled, her eyes now focused below my waist. "Looks like Mr. Johnson's ready, willing, and more than able."

I ran to the bathroom, slammed the door, put my back to it and closed my eyes. Toots had never done anything like this before. "Why are you doing this now?" I cried. "Can you please not do this?"

When she spoke next, she stood in front of me, in the bathroom. "We haven't done this before because you were still grieving and it was inappropriate. Now that you've had a chance to speak with Debra Ann and she's forgiven you—you see, I was there, remember? Now it's absolutely appropriate. Don't you think? Come on, Slick, open those beautiful eyes of yours."

I opened my eyes slightly. She stood there unabashed, and for the first time, completely naked. I scrunched my eyes tight and groaned long and loud.

The cell phone rang in the other room.

"Don't answer it," she said. "Take me right now, Bub. Bend me over the sink and take me like I'm your love slave. I know you want to."

My heart started to flutter. I opened my eyes and locked them on hers, fighting the strong urge to look down her body. It hurt something fierce to say it. "You're a hallucination. You're a hallucination."

A large tear bulged then rolled down her cheek. Something else she'd never done was cry.

Before the tear fell from her face, she began to fade away.

IN THE BEDROOM the phone stopped ringing.

I stripped off my clothes, stepped over to the shower, bent over, and turned the water on. I let the water get hot before I stepped over the tub's edge into the bath. I peeked around the curtain. The room was empty. It was an emptiness I felt to the core. "Okay," I called out. "I'm sorry. Please come back."

"Pass me the soap, I'll get your back," she said from

behind me. I could hear the smile on her face before I turned to find her naked and beautiful.

I said, "To be fair to you, you have to know that I love Debra Ann."

Toots said, "We'll see about that."

I handed her the bar of soap, turned around, and put both hands against the cool tile wall. I closed my eyes and envisioned Debra Ann and the last thing she'd said out in the desert, out in front of Xaviers':

'I like it that you call her Toots.'

12

TOOTS KNEW I couldn't feel her touch. She said, "Hey, big boy, turn around."

I did but kept my eyes closed, trying to conjure up Debra Ann. Only her image wouldn't materialize. I couldn't push out Toots' wet nakedness. The water sprayed on my back and half-shot over my shoulder.

"Come on, big guy, open those pretty baby blues."

I did. I wanted to take her in my arms and kiss her. I wanted to so badly the emotional pain rose up in my chest. And this was Toots, not my Debra Ann.

She stood at the back of the shower with a soapy washcloth, the water sluicing down her body. The water and soap suds made her breasts slick and continued on down between her legs in a soapy stream. My eyes followed the path of the water.

She giggled. "You like this. I can see you like this. Go on, touch yourself. Don't be so old fashioned. It's not taboo like it used to be."

I shook my head no and kept my hand away from my erection. I couldn't believe this was happening. Sex with a hallucination. No, no, that was taking it too close to the edge. I tried to close my eyes but couldn't.

She giggled and massaged her breasts with the soapy washcloth, her large areolas darker now with the water. "Like this," she said. "Do it like this." Her free hand moved down between her legs, her fingers sliding, parting—

My fluttering heart leapt hard against my chest, hard enough to shoot an electric jolt up in my throat and down to my toes. My vision blurred. Toots' image sparked blue, sputtered, and blinked out, and Debra Ann appeared.

"Take it easy, Will," she said. "Take it easy, or you'll faint and drown in two inches of bath water."

Guilt for what I had been doing with Toots made me shrink mentally and physically as my erection ran for cover and found nothing but wet thatch. "I'm sorry, Debra Ann, it's not what you think. I was just--."

"Hush now. You have bigger problems. Someone's in our house. Keep still."

"WHAT? WHO?"

She stepped in close, her clothes getting soaked, the beige silk blouse turning see-through. Her areolas were round and dark. She put a finger up to my lips leaned in close.

"Shhhh."

Her breasts pressed against my chest. My erection instantly returned, harder, more alert than before. Dizziness spun around with the water. I couldn't focus on her words, the danger she spoke of. Her hips moved in. When we connected—her pelvis to my erection—my body let go, shuddered, and convulsed. I let out a long, low groan.

Then the bathroom door suddenly kicked open. Soaked, Debra Ann reached up, clamping her hand over my mouth.

Her words finally sank in. *Someone is in our house.*

I immediately turned angry, the longtime cop in me taking over. How dare someone violate this house and put my wife in danger.

Debra Ann whispered, "Remember, when you're in this state, your heart is always on the verge of total meltdown. You're going to need one of your pills soon. And Will....you're invisible."

The black blade of a carbon steel knife punched through the shower curtain like the sword penetrating a magician's box. Then the shower curtain was jerked aside. The intruder was wearing a black ski mask, revealing only cold brown eyes. His lips were thin and a little too pink in contrast against the black knit.

My instinct was to grab his arm and twist him up into a wristlock, but good sense won out. What if he wasn't alone? I moved Debra Ann around behind me away from this armed intruder. This was a burglar plain and simple, a perpetrator of a home invasion looking for a quick score to fuel his drug habit. He had heard the shower going, and afraid of being caught, came forward to silence any witnesses.

The suspect yanked the plastic curtain down to get a better look, surprised he'd found no one in the shower. He carried a lot of power through his shoulders and arms. Good thing I had not grabbed onto him. I suddenly felt vulnerable, naked and soapy and wet. I found myself holding my breath, which I could ill afford, with a body already starved of oxygen.

He stepped back, looking around the small bathroom for other places to hide, and found none. He spun and exited.

I got out to grab a towel, ready to go after him. I'd get my gun and pistol whip him, knock him unconscious, and cuff him. Then I'd jerk that mask off and find out who he was and call the police.

The floor was wet. I grabbed a towel swung it around my hips, took a step to go after him, and slipped on the wet floor. The water sports in the shower must have overcome the plastic curtain. I let out an inadvertent, "Whoa," and grabbed onto the sink before I fell on my kiester.

Debra Ann jerked the towel off. It fluttered to the floor as the crook reentered the bathroom at a run. I leaned up against the bathroom sink and sucked in my stomach to avoid contact. He radiated heat, possessed an animal instinct to kill that was palatable. So close, I should have been able to smell him. Why couldn't I smell him?

The man looked down at the towel, puzzled. He gazed right through me, caught his reflection in the mirror, held it for a second, spun and fled.

I followed along, my heart complaining about the exertion. He was younger and strong and cut through the quiet house in long bounds. His free hand went to his pocket, pulled a cell phone, and hit speed dial.

"He's not here."

It stopped me cold. This man had come for me. He'd come to kill me.

Worse, he was there on the orders of someone else.

13

MY BODY SHOOK from the chill as the adrenaline bled off. I stepped back into the bathroom for the towel and dried off, thinking about how I'd explain what happened to the police. An intruder entered the house, tore the shower curtain down, and somehow missed a naked man hiding in plain view? No way. Wouldn't fly.

Of course, I could make something up, but—

I dropped into the chair in the living room, the front door still wide open, as I realized what had happened out in the desert in front of Xaviers' had not been a dream or a delusion brought on by an over-taxed heart depriving the brain of oxygen. I'd really turned invisible.

Through a fog of confusion, I heard my cell phone ringing, back in the bedroom. The blasted thing quit before I could pull my thoughts together. Then the phone jingled again, indicating a voice message.

According to the missed calls index, three had gone unanswered. I hit play.

Wolford's voice came first: "It's nine-fifteen. Where the hell are you?" I glanced at the clock radio; it was now 9:45.

Toots was lounging on the bed smoking a Benson and Hedges, totally naked. "Was it as good for you as it was for me? Huh, Bub?" She growled like a tiger and showed her claws.

I swallowed hard and tried to focus, tried to look away

from her but couldn't. I pushed the button for the next message. Wolford said, "It's nine thirty. Where are you, asshole?"

Toots said, "He's a real punk. Forget about him, sweetie." She patted the comforter. "Come to bed, honey. I guess that doc was wrong about you and Mr. Johnson. You still got it. Whew."

"Please don't call me honey." Debra Ann called me honey.

The third message from Wolford: "I don't like to be stood up. You don't know who you're screwing with, mister."

I dialed him back. He picked up on the first ring. "Too late, asshole. You just blew a golden opportunity. I was going to pull your nuts out of the fire. You blew it, pal."

"Walt, I'm sorry, I don't know what happened. I just laid down for a nap and didn't wake up for nine hours. I've never done that before. I guess I'm still recovering. I'm sorry."

I suppressed the urge to tell him what had happened. I needed to tell someone. But what if he'd been the one Ski Mask was talking to on the cell as he fled our house?

Silence for a long moment.

Wolford said, "You were asleep, really?"

"Yes, I came right back from the station, like you said, and laid down. I was out cold."

"Oh, well…ah, I guess I'm sorry, then."

"Are you still at the Tick Tock? I can be there in twenty minutes."

"Yeah, I just pulled out of the parking lot. I'll turn around and go back. This is important."

It grinded me to say it, but I had to. "Thanks, Walt, I really appreciate this opportunity."

"Yeah, just get here. I've wasted enough time already." He hung up.

"What a peach," Toots said. "The man's a real peach."

I got dressed, throwing on what I always wore to work while in Specialized Investigations: a suit and tie with black wingtips. Tonight the suit was dark blue with a thin gray pinstripe, light blue dress shirt with a solid red tie. After all, this was an actual assignment of sorts. I checked the mirror and realized this had been the suit I wore the night Debra Ann burned. I had not worn it since. I had just passed a crossroads.

Out in the living room, I put the department issue Glock .45 in a paddle holster on my hip, clipped the sergeant's badge onto the belt, and grabbed the car keys. After a moment's reflection, I unhooked the badge and set it back on the table, a slight tremble in my hand. I hadn't felt like a cop since the meeting in Sheriff Novak's office when I admitted to the theft. Who was I kidding?

That's when I noticed the scent of tar and nicotine. I didn't smoke. Never have. Neither had Joan or Debra Ann.

At the entrance to the kitchen, Toots stood leaning against the wall, her hip canted at a sexy angle as she puffed her Benson and Hedges. She was fully clothed now, back in the red diaphanous dress and black spiked heels. She'd reapplied the red lipstick I must've kissed off of her lips in the shower.

I'd never noticed it before, but she was braless in the dress. She took the cigarette from her mouth between two fingers and pointed at me, the smoke curling up into her face, making her squint. "Bub, if I were you, I'd double check your equipment. I think there's been a weasel in the hen house."

I pulled the Glock and press checked it. The magazine was full but there wasn't a round in the chamber. I tried to remember the last time I'd checked the weapon and couldn't put a date or a time to it. My memory had gone mushy since the incident in the desert. But I always, always, kept one in the chamber.

Toots took a step into the living room, scooted onto the table that held the phone, feet off the ground, her legs swinging. "If it were me, tonight, I'd be very careful of someone trying to coax me into a gunfight."

"Well, you're not me."

She was a hallucination; my subconscious, but I asked her anyway. "Do you know who it was who came into the house and tampered with this, the guy with the big knife who wants me dead?"

"As a matter of fact, I do."

"Tell me."

"You don't have to worry, I got your back. I'll tell you when the dude's sneaking up on you with that machete. And when he does, I'll ace him out." She sliced the air with her hand imitating a karate chop.

"Quit jerking me around here and tell me, Toots. This is important."

"You saw and heard everything I did. You saw his eyes, heard his voice. I have confidence in you; you'll figure it out."

"I know the guy?"

She put her finger to her nose. "Give the cowboy a kewpie doll."

"I'm not messing around here. I want you to tell me right now."

"Bub, a little bit of sex and all your brains shoot out your little head along with the baby batter. You're better than this. Think about it. It'll come. If I know it, then you know it, too."

She'd heard the conversation with Debra Ann, all right. Toots had never mentioned anything about being an aberration of my subconscious; she'd gotten it from Debra Ann.

I held up my hand, my index finger separated from my thumb by an inch. "I'm *this* close to calling you a hallucination and meaning it. It'll send you away. You want to go away?"

"You want me to go away, Bub? You say it enough times and one day you're going to get better and I'll go away for good. That what you want? You better think about it." Tears welled in her eyes. "I just thought…well, I thought we passed a milestone or something, back there, in the shower. Wasn't it good for you? I thought…well, I thought we might be like penguins and we would be mates forever."

I gulped hard and closed my eyes. "Never mind." I racked a round into the chamber, holstered the gun, and went out to the car.

I didn't know whether she was following me. Didn't want to look back.

14

THE TICK TOCK sat sandwiched between Andy's, an upscale steakhouse, and an English pub called The Underground. All three were on Restaurant Row in the city of San Bernardino. Ten o'clock at night and the place was hopping. Some of the cars, like the plain-wrapped sheriff units, were familiar. This was a Sheriff's Department watering hole. Odd, I thought, that Wolford would pick such a visible place.

Clocks hung from the walls and on shelves, the motif linked to an elaborate and extended happy hour with deep-fried specials and sugary cocktails. Cops were known for drinking on the cheap. The entry, where the hostess stood, rattled with ambient noise from the timepieces, but the noise faded when I passed into the crowded bar, the sound merging with contented drinkers' conversations and clinking glasses. The floor was tongue-and-groove planks covered in wood shavings. The step-up booths, recessed and dark, showed only glimpses of suited legs and legs with nylon stockings and high heels, their owners but dim shadows.

The hustle and bustle alone was fatiguing and made me want to lie down and sleep, sleep for a year or two. I fought the fatigue. I needed to get this done and get out. Scanning the crowd, I recognized some faces; people who, when they recognized me, turned away and went back to what they were doing. Some smirked, others scowled. They didn't want to be seen in public talking with the likes of me. I was a common thief about to be tossed out on his ear, a cop morphing into one of *Them*, the criminals they were sworn to chase. It made me sick to my stomach. I didn't want to be one of *Them* and would give anything to be back in with the hunters of those men.

Toots turned to me and said, "Don't let these dipshits get to you, Bub. They don't know all the circumstances and if they did, they'd classify them as extenuating. You know, like Novak. Probably even pat you on the back for it. Trust me on this."

I caught Mike Bland's eye. He immediately turned to the bar and put his back to me. We'd worked as station detectives at Highland station when it first opened and after hours had hoisted many a beer.

Toots saw the move, hustled over, wiggled in between some other drinkers and got right in his face. "Hey, hey, buttlicker, do you know what this guy just did, not four days ago? Four, right, Bub? It was four, wasn't it?"

"Toots, don't." No one heard me over the din of conversations, the boisterous war stories.

Toots said to Bland, "That's right, Buster Brown, he went into harm's way to save a dispatcher, put his own life at risk, and—"

I couldn't listen, so I moved on down the line, searching for Wolford. Toots was wrong about that; I hadn't saved Sara Lang's life. She had died anyway. Mine was nothing but a futile gesture.

Further down the bar, Wolford broke away from a group of lawyers from the District Attorney's office and wove his way through, a smile large on his pudgy face. The irony of it: the way he socialized with the folks who, once he was caught, would prosecute him and throw him in prison. He held high a tumbler with an amber liquid, Crown Royal neat, the only cocktail he ever drank. And if memory served, he drank a lot of them. He wore relaxed denim pants with a salmon-colored, long-sleeve dress shirt and gold cuff links of little Sheriff stars. The man was a walking contradiction. He'd always portray someone who lived and breathed the Sheriff's Department, yet in reality he was no better than a common crook. Not even a good crook if he couldn't hide his money any better than he had. Not the way Novak got on to him so easily.

Wolford patted me on the back, his eyes glassy with drink. "Glad you could make it. Really, I mean that." He said it loudly over the clamor, louder than need be. A show for my benefit, letting everyone know *he* at least, was my friend. I might have believed his magnanimity genuine had he not glanced around, his smile turning fake, to see if anyone had been watching.

He guided me over to a booth filled shoulder to shoulder with fresh-faced young men sporting buzz-cut hair, all of them drinking tall schooners of beer. He held his thumb up. "Beat it FNG's, real cops need the space."

Toots said. "FNG's?"

I said, "Fucking New Guys." Wolford looked at me when I said it aloud.

The young men didn't even blink and started to slide out.

Toots waited patiently for a spot, moving out of their way. "Hey, you think if he throws a stick these guys would go fetch?"

Wolford glanced back at me. "Remember back when *we* were rookie jail Deps going out to the bars where the real cops drank? A whole lot of water's passed under that bridge, huh, bro?" His voice was loud enough for the eager young men to hear. His pompous arrogance made me uncomfortable.

Toots said, "Since when has he been a real cop? And *bro?* Where does he get off calling you bro? The nerve. I can't wait till you arrest him and get to say peek-a-boo, asshole."

I did remember being young and new and ignorant to the ways of the world. The nostalgia only served to enflame my guilt and remorse for having gone down the wrong road. One poor decision had sent me there. Maybe my subconscious had made the decision to take the money. Maybe I no longer wanted to be a cop and didn't realize it. I'd been unable to save Debra Ann, my own lovely wife whom I adored. Cops were sworn to protect, and I couldn't do my job as a cop or as a husband.

Toots found her opportunity, slid in, and hooked her thumb toward Wolford. "Don't let tub-o-guts here get you down. All this shit's going to work out. You're going to be back on top again, soon. Trust me on this."

How could she possibly know that? She only knew what I knew.

I said, "I wish you wouldn't use that kind of language."

Wolford shook his head. "I guess I'm getting used to you talking to your imaginary friends."

What he thought no longer mattered. I was through, my job over. I casually reached up to my inside suit coat pocket and surreptitiously activated the digital recorder. "They're not my little friends. It's my wife, Walt, Debra Ann, who I'm talking to." If I tried to explain Toots instead of Debra Ann he'd have thought me crazy. So Debra Ann would have to do.

Wolford froze and stopped his progression, sliding in the booth. "I'm sorry, Bill." His expression showed genuine remorse, and for a fleeting moment I wondered if I could go through with setting him up.

Sheriff Novak had installed an 800 line, an anonymous voicemail, where anyone could call and report anything they wanted concerning the department. An anonymous informant had called in and said two Sheriff's Captains were deeply involved in "corruption at the highest level," and that "the bastards need to be taken down before the cancer spreads." And: "It's gonna spread, trust me on this. It already has." The anonymous voice said these captains were "giving the department a black eye. They need to be taken down hard."

In a department of three thousand deputies, Novak had 26 captains. Novak had worked in narcotics as a deputy, then as a detective, and then again as a sergeant before moving on to administrative assignments. He wasn't a stranger to financial crimes. He'd conducted the sub-rosa investigation on each and every captain. Only one of them bubbled to the surface: Wolford. Wolford had purchased a home with fifty percent down in Highland, a city east of San Bernardino. The house cost nine hundred and fifty thousand dollars, which meant a down payment of four hundred and seventy-five thousand dollars cash. On a captain's salary, if he'd been frugal or if he'd sold another house, he could've pulled it off. But he wasn't and he didn't. Novak also found a paper trail to a vacation home in Lake Havasu, purchased two years before in his wife's name, another eight hundred thousand dollars. They'd paid cash for the house.

Whatever Wolford was into, he'd been at it for at least two years. Novak's dilemma was that he couldn't uncover the second captain who had been obviously more cunning than his partner Wolford. Without knowing the other culprit, Novak couldn't assign the investigation to an investigator who might be reporting to the unknown captain. Novak had a choice: call in the state guys to handle it, an outside agency to clean his own dirty laundry, or find someone he could trust. As it turned out, I strolled right into his office and confessed to a large theft. The way he put it, "A theft with extenuating circumstances." I'd taken the money from a dope trafficker and donated it to a good cause. The way Novak put it, who better to trust than a "semi-crook," legally in the wrong but at the same time on firm moral ground? Once the other captain was ferreted out, Novak would let me quietly walk away from the job. But Novak also needed enough evidence to prosecute. And he *was* going to prosecute. I had never seen him so livid.

The waitress came to the table. Wolford slurped down his Crown Royal and set it on her tray. "Another one of these, baby doll. What'll ya have, Bill?"

Toots said, "You call him Bill one more time and I'll cut your nuts off, whatever nuts you have. Bub, you think he's got any stones down there?" She smiled at me, trying to solicit a chuckle.

"I'll have a coffee, black."

"Bub, no caffeine, remember? The old ticker?" She patted her breast, her braless breast. For the last two years, how had I missed the braless thing?

"Ah, make that decaf, please." The waitress left.

Wolford stared, a sick little smile on his mug. I read it as gloating, that he had me over a barrel and was about to pull me down into the muck with him.

Toots saw that I was looking at him and said, "I hear ya, he's got more chins than a San Francisco phone book."

I ignored her.

Wolford finally spoke. "Before we get into it, I gotta ask you. Did you have any contact with Abel Jenks today?"

15

I NEVER WAS a good liar. I tried not to break eye contact but couldn't help it and looked away. "No, of course not. Why?"

"So you weren't out at the Taco joint today threatening to kill Abel Jenks?"

"Hey, Fatso, he said he wasn't there. Let's move on to putting the noose around that chubby neck of yours."

I said, "No, what are you talking about? What happened? What taco joint?"

Wolford said, "Jenks is a bona fide psycho. You must've put the fear of God in him some time ago and it's just now resurfacing like some repressed memory or something. Dewitt tackled him today and that gung ho ex-marine Mannerly tasered him. And strangely enough all the little prick wanted to do was file a criminal complaint against you. Hell, Dewitt said you weren't even out there, but the little puissant insisted on the complaint."

"Nope, wasn't out there. But I have to say if I had been I might not have been able to keep my hands from the pedophile's throat."

"I know, you guys go back and you have history. Anyway, what he did manage to do was convince a judge, through his attorney of course, to issue a temporary restraining order on the entire department. No one's allowed to go near him until there's a hearing on the matter next week."

"That doesn't sound good."

Wolford waved his hand in the air. "He'll have to prove you did it and if he can't prove you were even there how can he get anywhere at all with the judge? I'm not worried about it." He suddenly changed tones. "Okay, now, I talk, you listen. Not a word, you understand. You only nod your head."

I nodded.

"I'm going to let you in on a very lucrative proposition. I need someone, a runner if you will, for a very important assignment; someone who I can trust and knows his way around a homicide suspect. You do this and you will be paid...." He pulled a cocktail napkin over and wrote on it: "5k."

He was being careful with his words in case I was wired, which was smart.

He nodded as if asking if I understood.

I nodded back. "I appreciate this, I do. But what exactly is it that I have to do? I'm not going to whack someone. I won't do that."

He sat back; his expression morphing into anger. He held up his finger and pointed right at my nose. "Watch what you say, Bad Bill, or this conversation is over."

"That's it!" Toots said and lunged over the table at him. I jumped to stop her. The waitress had walked up and was setting the drinks down. I caught myself and reached for the coffee. It still looked funny, the abrupt movement for a cup of coffee.

"No, Bub, I warned him. That's it. I'm going to wrap some barbed wire around his nuts and drag him around the block."

Wolford took his drink, continuing to stare at me. I sipped the coffee and said to Toots, "It's always the nuts with you."

Wolford said. "What? What did you say about nuts?"

"Nothing. Go on. Continue, please."

He muttered under his breath, "I'm the one who's crazy, using a guy who's nuts." He shook his head. "You do a couple of these and it works out, then you'll be brought into the fold and given a regular salary whether you do the running or not.

Are you in? I need your answer before you walk out of here tonight. If you're in, you'll be notified later with the details of the assignment."

Toot's picked up my coffee and before she sipped it said, "What's with all this spy bullshit? What does he think this is, Casablanca or some shit like that? What a tool."

"I'm in, but I have to say I'm a little hesitant not knowing what this is about. What I'll have to do."

"Trust me on this. It's a milk run. And once you see what it is, you're going to think it far below your skill set. And it is, but once you're brought into the fold and understand the entire…er, setup, you'll know I'm doing right by you. In fact I think you're going to be stunned at how simplistic this deal is."

"Why me?" This was a question I thought I should ask if I'd had no prior knowledge of anything Novak had briefed me on. I had to play along until I was 'brought into the fold.'

"Why do you think? Because we came up together, worked the streets together. We were partners and you're in a bind right now. This is what partners do for each other."

"Oh, gag me."

She was right. There was no way I believed him. There had to be a subtext here, an ulterior motivation.

"Thanks, Captain, and I mean that. I can't thank you enough."

He slid out. "Just do this thing right and we'll talk again. You won't regret it. You'll be notified." He slugged back his drink, set the glass down on the table, and was gone.

I sat a minute, short of breath. I didn't realize the anxiety of the meeting had elevated my pulse. My heart didn't like the stress. I leaned back, closed my eyes, and focused on relaxing.

"Will? Will Donnelly?"

I opened my eyes to find a woman standing in front of the booth. She had short red hair and bright hazel eyes. Her lips were full and lightly masked with a soft, unassuming lipstick. She had a light spray of freckles across her nose and under her eyes. She wore a nice stylish dress with a belt at the waist. The entire package made her very attractive. But if you took away one or two of these attributes she'd sink into mediocrity and fade away into a crowd.

She held out her hand to shake. "Oh, my god. You don't recognize me, do you?"

Toots said, "I do. Bimbo alert. Grab your Johnson, Bub, grab him and hold on, 'cause this sleaze is here to take you for a ride."

"No, I'm sorry, I guess I don't. It's been a long day."

The woman slid into the booth, all the way around until we were almost touching, bold and presumptuous. "That was really something, what you did out in the desert."

I smelled mint with an alcoholic beverage chaser.

"She's a groupie looking for a quick poke in the whiskers. Don't fall for it, Bub. It's a come-on, nothing but a cheap come-on."

With a closer examination, she was about my age. I said, "Don't keep me guessing. I already feel like a big enough fool."

"I don't know if I should be mad or what I should feel, really. Will, it's me, Mary."

"Mary?"

"Oh, shit," Toots said. "Internal Affairs Mary."

"For crying out loud, it's me, Mary Rhymes. Now, I *am* going to be mad."

16

MARY HELD UP her hand to flag the waitress who stood amongst the throng across the room—close to ten men grouped around a small table—frantically taking down orders.

Mary smelled so nice. I hadn't seen her in twenty some years; hadn't thought about her, not during the time of Joan and then Debra Ann. She'd dyed her hair red. With Mary sitting close, she sparked that old flame. I knew it was my messed-up situation and the need to talk to someone, the need to be emotionally close. What did I have to lose?

"Watch her, Bub, she's here to work you like a beef rib. If you know what's good for you, you'll kick this dried-up wench to the curb. Do it right now, Bub. Tell her, Bub, tell her about me. Tell her what we just did in the shower, how good we are together."

Mary turned, looked me in the eye, and picked up my hand. "I heard about your wife. I'm so sorry for your loss."

A lump rose in my throat. Even after two years, I didn't know what to say and felt guilty being close to this woman when I still loved Debra Ann the way I did. I looked away. "Thank you."

Mary's soft touch found the gold wedding band on my hand and turned it round and round. I liked her touch and looked back at her.

Mary smiled. The amount of alcohol she'd consumed soon became evident in her eyes and expressions; she'd clearly learned to mask it pretty well. She wasn't entirely in control of her emotions; the alcohol was impairing her good judgment. If she was in her right mind she wouldn't be sitting with, let alone talking to, a department member with pending discipline. Too big of a conflict with her being the head of internal affairs. She said, "Remember that night we went to the movies and parked in that underground parking structure in LA. We started kissing and one thing led to another. We crawled into the backseat." She looked away, a red blush rising up her neck. She laughed. "We missed the previews and half the movie. You remember that, Will?"

I had forgotten. The memory rose up bright and beautiful as a high point in our relationship. She'd always been a kind and considerate lover.

She asked, "What was that movie, anyway?"

I didn't remember and felt sad the memory had tarnished to such a degree.

Toots said, "It was *Fatal Attraction*. Run, Bub. Get up right now and run for your life before she comes at you with the metaphorical butcher knife like Glenn Close and eviscerates you emotionally."

I said to Mary, "You probably shouldn't be sitting here, not with me."

"Oh, please...." She slid back around and out of the booth. "You and I, we're old partners. We came up together, worked the jail. Don't worry about it." She waved her hand. Standing, she swayed on her feet. "I'm going to the ladies. When the girl comes around can you order me an Old Fashioned?"

Mary moved off. I whispered to Toots, "Can you go with her to make sure she's okay?"

Mary's head whipped around. "You talking to me, Will?"

"Ah, no, no."

Mary nodded and disappeared into the crowd. Toots said, "Bub, you're playing with fire here. She might be that second captain you're looking for and if she is, she's playing you to see if you're going to report to Novak on her partner. Wolford's contact. Think about it Bub, if her partner's that fat-ass Wolford, do you really want to kiss that mouth of hers? Do you really want to do the nasty with Wolford by proxy?" She shook herself. "Ugh, I can't even imagine."

Toots' words hit home. Not the sex part. But Mary used some of the same words Wolford had. I got up, tossed some cash on the table, and wove my way out of the bar. The fresh night air was invigorating after the hot, close bar.

I had the key in the door when Mary from behind said, "Will? Will, where are you going? Why'd you run off that way?" She walked unsteadily on high heels to catch up. Before she got to me she miss-stepped and lunged. Fell into my arms, her body hot and inviting. She looked up. "Thanks."

"Oh, gag me. She did that on purpose. That entire move was done on purpose. Can't you see it, Bub? Toss the ho to the ground and let's get out of here."

Mary gently pushed away and straightened her dress. "Sorry, Will, this is no way for a captain to act. I don't usually drink so much. It's a special occasion."

"Bullshit, Bub, she's not as drunk as she's letting on. This is all part of the web this black widow is weaving. Next she'll have you tied up with that long beak of hers, piecing your neck and sucking your blood."

I said to Toots, "Would that be so bad?"

Mary looked at me funny.

I waved off my comment, said, "You're in no condition to drive. Let me drive you home."

Toots pulled back and slugged me. I cringed, waiting for the blow even though I knew it would pass right through.

Mary put a hand on my arm. "Are you feeling okay?"

"Sure. Come on, this is my car."

I opened the passenger door for her. On the seat was a cheap briefcase. Taped to it was a white piece of paper with "*Bad Bill*" written in red ink. These were instructions from Wolford. Mary didn't say anything. I reached in, picked up the brief case as if the thing meant nothing, and tossed it in the backseat.

Mary got in. I closed the door. Toots' eyes brimmed with tears. I hadn't meant to hurt her. I whispered, "Come on, don't be that way. Get in the back." I opened the back door for her and let her get in. Mary swiveled in her seat. I reached in and adjusted the briefcase as a cover.

In the car with the engine started, I said, "I'm sorry. I don't know where you live?"

Mary watched me with a confused expression. "Highland Ranch. Take Baseline out to Green Spot road."

Toots said, "See, I'm right. That's where Wolford lives. He lives in Highland, right?"

I drove out Hospitality Lane and north on Waterman. In the rearview Toots sat with her arms across her chest, her bottom lip out. She said, "You going to kiss her good night?"

I didn't answer. Mary had already seen too much eccentric behavior.

"I'll tell you right now, Bub, she's like one of those pretty red apples, all shiny and bright on the outside, but as soon as you take a bite she'll turn all mealy and mushy right in your mouth."

Mary looked over her shoulder into the back seat. "Is something wrong? Is someone following us?"

"No, everything's fine." I switched my attention back to the road and turned east on Baseline.

Mary said, "To be honest, Will, I probably could've driven home but I wanted to talk to you."

"I kind of figured as much."

She put her hand on my arm.

Toots leaned over from the back seat, her mouth gaping. "Come on now, no touching."

Mary said, "You know I shouldn't be talking with you at all, but I couldn't live with myself if I didn't say something. I thought about calling you and every time I picked up the phone I put it down when my good sense took over. Tonight, when you came into the bar, I took it as fate and knew I had to say something."

Toots leaned back, her arms across her chest again. "She's lying. All she wants is another go at Mr. Johnson. You know I'm right, Bub. You do her and you'll regret it the rest of your days. Trust me on this."

I said nothing.

Mary said, "We're finished with the administrative investigation, our end, and Novak has instructed captain Coleman from Special Investigations to do the criminal. Which really stinks. Coleman's your captain and he's a friend of yours, isn't he?"

"There's nothing unusual about that. Novak is following procedure and so is Coleman."

"I know, but when they interview you on the criminal don't say anything. Lawyer-up. Let your attorney develop a strategy and stick to it."

"There's nothing a lawyer can do. I stole the money and I have to pay."

"You'll go to prison, Will."

Toots leaned forward again. "That's not true, is it, Bub? Is it?" Toots was my subconscious and I guess I had always been kidding myself about the prison part. Toots leaned back and smirked. "Huh."

I looked in the rear view at her. She chuckled a little. "How in the world are they going to keep the invisible man locked up? Huh, Bub? Tell this little witch that, huh?"

That was a valid point. Toots sat the briefcase on her lap and opened it. Enthralled, I watched her in the rear view. I really wanted to know what the envelope contained, what Wolford had in store for me and what kind of criminal conspiracy he was wrapped up in. Toots held something out of view on the other side of the briefcase. "Well, I'll be a monkey's uncle. This is really bizarro, Bub. You're not going to believe this."

I started to sweat. We rode in silence, Mary looking out the passenger window, obviously thinking about something. She finally said, "You know I'm up for Deputy Chief when

Rankin retires next month. I got a shot, a very, very small shot." She held up her thumb and forefinger, an inch apart.

"That's great. I have no doubt you'll get it. Congratulations. I don't know anyone who deserves it more."

She turned in her seat. I sensed she was looking at me. "You know," she said, "now that I've made it, I don't know if the sacrifice was worth it."

"What do you mean?"

"I loved working the streets, chasing the crooks. I gave all that up to follow an administrative career. Now it's too late to go back. I miss it. And I regret my choice."

I didn't know what to say.

She continued, "You did it right. You followed your dream. You worked Specialized Investigation longer than anyone on the department. Hell, you ran that division and Coleman owes you big for it. Now he's the one nailing your coffin shut."

I turned onto Green Spot Road.

Toots said, "Yeah, that's right. That same division he worked so hard for is now trying to throw his ass in the slammer. That's gratitude for ya. She's right about that, Bub. She gets some points for that, Bub."

She said, "Make a right up here, two streets, then a left."

We both watched the houses pass by. She said, "There's something else I regret even more." Then: "Right here, pull up in front of the house with the faux rock fascia."

I stopped the car and put it in park. I knew what she was going to say. I said, "I know."

"You do?"

"Yes."

She said, "When this is all over, do you think we could go out, I mean to a nice dinner or something, maybe drive into LA to see a movie?"

"Sure." I couldn't believe Toots hadn't interjected with some snide comment.

Then she did. She leaned forward and whispered, "I can't believe it. This ho's flipped; she's gone to the other team. She's a carpet muncher."

Now, this was the Toots I knew, trying to cloud the issue with whatever she could in order to distract me. How wrong could she be?

Mary waited a long second, opened the door, and got out. I leaned over and said. "But I don't want to lead you on." She leaned back in to hear the rest. I said, "I still love my wife Debra Ann, and I don't think that's going to ever change."

Ordinary Mary smiled. "I wouldn't want it any other way."

17

THE WOMAN AT the gate peered over my shoulder, searching for the second passenger, when I handed her two tickets to Houston on United flight 246 out of Los Angeles.

I said, "It's okay, I bought the extra ticket because I like the elbow room."

Truth was, I hated to fly and needed Toots next to me for moral support.

Cooped up with three hundred people in a thin-skinned metal tube, propelled at five hundred miles an hour, by jet engines, was not my idea of a good time. I'd flown only one other time in my life, to extradite a rapist from Arkansas. That trip was a white-knuckler as well. I said I'd never do it again and yet there I was, high-stepping it down the skyway with a small carry-on that contained a briefcase with a cell phone, a cheap laptop, some cash for expenses, and an address.

The instructions in the envelope marked *Bad Bill* had been explicit: fly to Houston, rent a car, drive to 1635 River View Drive, knock on the door, and identify yourself as a sergeant with San Bernardino County Sheriff's Department to one Henry Octavio Sanchez. I'd instruct him to go inside where we'd sit at his dining room table. Once we were alone I'd use the cell to get further instructions. I had to be there at exactly 8:00 p.m. or the deal was off.

A couple problems. Firstly, I didn't know what the deal

was, and secondly, the timetable was subject to too many variables: possible delayed flight, the time necessary to rent a car, and then the time needed to find the address. A lot could go wrong. And according to Murphy's Law, it would.

I put the carry-on in the overhead and sat in the middle seat, leaving the seat by the window vacant for Toots. I had no desire to look out the window as we left mother earth. So I sat back, closed my eyes, and tried to concentrate on keeping my heartbeat at a reasonable pace.

After a few moments Toots whispered into my ear. "Take it easy cowboy. You're right on the edge. You go invisible here, you'll panic the entire plane and make the afternoon news nationwide. Here, take a gander at these. They used to always calm your nerves."

Before I had the chance to decide what she meant, I peeked. She'd leaned over to let the swoop neck of her red diaphanous dress dip open to expose two exquisite breasts. "Can you hear them, Bub? These puppies are yapping for some attention."

"Oh, and like that's going to calm my heart. Are you crazy?"

A gray-haired woman scooted into the aisle seat next to us just in time to hear what I said and gave me a wary eye. I put my head back and closed my eyes, which were stinging from sweat.

Tough, let the old gal think she's sitting next to a psychopath.

I needed to focus or else the inside of the plane was going to get real loud with riot and panic.

A moment later the old woman put a warm hand on my arm. "Excuse me, son, is anyone sitting there? I'm sorry, but I get queasy sometimes when I can't sit by the window."

I opened my eyes and looked at her. On the other side of me Toots said, "Come on, Bub, I've never sat at a window before."

I didn't need any of this. First and foremost I needed to focus.

"Sure," I said, and wiggled until I got to my feet. The old

woman pushed herself out of her seat, stepped into the aisle, and I let her pass.

"Okay, then, I want the aisle. I get the aisle, Bub." I didn't argue. I sat in the middle seat, my oversize shoulder nudging the old woman. She leaned away closer to the window and said, "Really?"

Toots said, "Bub? Bub?"

"Be quiet, would you. Just sit back and enjoy the flight, would you, please?"

The old woman said, "Well, I never."

I shrugged, closed my eyes, and tried to go to sleep. Toots had been right: the after-image of her lovely breasts did have a soothing effect.

I WOKE TO the plane touching down hard in Houston, the side of my chin wet with drool, my head resting on the old woman's shoulder. The old woman shoved me as I sat forward.

She said, "That was the worst flight I have ever taken in my life, thank you very much."

"Sorry, I have this condition. I'm tired all the time and—"

"Just let me out. Let me out."

Toots got up but was shoved back toward us as passengers cluttered the aisle to retrieve their carry-ons from the overheads.

"Rude," Toots said, and shoved back.

I felt strangely refreshed.

Half an hour later we were in a rented Ford Taurus headed to River View Drive. Toots squirmed in the passenger seat. "You're not the least bit interested in what this is all about?"

"Of course I am."

"We're walking right into an unknown situation, blind. We have no idea what's going on here."

"The way I see it, we don't have any options. Not if we want to find out what Wolford is up to, and more importantly, uncover the other captain. What's really interesting is that they're using the department in their scam. I'm supposed to identify myself as a sheriff's sergeant."

"Why didn't you call Novak and brief him on what we're doing? I mean, we're out of state where your police powers are null and void."

"What could Novak do? This isn't a sanctioned investigation. It can't be, not if he wants to keep it completely quiet. For all we know the Under Sheriff is involved. If we were sanctioned by the department we'd have to get letters to the airline to carry a gun, interdepartmental notifications, detectives at the other end to assist. There would be too many people in the loop and word would get out. No, I thought about it, and it's much better this way."

"Watch it," she said, "this is our turn."

I turned onto River View and as I did my heart started to beat faster with anticipation of the confrontation.

To the right all the homes sat back from the street with crushed-shell driveways. The lots had to be half acres. The homes were all well groomed and manicured. Most were red brick with inviting lights on in the windows. Across the street from the houses the river ran quietly with gray docks like so many teeth slotted with sail and motor cruisers.

"Nice digs," Toots said. "What do you think these pads are worth?"

"I don't know California real estate prices, and you want me to guess at houses in Texas?"

"You don't need to get snippy, Bub. I told you not to take that money. Remember? I hate to be an *I-told-you-so*, but guess what?" She paused. "Oh, there it is, the house we're looking for. And that must be Sanchez out front."

I checked the clock on the dash. Seven-forty. We were twenty minutes early.

She said, "Look at the way that guy's giving us the eye. He's a full-on predator. I told you, you should've brought the Glock. Now, if it comes down to a violent confrontation, all you're going to have in your hand is Mr. Johnson."

FIRE AT WILL

She was right. The man had thinning black hair, and was dressed in black slacks and a white long-sleeved dress shirt. As he watered his lawn, he kept his gaze on us.

I had no choice; I pulled right into his driveway, the tires crunching.

We'd just have to kill some time with small talk until eight, the time designated for the phone call.

As I got out, Sanchez stepped backward, never taking his eyes off of us. His hand went behind him, fumbling for the spigot, and shut off the hose.

"Mr. Sanchez? Mr. Henry Sanchez?"

He said nothing and quick-stepped backward toward the open front door. He didn't turn to enter but backed up as though he were afraid I'd pull a weapon. He disappeared into the dim recess. Then inside lights went off.

Toots said, "Oh, shit."

"Yeah."

18

MY HEART BATTERED against my ribs at the thought of going in after Sanchez. I took out the nitro bottle, shook a small white pill into my hand and hoped the sweat wouldn't dissolve it. We stopped at the threshold to the front door.

Toots said, "All right, what're we going to do now, Barney Fife?"

I ignored her and spoke loud enough for Sanchez to hear. "Henry, my name's Will Donnelly. I need to talk with you."

From deep in the house came, "Talk about what? What is it you want?"

Hell if I knew.

Toots said, "Ask him why he ran when he saw us, huh? Ask him that, Bub. He showed a consciousness of guilt if you ask me."

I ignored her and said, "I have something to show you on my laptop." I hadn't been able to get into the password-protected laptop, but common sense dictated that I'd get the password during the phone call, and then Sanchez and I would find out together what this was all about.

"Just go away."

"I can't go away."

"Why?"

"I just can't."

He said, "I have a gun."

"Oh, shit, Bub, we have to back off and call the local cops."

"I told you, we can't do that."

"Who are you talking to out there?"

"Nobody. Listen, I'm with the Sheriff's department. I don't have a gun. I just need to talk with you, then I'll go away."

"You're talking right now, so talk."

"Someone's going to see me standing out in your front yard here, speaking to the side of your open door. Your house is dark. They're going to call the police. I don't think that's something you want."

"You bet your ass he doesn't want that."

"Sssh."

Sanchez said, "I thought you said *you were* the police."

"I am, but it's complicated."

"That's good, Bub. Keep going on that tack."

My heart pinged and with each ping a pain shot down my spine into my leg and down through my foot. I put my fist to my chest and stifled a groan. "Listen," I said to Henry Sanchez, "I'm not going to be a cop much longer."

This hurt to say, especially to a civilian, someone who didn't understand the brotherhood to which cops belonged. "You see, awhile ago I took some money...and...and they're going to file charges on me when I get back."

The lights came on. Henry Sanchez crouched in the dining room right at the pass-through to the living room, aiming an old Winchester repeating rifle. "Come in and close the door."

"Bub, you go in there and he's got you. He can ace you out, drag your sorry carcass down to the river, and toss you in."

I went in anyway and closed the door behind me.

Sanchez came out of his crouch, leveling his rifle at my navel. Motioning with the weapon, he said, "Go in there and sit down. Who are you talking to? Are you wired?"

"No, this isn't a sanctioned visit. I'm here on my own."

"Oh no, Bub, you shouldn't have told him that."

Sanchez stopped following and froze with a confused

expression. The pinging pain increased the tempo of my heart, shooting down my leg.

"Bub, you better sit down before you fall down."

I sat on the couch. The briefcase banged against my knee as sweat beaded on my forehead. The nitro pill had turned to paste in my other hand. I had to put my head back and close my eyes or risk…I couldn't even think about what I'd turn into.

Gradually the clock slowed to match my heartbeat. No, it was the other way around. I opened my eyes and noticed a blank spot over the fireplace mantle with two pegs where Henry had pulled down the Winchester. On the couch next to me sat the briefcase, open; the laptop was on the table. Next to that was my open wallet with the gold star exposed, declaring my membership—my soon-to-be-terminated membership—in San Bernardino County Sheriff's Department. Sanchez had been busy. Toots sat across the coffee table in an easy chair, legs crossed in a casual manner. "Nice to have you back, Bub."

"How long have I been out?"

Henry Sanchez leaned against the dining room table, the gun pointing at the floor. He looked tired. He checked his watch, said, "About twenty-seven and a half minutes. Now, tell me, why are you here?"

"He searched you, Bub, head to toe. For a moment I thought maybe he was going flip you over and make a woman out of you. Thought he might tie you up, but he doesn't think you're a threat because of the condition of your heart."

"This is going to sound crazy," I said, "but I don't know why I'm here. I was given instructions to find you and once I did, I was to make a phone call at exactly 8:00 p.m."

"You need a pacemaker and probably an implanted defibrillator. That banged-up heart of yours can shut down anytime for the least little excuse."

"And you know this how?"

"He's a doctor, Bub. Works the ER at the local hospital. He's well liked. Everyone calls him Hank and invites him over to their houses for barbequed hot links and Pabst Blue Ribbon.

He plays the guitar, does a great rendition of *Bridge Over Troubled Water*."

Henry Sanchez said, "If you don't know, I'm not going to tell you. You apparently haven't done your homework before flying out here. I'm going to ask you again, why are you here?"

"You're an emergency room doc, here in town."

That information let the air out of him.

"Bub, he thought you knew nothing about him and for a few minutes there he was scheming to kill you and drop your sorry carcass in the river across the street."

"But why?"

Sanchez thought I was talking to him and said, "I didn't think anyone would find me here. It's been a long time, a very long time. I changed my name, came to this little town outside of Houston.... How the hell did you find me?"

"I didn't find you. Wait, what time is it?"

"Time no longer matters to me. Not now."

Toots said, "Eight-fifteen."

I sat forward too fast. The air in the room turned thick and the floor tilted. I fought through it, grabbed the cell phone, and pushed the pre-designated number. On the other end the phone rang once and then someone picked up.

"You're late. Is there a problem?"

I couldn't tell if the voice was Wolford's.

"No, no problem. Everything is the way you asked."

The man on the phone paused a long moment. "Okay, open the laptop and power it up."

"That's done already."

"Type in the password, 'Extortion', with capital E."

I watched Sanchez out of the corner of my eye as I followed instructions. The letters appeared as little asterisks, but he'd watched my fingers dance on the keys and followed their path. He sat back. His expression fell.

The screen loaded automatically to Skype. Two people in ski masks sat at a small round table. From the background—the cheap painting on the wall, the drab curtains—it looked like a dive motel room. Both people wore gray trench coats and gloves. The one man put the cell phone down and said, "Now move the computer so we can see Mr. Sanchez."

I shifted the screen so the camera in the laptop picked up Sanchez.

I watched over the top of the laptop and listened.

"Mr. Henry Octavio Sanchez, after thirty-one years, five days, and sixteen hours, justice has finally caught up with you."

Toots moved around to watch both the screen and Sanchez. All the color had drained from Sanchez's face.

Wolford, or the man who I thought was Wolford, slid a second laptop into view and lined it up perfectly with the camera while keeping the extortionist center frame. "Here's a little slide show presentation we put together just for you." Wolford pushed a button. Graphic photos of murder scenes floated across the screen. The background, the furniture, the color of carpets, curtains, the decor of these photos set the date thirty years before. The last piece of the puzzle. I now understood my role in Henry Sanchez' house.

Wolford spoke. "Thirty years ago, Mr. Henry Sanchez, you were a serial killer. While attending medical school in Los Angeles, you killed one prostitute every three to four months for six years. Your killing ground spanned three counties."

I looked over at Toots. Her mouth hung open, her eyes wide with shock. My heart fluttered and bounced hard against my chest. The lights in the living room sparked blue. Toots turned translucent and faded away. Debra Ann appeared in her place. She rushed over. "Quick, your clothes."

I didn't have much strength with my heart doing the mambo. She helped with my pants as I pulled my polo shirt over my head. Sanchez stared mesmerized at the screen, unable to look away from his accusers.

Wolford said, "Cold case detectives finally caught up to your cases and reexamined the San Bernardino County's murders. They ran DNA and got a hit, on guess who. We," he pointed to his partner who had yet to say anything, "have decided that it is better for the suspect we uncovered to pay back society, but not with years of his life incarcerated, doing nothing, wasting away. No, we've decided it would be better for you to give back to society a small iota of what you stole. So for the rest of your life you will pay us a monthly stipend that will leave you living just above poverty. That will be your penalty. We've done our homework. You are to wire twenty-one thousand dollars a month to—"

Sanchez brought the Winchester up and shot the laptop. The explosion lit up the walls and clogged my ears with a loud ringing. The laptop crackled and popped and was flung across the room with the unexpected violence. Sanchez came out of his trance, leveled the rifle, chambering another round, and swung it to where I had been standing.

I'd moved and was naked with the exception of my black socks. I froze, too scared to move. He looked down at the pile of my clothes, confused for a moment. He swung the rifle around to cover the room. "Where'd you go? Why'd you take your clothes off? I'll find you, you sick little pervert." He rushed from the room and out of sight down the hall.

Debra Ann put her warm hand on my arm. *I could feel her.* I took her in my arms and kissed her long and deep. I didn't care about the mad man with the rifle looking to kill me. All I wanted to was to hold her and never let her go. She melded to my body, hers hot against mine. I didn't want it to end. I savored every moment of her presence.

She pulled away, breathless. "Babe, your socks. You have to take your socks off."

"Not now."

Henry Sanchez rushed into the room, eyes wild. "I heard you, you're in here."

I carefully moved Debra Ann behind me to shield her from the armed psychopath.

The movement of the socks caught Henry's eye. His mouth dropped open. He was puzzled, sure, but Henry Sanchez was also a stone killer with keenly honed survival instincts.

He pointed the Winchester at me and fired.

19

THE LARGE CALIBER rifle round tore into my side and spun me around. I fell back and flipped over the couch to the other side. Sanchez leveled the rifle and fired again and again through the couch. The bullets buzzed over my torso and head and thudded into the wall. White smoke billowed with bits of stuffing floating in the air. I lay there unable to move, my heart trying desperately to catch up to the situation.

Debra Ann said, "Your socks. Get them off!"

I couldn't move. I had just enough strength to work my lungs. I'd been shot. No pain from the wound, though, only a searing heat that intensified, doubling and tripling with each second. Something tugged at my socks. Debra Ann. She tossed them aside as Sanchez peeked around the end of the couch. When he didn't see what he expected—a wounded and/or dying man, he looked startled.

Debra Ann said, "The blood, he's going to see your blood as it leaves your body and materializes."

I pressed my hand harder into the wound and gathered my knees underneath me. She was right. Blood appeared in a widening puddle on the spotless white carpet. I coughed. Sanchez jumped back, leveled the gun and aimed it right at me. A good guess based on the blood.

"Will!"

I fell and rolled out of the way. Another explosion from

the gun. Sanchez levered the gun. How many rounds did the rifle hold? I came up on my feet, grunting with the effort, the heat from the pain turning difficult to manage. I was trapped behind the couch without options and nowhere to move. I sucked in my gut and inched my way beside Sanchez. He was less than a foot away. Sweat ran in rivulets down the sides of his pale, acne-scared face. His eyes were wild with desperation.

"What's going on?" he said. "Where are you?" He moved his foot to rub the blood puddle in his white rug. "What the hell's going on? This isn't possible."

Debra Ann said, "Tell him you're a ghost from one of the women he killed and you've come to exact your pound of flesh. Say it, Will. It's your only weapon now."

I didn't want to play in this invisible world. I didn't want to accept those rules, that unbelievable reality. I shoved Sanchez hard.

He leaned over with one hand to catch himself on the couch as he fell. He yelped from the touch but kept a loose grip on his rifle, enough to swing the weapon around to where I stood and pull the trigger.

Click.

On his back on the couch he levered and fired again. *Click. Click.* In a panic he jumped up and ran out of the living room, down the hall and out of sight.

Debra Ann said. "He's going for another gun. He's going to track you by your blood."

Splotches, red on white—macabre Rorschach blots on the carpet—trailed where I had been right up to where I stood. I thought about picking up a couch pillow to hold against the wound but realized how stupid that was. He'd see the pillow suspended in the air, a perfect target. *Suspended in the air?* I was accepting my fate and didn't like it.

Debra Ann said, "You have to move. You have to do something. Don't just stand there and wait for him to come out and shoot you dead."

For the briefest of moments I thought about my demise as a solution to all of my problems. Then the survival instinct kicked in. I picked up the poker from the set next to the fireplace, went to the dining room table, set the poker on the chair, and then I sat on the table edge. I held my wound at my side, pressed hard, and tried not to let the blood—which was subsiding now—drip on the floor or table.

Sanchez rushed out of the hallway with a brown leather grip in one hand and a small handgun in the other. Outside, sirens pierced the quiet night, penetrating the walls.

In his rush he had not seen the poker lying across the arms of the chair. Henry stepped close to me, his gun pointed toward the living room, searching for the threat.

I picked up the poker, the weight of it almost too much. I hesitated. In all the years on the Sheriff's Department I had never shot anyone in the back. With his back to me I couldn't hit him with the poker. I slid off the table, intent on slowly easing into a bathroom or bedroom to hide until he left.

The sirens came closer.

The warmth of a long bead of blood rolled down my naked hip, down my leg to my foot. I suppressed another cough. Henry whirled around and brought his little gun to bear. I raised the poker in self-defense. Still I couldn't do it.

He looked surprised to see the poker suspended alone in the air, poised to take his life. Then the light in his eyes shifted, and he morphed from fearful prey into the predator who'd killed all those women thirty years ago.

A warm hand wrapped around mine. Debra Ann. She swung with mine as Sanchez tightened his finger on the trigger.

The thunk reverberated up my arm.

Sanchez wilted to the floor with a new slot down the center of his forehead, his eyes wide, looking at nothing.

20

MY HEART CONTINUED to calm as we drove away. I rolled the windows down to let the sultry night air flow across my damp skin. Two cop cars zoomed past with lights and sirens.

I had just killed someone. The guilt weighed heavily on my already over-burdened heart—a weight that threatened to smother me.

"I don't know why we're running," I said. "My fingerprints and blood are all over the place."

"Just drive. I took care of the fingerprints, and if they don't have a comparison in the computer, they can't track you with DNA."

I was still naked. Debra Ann was gone, Toots left in her place.

"Head for the country, Bub. You don't want to pull into the Quicky Mart naked as a jaybird and have some little twelve-year-old girl eating a banana popsicle say mommy, look..."

"Do you mind? I think I have this."

She puffed out her lip.

I said, "I'm sorry. Really, I am. But can you give me a break here? I'm a little stressed out."

I finally pulled onto the highway. The long uninterrupted road was soothing. After twenty minutes we came to a rest stop and pulled all the way to the back, away from the five or six other cars in the lot. I didn't want to risk getting out. I reached into the back to get a fresh set of clothes from the carry-on. The wound in my side reminded me I'd been shot with a large-bore rifle. I chanced turning on the dome light. Luckily the round had hit at a good angle, right in the fat of the love handle. Nothing vital there. The puckered purple and blue wound had stopped bleeding and only oozed.

"A large-bore rifle like that and the round didn't even punch on through," I said. "The lead ball is still in there around the back side. I can feel it. It's just under the skin."

Toots crossed her arms over her chest, still mad at the way I'd talked to her. She said, "Not surprising. That gun was an antique. Those bullets were seventy-three years old and loaded with old black powder that had lost its potency. Otherwise you'd have been stuffed and hung on that killer's wall. A real trophy. A jerkwater cop from the land of fruits and nuts. You strolled right in there with nothing but Mr. Johnson in your hand. I can't say I didn't warn you."

I struggled into my pants, strength returning more and more. I started to ask how she knew about the bullets and the age of the black powder and remembered something more important. "You said she took care of the fingerprints. How did you do that?"

"Really? You want me to spell it out for you? Think about it for a minute, would ya? Really, Bub? Come on."

I took a pair of clean boxer shorts, folded them up and gently pressed them against the wound. With the spare belt I wrapped it around my waist to hold the boxers in place.

"Okay, I'll take a stab at it. When…when I'm in that other place…invisible, I mean, time sort of expands and contracts, right?"

"This is your story."

"Or maybe it's not time that's different, maybe it's my mind shielding things… No, wait, only allowing certain things to register in my brain as memory. *I* was the one who really cleaned up the place."

"You're smarter than you look, Bub."

"So, if that's the case, then maybe my brain is making this invisible thing more real than it is." I looked into her eyes, sad. Not for her but for myself. I really was off my nut and now officially met the requirements of Welfare and Institutions Code 5150. I was a *danger to myself and others.*

Toots carried on as if there was nothing wrong. She couldn't read me as well as Debra Ann. "Time isn't linear when you flash invisible, and—"

I held up my hand to stop her. "That's okay. I can live without knowing how it works." Now I was hiding the truth from a hallucination. "No, that's not true, I know how it works. I've crossed that fine line the shrink told me about. I've wandered deep into no-man's land with no way back."

"Who pissed in your Wheaties? Snap out of it. We still have a long way to go before we're home."

I put on my shirt as my side started to stiffen. When I looked over at the passenger seat, Toots was gone. Panic struck strong enough to almost shift me back to that *in-between place*, until I glanced up in the rear view and spied her in the backseat rummaging through the grip.

She didn't look up, her arm deep in the bag, "We better shag ass. We've been here too long. Make for the airport; we have to get back."

"Why?"

She stopped what she was doing and looked up into the mirror. "Come on, Bub, we've been over this. Whatever I know you know."

I started the car and shifted into drive. "If you truly know what I know, then you'll realize I am on the razor edge of insanity and I'm about to toss your skinny ass out on the highway. Now tell me."

I checked the mirror again. She was gone.

I started when she abruptly appeared in the front passenger seat.

Her tone softened. "You'd do that to your wife? You've never talked to me like that before. You're not very nice."

"I'm all out of nice. For crying out loud, Toots. I'm in pain here and I just killed a man."

"Say you're sorry."

I had to grit my teeth to get it out. "Okay, I'm sorry."

"You're forgiven." She leaned over and kissed me on the cheek. She was a hologram and I didn't feel it. She said, "If you let your brain relax, the answer will bubble to the surface."

"Toots, tell me now."

"No."

I slammed on the brakes, reached over past her and threw open her door, the wound crying from the abuse, having reached too far. "Get out."

She stayed seated, crossed her arms again, looked straight ahead and said, "All right. But I don't know how *we* know this."

"Tell me."

"It's Abel Jenks," she said. "He's grabbed another little girl."

21

AS I WALKED down the jetway at Ontario International Airport, I spotted Sheriff Novak standing at the end of the gate, with a grim expression and the pallor of a man who hasn't slept.

Toots said, "Shit, how did he know we were on this flight?"

I stopped in my tracks, leaned up against the wall for support as fellow passengers flowed by. Novak and I stared at each other.

I was empty handed. I'd left the carry-on in Texas, the bag too heavy to tote, and what did it matter, anyway? I'd killed someone. I half-expected the law to be waiting for me at this end; wanted them to be there, needed them to be. I didn't require clothes and toiletries where I was going.

I'd stopped at FedEx in Texas and shipped the brown leather grip belonging to the dead doctor, his "Go" bag. What he would need if someone came knocking at his door, like an invisible man and his vulgar mouthed wife. Money and an ID to take it on the lam.

Novak wore black polyester slacks with a large, silver rodeo belt buckle and a blue long-sleeved shirt with a black bolo tie. He had on the black cowboy hat that he always wore when he was going to fire someone or take them into custody.

After all the passengers were off the plane, a flight

attendant came by and said, "Sir, you're going to have to vacate the jetway."

I didn't look at her, just kept watching Novak, waiting for him to make his move.

Toots said, "Run, Bub. I'll distract him; you take off down that way."

Ludicrous, I thought. How could she distract anyone other than me?

I pushed off the wall and walked with heavy steps. I wanted to go. I'd killed someone as a civilian. Killed him while trying to extort him.

"*Run*, Bub." Her voice rose almost to a screech.

"Hello, Sheriff."

"How's it going, Will? You look like hell."

"You here as a welcome home committee?"

His eyes cut away, and I followed his gaze. Two deputies from his elite Violent Crimes Team stood thirty feet away with their hands crossed casually in front as if on stakeout in church. I smiled and looked back at Novak. "Don't feel bad, boss. You didn't do this. I brought it on myself."

"What are you doing, Will? Why are you coming off a flight from Texas?"

"What?" I was confused. Why was he there if he didn't know what happened?

Toots said, "He doesn't know about Sanchez. How come he doesn't know about Sanchez? What the billy hell is he doing here, huh, Bub?"

I said to Novak, "Who told you I was on this flight?"

"Does it really matter? How come you left the state without telling me?" He didn't wait for an answer. He looked to his boys and nodded. The boys uncrossed their hands and headed over.

I looked back at Novak. "It does matter. It matters a great deal. Who told you I was on this plane?"

"*We*, Bub, that *we* were on this plane."

I held his eyes as he said, "Captain Rymes."

Toots took a step back, her mouth agape. "She's the other

captain, isn't she, Bub? That's proof right there. Ordinary Mary's in up to her wrinkled old chicken neck."

Deputy John Haynes and Buck Dobbs came up on either side of me, their expressions solemn. We'd worked cases together. I felt badly for putting them in this position, but I still held Novak's eyes. I watched as the implication dawned on him.

He said, "No, bullshit. Is this on the up and up? Bullshit, Will." He'd made the leap and couldn't believe that the second captain he was looking for held one of the most important commands in the department.

I didn't want to believe it. I said, "There isn't any hard proof."

Novak put his hands on his hips, spun, and walked away. "Son of a bitch," he said, loudly enough for passengers in the terminal to turn their heads.

I stood still with Buck and John. Novak spun around, gritting his teeth, seething. "You God damn sure about this, Will?"

"No, I'm not."

Novak looked at Buck and hooked his thumb over his shoulder. "You two follow behind far enough so you can't hear. You understand? Way back, damn it. You're not to hear one word, you understand?" Novak took me by the arm in a firm grip that pinched the flesh. "Come on." His action tugged on the wound, and I felt it open and turn wet.

As we walked down the terminal, I told him the whole story about the meeting at the Tick Tock with Wolford, the flight to Texas, the Skype conversation with the two masked captains. Then I hesitated, the guilt clogging up my throat. Finally, I told him the shameful part. The part about the killing.

Novak stopped us. "So that's it. That's what this whole thing is about? Blackmail using cold case DNA? Son of a bitch." He pulled back and kicked at air. "When the press gets a hold of this we're going to look like a bunch of monkeys fucking a greased football."

Toots said, "You hear that, Bub? You lay your heart out

on the table, tell him how you had to kill that poor son of a bitch back there, and all he can think about is how bad it's going to be for his beloved department. What a dick."

We stepped out through the automatic doors into the warm, dry night air.

I said, "Quiet."

Novak said, "What? You say something?"

I didn't have to answer. My old commander, the man whom I let down the worst when I took the money from the *narcticos*, Captain Coleman, pulled to the curb in a black Crown Victoria. He got out and started to walk around the front of the car. A uniformed airport policeman came up and confronted him. "Sir, you can't park here. You're going to have to move it."

Coleman reached into his suit coat for his badge case, and flipped it out, flashing his gold star without looking at the guy. The uniformed policeman took a step back and spoke into his lapel mic. Coleman wouldn't look at me; he walked right up to the sheriff. "We have a situation out in Joshua Tree."

Novak said, "What is it?"

Coleman cut his eyes toward me without really looking.

Novak said, "You can talk in front of him."

Novak's words bolstered my ego. He still trusted me enough to let me hear this.

Coleman said, "It's an Amber Alert. A twelve-year-old girl, Donny Martin, has gone missing from her mother's house in Yucca Valley. I scrambled two teams from narcotics and I pulled two from gangs."

Novak said, "Okay, this isn't good, but you could have notified me by phone. What am I missing here? Why did you drive all the way over here to make the notification?"

I answered for him. "Because Abel Jenks snatched her."

They both looked at me like I'd grown a second head.

Coleman took a step over to me and got right in my face. I smelled Lupe's Green Burrito Special, Coleman's favorite. She didn't charge cops for eating at her place. He said, "How do you know that?"

Toots said, "You want some help on this one, Bub?"

"Yes," I said, "that would be nice."

Coleman said, "What's nice? You're off your nut again, aren't you?"

Toots said, "Okay, but you're going to have to apologize and promise you'll never, ever, call me a hallucination again."

"I promise."

Coleman said, "You promise what?"

Toots said, "You figured it out in your subconscious using simple math. One plus one equals two. You know Jenks better than anyone and what he's capable of, and when you heard his attorney got a restraining order against the cops from going anywhere near him, you knew he would feel safe for the first time in two years and make another snatch."

I held Coleman's eyes and said, "I meant, I'm sorry for what I did while working under your command. I promise you it will never happen again, and I will do everything in my power to make it right."

"You got a lot of nerve, asshole." He brought his finger up just under my chin. "You bet your ass it'll never happen again. I don't know why you're out walking around. If I had my way, your ass would already be in the can doing hard time."

Novak stepped in between us. "You know something about this, Will? Tell me now."

I broke eye contact with Coleman and looked at Novak. "We empowered Jenks when we let him put a restraining order against us. He's a degenerate child molester. What else was he going to do?"

Coleman said, "That's it? That's how the great Sergeant Will Donnelly knows who kidnapped a little girl? What a bunch of shit."

Novak said, "I believe him. I think there's a good chance he's right. Split your teams. I want half of your manpower all over Jenks."

Coleman said to Novak, "Jim, you going to be a backseat driver on this investigation? You've never done that before."

Now Novak was mad. "And you never found Peggy

Kellogg two years ago, did you? So yes, I think it's about time I take a more active role in supervising your faulty leadership."

I turned away. I couldn't look while my old boss was dressed down in front of subordinates. Buck and John both flinched when Novak said, "Faulty leadership."

Novak turned back to me. "You know this Jenks that well, I want you on this."

"No way," Coleman said. "I won't stand for this charade any longer. He gets booked right now for embezzlement and grand theft, or I'm calling Herb."

Herb Gold was the District Attorney for the county. Coleman golfed with him every Wednesday.

Novak's face bloated with anger. He took a long moment, then said, "Buck, you take Will here to West Valley and book him. John, you and I are driving to Joshua Tree."

He stepped over, took Coleman by the arm, and led him away. Not far enough, though. Coleman jerked his arm out of Novak's grasp. Novak said, "You find this Donny Martin alive or Monday morning you'll be captain of headquarters' facilities maintenance supervising janitors. You understand me?"

Buck said, "Come on, Will, let's get this over with."

22

WE WALKED ACROSS Terminal Way into the parking lot.

"Bub, I don't like jail. I don't like the food. It's all starch. I don't like the tiny, smothering cells and I don't like the orange jumpsuits they force us to wear. They make my ass look fat."

I said, "That's awful narcissistic of you."

Buck said, "I don't think it's right you talking to me that way. I'm just doing my job."

I said, "I don't want to ruin your night, but I think I should tell you, the jail's not going to accept me without a hospital clearance."

"Why? This some sort of trick?" He stopped, took some cuffs from under his shirt, pulled my hands together and slapped them on me.

I didn't blame him. He was just doing his job. According to protocol, I should've been cuffed right away. I was grateful he let it go this long.

"No, look," I said, "under my shirt, left side above my waist."

In the dark, he pulled up my shirt, which was wet and sticking to my abdomen. My boxers were dark red with dried blood and stuck all on their own, the belt having slipped down. At the bottom of the shorts a trickle of blood ran into the top of my pants.

"What the hell?"

"I've been shot."

"The hell you say? Who shot you? Geez, I'm sorry Will. You didn't tell me that. Does Novak know?"

I'd told Novak about clubbing Sanchez but not about how he'd shot me. It didn't seem right to spread my tale of woe when a man back in Texas lay dead. "To tell you the truth, no. I think he has enough on his mind right now."

No cop liked a hospital check. It meant hours and hours of waiting. Buck must have thought he'd dump me off at the jail and run out to Joshua Tree to get in all the action and overtime.

We came to a black Dodge Charger. Buck opened the front passenger door for me. Toots already sat in the seat with her red diaphanous dress, braless. She leaned over, purposely exposing her breasts. She said to Buck, "What do you think about these, Cowboy? Bub, I'll distract him, you knock him out, and we'll run for it."

I said, "Get in the back."

Buck said, "What?"

"I said the bullet's in my back."

"Oh." He nodded. "If you promise to be cool, I'll take the cuffs off."

"Where am I going to go? No, you don't have to keep me cuffed."

Toots climbed over into the backseat—something a classy woman like Debra Ann wouldn't have done. Her dress hiked up past the back of her knees, exposing lots of thigh with a black lace thong cleaving a beautiful bottom. I groaned at the sight.

Buck held the door waiting for me to get in, not entirely sure I wouldn't lam it right through the airport parking lot. "You must be really hurting," he said, in answer to the groan. "We'll get you to the doctor ASAP."

I got in and looked straight ahead, afraid she might try stripping down for her next stunt. She said, "What's the matter with this guy? He got ice water in his veins? What do I have to do to distract him, strip naked and dance on the hood of this car?"

I turned. "That's utterly ridiculous. He can't see you. And besides, I've made up my mind I'm not going to try and get away."

Buck had opened his door and was getting in. "I believe you." He started up and chirped the tires backing out.

I was still turned to the side where I could see her. She had her arms crossed, supporting her loose breasts, her lip out in a pout. She said, "If *she* were here, I know you'd be doing whatever she asked you to do."

For a moment I opened my mouth to tell her that wasn't true but stopped; of course she was right.

We drove in silence for a while. Something was eating at Buck. His expression, his body language gave it away. After almost three decades as a cop I'd learned to read people. I said, "What's bugging you?"

I thought I knew. He was going to ask me how I could have taken the money and given cops everywhere a bad name.

He looked away from the dark night, flashing bright with streetlights in a black-and-white kaleidoscope of parked cars and trees and run-down houses. "I'd really like to know what's going on between you and Novak."

This caught me unaware and I could only answer with, "What? Why?"

He watched the road for a moment, obviously thinking about how to frame it. Finally he said, "Don't take this the wrong way. I like Novak, you understand, and would go to the wall for him, but I work for Coleman, and…and something's going on that's tearing the guts out of Coleman."

You can't hide things from cops, not for very long. It's their job to be suspicious and hyper-aware of their surroundings.

From the back seat Toots said, "Ask him how Coleman knew Novak was at the airport picking you up."

Her words struck like a fist to the stomach. Then I relaxed. "Did you or John call Coleman and tell him you were going to be picking me up at the airport? Of course you did; you work for him."

Buck shook his head. "No, that's what I'm talking about. Did you see the way Coleman gave us the hairy eye when he got out of his car. He didn't know anything about our assignment tonight. Novak called us directly and told us not to tell anyone, and he was specific. He said not even Captain Coleman. Man, do I feel like the last turd in the toilet bowl, going behind Coleman's back like that. But what were we supposed to do? The Sheriff called and ordered us."

Toots leaned forward and moved the flat of her hand in front of my face. "Hello? You hearing what I'm hearing?"

I ignored her and said to Buck, "Okay, let me ask you this again. How did Coleman know Novak was at the airport picking me up?"

"Why is that important?" He turned into the parking lot of Arrowhead Regional Medical Center and drove to the emergency entrance in the rear.

"It could be very important."

"Tell me why?"

"I can't do that." I thought about how Coleman had been disrespectful to Novak. Coleman had always been a model of leadership protocol. He would never have a scene with his boss in front of subordinates.

"I don't know. I guess Novak called him just like he called us."

"That doesn't make sense, not after what you said about Novak ordering you not to say a thing about it to anyone, including your captain."

"Mine is not to wonder why, but to do or die. Novak probably wanted to tell Coleman himself."

23

THEY X-RAYED ME, and the physician's assistant excised the lump in my back, removing the lead slug from Sanchez' rifle. Buck took the slug as evidence even though he didn't have knowledge of any crime. He was a good cop. Buck never let me out of his sight and had even handcuffed me to the wheelchair when they took me to x-ray. I expected at any moment for Buck's cell phone to ring and to watch his expression as he was told I was now wanted for murder out of Texas.

Through the entire process Toots remained strangely morose. I was in the unused trauma room waiting for the doctor to check my chart, approve it, and clear me for booking. That wouldn't happen, of course; the doc found my heart condition and gave me some meds. He had no choice but to regulate me to the hospital ward. In a few minutes, once the paperwork was complete, they would roll me to the elevator and take us to the fourth floor, the jail ward.

Buck's cell phone rang. He looked at the incoming number and stepped out of the room to take the call. I should have been tense, afraid of the news, but I was calm and resigned to my fate.

I said to Toots, who was standing by the bed holding my hand, "Why are you so bent out of shape?"

"Oh, no reason." She said, "You're just rolling over and

playing dead, giving up, when you can get out of this mess if you'd just use your head for five minutes."

"What...? Are you crazy? I'm lying here gunshot, on my way to prison. I'm locked in tight to a three-hundred-thousand-dollar theft that I did commit and deserve to go to prison over. And if that isn't enough, I killed a man in Texas. That has to come around soon and bite me in the ass. Give up? Hell, Batman couldn't extricate himself from this mess."

"Your right about that. Batman you're not. You're nothing but a weepy, broken down crybaby. Oh, does the baby need his diaper changed?"

"Stop. Just stop it right now."

Buck came back in through the hard door. Toots said, "Here we go, you're going to get your wish. Now they'll put you in a red suit, *High Security*, because you're wanted for interstate flight to avoid a murder charge. It's too late now. We're going to be locked down in a Texas shit-hole prison. You know they execute everyone in Texas. You jaywalk for the fourth time, they send you up the river without an appeal and then execute you for it eighteen months later. No appeals process. Boom, you're gone. But I guess this is what you wanted, right?"

Buck came in and sat in the seat he'd been in for the last four hours, his expression glum.

After several long minutes of him staring at the wall I couldn't take it anymore. "Well, was that Texas on the phone?"

"Huh? What? What are you talking about?"

"The phone, who were you talking to?"

"Oh, John, my partner."

I let out a lungful of air I didn't realize I'd been holding. "What's going on?"

He looked at this watch. Two o'clock in the morning by the clock on the wall. He said, "They got a deputy district attorney out of bed and ran this thing with the restraining order by him. He said we can't, for any reason, go anywhere near Abel Jenks. Not before there's a hearing with a judge tomorrow morning. And maybe not even then if the judge rules against us." He looked at his watch again. "I mean this morning, but not for at least eight more hours. They got nothing on this missing girl. Nothing. Every minute counts, but I'm not telling you anything new. Their best lead is Jenks and they can't even work that. Donny Martin doesn't have a chance in hell. The system's working against her on this one."

Toot's perked up. "She does have a chance, Bub. She does if *you* go after Jenks. You're the only one who can right now."

"And how do you expect me to do anything about it?" I held up my hand with the cuff attached to the bed.

Buck said, "Don't be ridiculous. That's not what I meant. No way can you get involved in this. The Sheriff himself ordered me to book you."

What Toots said started to work on me.

Buck shook his head. "Remember, two years ago I was new to the teams and worked the Peggy Kellogg grab. I still can't get that picture of her out of my head. You know the one that we were showing around, the one where she was playing at Deep Creek. She was on a tire on rope tied to a huge cottonwood, swinging out over the creek about to let go. She had the biggest smile and her eyes were so bright and alive." He shook himself out of the trance. "Now it's Donny Martin's turn. It's not right; it's just not right. If I had the chance I'd take a bull whip to that Jenks."

I did remember the picture he was talking about, but hadn't until he'd brought it up. I'd stashed that memory away. Not really stashed—smothered, more like. The death of Debra Ann had seen to that. Her death had happened at the same time.

Toots said, "You going to lie there feeling sorry for yourself, or are you going to do something about it?"

I had nothing left inside me except desolation, a vast open field of dried-up hope and ambition and motivation.

"You're a butt-licker, Bub. Do I have to remind you, Jenks was the guy you were chasing when you should have been at the anniversary dinner with…with her? It's because of him that you were late to the dinner. And because you were late—."

"Okay, *enough*."

"Enough of what, Will?"

"Could you ask the nurse if I could have a glass of water?"

"Sure." He got up and left.

"Now, how do you expect me to get out of this? You can't pick the lock on these and I can't just—" Then it hit me, what she wanted me to do.

The invisible thing.

Something I didn't want to accept as real. She was right, though, I needed to get involved. A plan had already started to form in my mind, how I could go at Jenks.

"Okay," I said, "I'm with you on this, but how do I get to that in-between place where…?"

She jumped back, smiled, and clapped her hands like a little girl. "That's simple. Just keep your eye on your beautiful wife." She started to move in a sensuous way, swaying her hips and running her hands up and down her body.

"It's not working. There's nothing, not even a tingle in Mr. Johnson."

"Okay, then I'll bring out the big guns." She eased her shoulder down and let the narrow dress strap slip off. The dress drooped, exposing one breast. "How's that, big guy? That get the ol' engine fired up?"

"I'm sorry, there's nothing."

She stopped swaying and pulled up her strap. "Oh, God, Bub, it's the heart meds. They must've given you a beta blocker or something like that. We could be in deep shit here. What're we going to do?"

"That's it, I guess, at least until the medication wears off."

"We don't have time for that. Every minute counts for Donny Martin."

"What else can we do?"

She smiled, but her eyes said she was sad. "There is one way. You're not going to like it."

"There isn't. I'm emotionally numbed by the drugs."

"No, there is one way."

"Quit playing games, I'm not following you."

"There's *her*."

"Who?"

"You know, *her*. Debra Ann."

Then I understood. Toots was referring to something I had hidden away in the deepest, darkest corner of my mind. Suppressed so tightly that it was the reason Toots existed in the first place. The *day* it happened.

The *day* Debra Ann died.

24

TWO YEARS AGO when Peggy Kellogg was kidnapped, never to be seen again, Joshua Tree station was still a hundred miles from anywhere. Rather than losing precious time driving back and forth from home, the county footed the bill for all the investigators, thirty-seven of them, to eat and sleep in Yucca Valley. The department command post, a forty-foot motor home purchased with seized drug money, was parked out in back of Joshua Tree station ten feet from the station's back door.

Everyone was beyond tired. We were exhausted. Five straight twenty-hour days, with only four hours to lay our heads down at the Safari, a fleabag motel on highway 62.

Captain Coleman had always monitored investigations without taking an active role. He trusted his subordinates to do their jobs; he trusted me to do my job. This time however, there was too much heat.

The first day of the investigation the media took up residency at the bottom of the street with live feeds to their radio and television stations and never let up. Unbelievable pressure was exerted on the county board of supervisors and passed on to Sheriff Novak, who in turn—though he had not said it outright—had passed it on to Coleman. The photo of Peggy Kellogg in the tire swing suspended over Deep Creek played again and again on the airwaves, dominating the market share. No one would easily forget her smile. Debra Ann had called every night and asked how I was holding up. She knew the photo got to me, no matter what I said.

Peggy had gone missing at a flea market she attended with her family in the middle of July, while the ambient temperature was a hundred and fifteen and the ground temperature off the asphalt pushed a hundred and forty-three.

The incident started out as a missing child. Two days later, after I examined a particular set of photographs snapped by a certain witness, the event morphed into a kidnapping.

The photos showed Abel Jenks furtively moving in and out of the crowds, carrying a pink iPhone, the kind a young girl would love to own; the kind a pedophile might use to lure a vulnerable and unsuspecting kid like Peggy Kellogg out of her comfort zone.

Since Jenks was a sex registrant and a transient with no known physical address, a warrant was immediately issued for him. We looked for him for three full days, in the hope that he'd lead us to Peggy.

The two air conditioners on top of the command post ran twenty-four hours a day, the noise a constant drone that I heard in my sleep, that four-hour nap out of every twenty-four. During that nap I'd lie on the swayed mattress at the Safari and miss my Debra Ann. Exhausted as I was, I slept little without her next to me.

Mannerly opened the motor home door and stuck his head in, his eyes shielded by the dark green lens of his aviator sunglasses, his expression flat, his tone indifferent. "I got Jenks. Where do you want him?"

Everyone had been looking for Jenks hot and heavy, and Mannerly never advised over the radio that he'd found him.

Coleman jumped up and ran to the door, his feet thumping on the hollow floor. "What? You did? Where'd you get him? Did you find the girl?"

The girl. Coleman, like a lot of the investigators involved, didn't want to put a name to the face to make it too personal. The descriptor *the girl* helped with distancing. I knew all about distancing, even then.

Mannerly stepped back to let Coleman out. I followed close behind.

"Good job," I said. "Put him in a holding cell. "Let him stew a little before I interview him."

Coleman quick-stepped over to the patrol car parked close to the motor home. Mannerly said, "I think he's going to need a hospital check." I looked down at Mannerly's hands. His knuckles were bright red, some of them skinned.

I whispered, "Oh, no, tell me you didn't?"

Coleman looked in the patrol car's back window, turned and yelled at Mannerly, "You son of a bitch."

Mannerly finally showed emotion. He smiled and said, "I know. The little turd resisted arrest. You believe that? Resisting arrest against me. I'm going to charge him for assault on a Police Officer."

Coleman rushed over to us and got in Mannerly's face. "Do you know what you just did?"

Mannerly apparently thought Coleman too irate to converse with and turned his green lens on me. "There weren't any witnesses. What's the deal?"

Coleman said, "I'm talking to you, asshole. Do you know what you did?" He pointed back without looking at the patrol car. "That's nothing but a piece of raw meat now. We needed him in a condition where he could talk."

Coleman fell short of saying that Mannerly had sealed *the girl's* fate. He'd sealed *Peggy Kellogg's* fate. Coleman said, "Get him up to the hospital now."

Captain Wolford heard the commotion and was told by someone that Coleman was going off on one of Wolford's deputies. Wolford came rushing out of the station's back door. "What's going on here?"

Coleman spun. "I'm bringing your man, here, this... this animal, up on charges. That's what's going on here. Look in the back of that patrol car. I can't tell which end is the man's face."

Wolford smiled, "Charges? I don't think so. I'm putting

him in for a citation. All alone, he did what thirty-seven of your investigators couldn't do. He brought in a kidnap suspect." Wolford nodded at Mannerly, "Get the punk up to the hospital and stay with him. Keep me apprised of his status and let me know as soon as he can talk."

Coleman's face bloated red. He stepped away from Wolford before he said something he'd regret. Coleman would never say anything in front of subordinates. He always adhered to strict leadership doctrine. He hit speed dial, probably calling Jim Novak. Twenty feet away he spoke into the phone at the same time he waved his hand at me and then pointed at the patrol car. He wanted me to handle the interview with Abel Jenks when Jenks was capable of talking.

I turned to Captain Wolford to ask him a question, but Wolford smiled and said, "So, Will, how long has it been? How's that lovely wife of yours, Debra Ann?"

"She's fine, fine. Captain, do you happen to know if your man interviewed – I mean had a chance to interview – Jenks before or after Jenks resisted arrest?"

Wolford smiled and said, "Jenks continually denied any involvement with the girl."

Wolford had just confirmed my underlying suspicion. Jenks had *not* resisted arrest; Mannerly had aggressively interrogated him trying to find the location of Peggy Kellogg. And to make things worse he had reported everything to Wolford before reporting to us. Wolford and Mannerly had colluded to violate Jenks' civil rights, not to mention the felonious assault under the color of authority. They were both exposed to heavy criminal and civil liabilities for what they had done. Wolford had done it because he wanted out of Joshua Tree station. If he found Peggy Kellogg, he'd be a hero. He wanted to be brought back into the fold, back down to a headquarters position where he had a chance at a promotion to deputy chief. I didn't know Mannerly very well but had seen the type enough times over the years. He'd done it for the love of violence. Wolford's and Mannerly's continued well-being now depended on each keeping his mouth shut over what had happened. Mannerly now owned a Sheriff's captain, a nice asset for a lowly patrol deputy.

Wolford said, "Good luck." He turned and headed for the station's back door. I watched him go. Something he'd said bothered me. Wolford and I had worked patrol back in our rookie years but we rarely saw each other now. The last time was….was when Joan and I were married. I stood there trying to think if Debra Ann and I had ever come into contact with Wolford and couldn't remember one instance.

Coleman materialized next to me, waving his hand in front of my face, interrupting my thoughts. "Will? Earth to Will, are you still with us?" Captain Coleman had calmed down; his pallor was back to normal: cheeks splotchy, marred with red veins, and a drinker's nose, bulbous and large. He held up his Blackberry. "Says here several months ago you put in for a tonight off and some dumb slob, that'd be me, approved it. Says here it's your anniversary?"

When he said it, my stomach dropped through the floor. With all the pressure, I'd forgotten about it. Debra Ann, being the stalwart cop's wife, didn't bring it up in our nightly phone conversations. What made it worse was that for the last five years there had always been a crisis where the Violent Crimes Team was needed for an investigation. Last year, I promised her that *this* year I would drop whatever I was doing and take her out to Le Chemine, the only French restaurant in Rancho Cucamonga.

I said to Coleman, "I can't take tonight off," and held up my hand toward the command post. "The investigation."

"You didn't see that hunk of raw meat in the back of the car. He won't be ready to talk until tomorrow, earliest. I'll need you rested for that. No, no, you go. Take eight, ten hours. Relax, take care of your wife, tell her you love her, and then get your ass back here, pronto."

Coleman was a good man.

"Thank you. I owe you for this, boss." He turned, waving his hand over his shoulder, and entered the command post, the blast of cool air conditioning reaching down to me. I pulled out my cell and speed dialed the love of my life, at the same time shoving down the guilt about leaving Peggy Kellogg out there all alone.

Debra Ann answered, "Will, is everything all right? Did you find her?"

"Never mind that. Put on your best togs. We have a reservation tonight that I promised you a year ago."

She paused a long time. I reveled in it, knowing her excitement, sensing it, feeling it. I enjoyed making her happy. I didn't do it enough.

"Are you sure, Will?" Her voice all but a whisper.

"Of course I'm sure."

Another long pause.

"What?" I said. "What's the matter?"

"Well, I mean, I love it that you remembered and that you want to do this very romantic thing—"

"But? What am I missing here?"

"Come on, please don't make me say it."

I was a bun-head. I wasn't seeing it and imagined all sorts of scenarios, all bad, all except the obvious one.

That was the worst she ever called me, a bun-head, and only in a playful manner. I said, "I'm sorry, honey, I'm a little tired and the old brain just isn't giving forth like it should."

"Tired? You're exhausted. Leave it to you to underplay the situation. You don't even realize it when you've given more to your mistress than...than to me." Her tone turned angry for a flash, a fraction of a moment, and then shifted back to the kind, loving woman I knew.

My mistress was the job.

She said, "I know this sounds selfish and narcissistic, but I couldn't live with myself if you pulled out of that investigation and...and—."

"No, no, it's not like that. Not at all. There's a natural break here in what's going on. Trust me on this. I'll explain it all when I see you, but right now you need to get ready and I need to get on the road. It's two hours of freeway time to get there."

"Sure, Will, I'll do it. I'll doll up for you. I love you."

"I love you, too."

"I'll see you there."

I said, "No, why don't I pick you up? That way you can have more time to get ready."

"Really, Will, you don't think two hours is enough to throw on a nice dress and a little make-up. What you must think of me."

"What I think of you is that I don't want you to have to rush. I don't want you to have to drive. It's not proper. I should drive you. Put a bottle of champagne on ice and I'll be there in two hours."

"Okay."

Silent air on the cell phone.

She spoke first, "Will?"

"Yeah?"

"I love you more than you know."

"Ditto, babe."

She clicked off.

I said it again to no one. "Ditto, babe."

25

ON THE DRIVE home, for the first time in five days, I didn't think about Peggy Kellogg. I thought of nothing but Debra Ann. How we'd met. How we fell in love and eloped to Reno. She was the night manager at the Tick Tock restaurant. I had just separated from Joan, pending a divorce I never saw coming, and knew I was emotionally vulnerable. The way a poet would put it, my injured soul was searching for solace in any form. Debra Ann stood in front of the podium just inside the door, talking with the hostess. She was dressed business professional and at first glance didn't catch my eye. Then she turned and smiled. Her entire persona transformed. She radiated a vibrancy and beauty unsurpassed by anything I'd ever experienced. The smile stopped me cold, the same as if someone had pulled a gun.

Women always scared me. I had a difficult, if not impossible, time talking to them in a social setting. That night, though, her smile invited me to say something. I asked her if I could buy her a drink. Her smile brightened even more when she agreed. We sat down in a quiet booth and talked. The rest of the hustle and bustle fell away. She would get up and leave periodically to handle a restaurant issue and come back minutes later. While she was gone and without any real justification, I felt an emptiness I never thought I'd experience, especially not in a new relationship. It wasn't until the restaurant and bar closed that I found out she was the manager. We were married six months later in between the organized Jose Domingo Beltran escape from our jail and the Glen Williamson triple murder.

That day two years ago, at the end of my long drive from Joshua Tree, leaving the Peggy Kellogg investigation, two hours after I had spoken with Debra Ann, I turned down our street and was confronted with disappointment. Her silver Honda Prelude wasn't parked in the driveway. She must've been watching the clock and knew about when I would arrive, because my cell rang.

"Hello, Debra, where are you?"

"I'm sorry, darling. My dress, the only one suited for the occasion, is out at the dry cleaners. I'm all ready except for the dress. I'm picking it up now. I'll see you there. Love you."

She hung up before I could reply. Of course I was a little disappointed. I pulled into the driveway, backed up, and headed to Rancho Cucamonga without going into the house.

The San Bernardino freeway eastbound slowed and then came to a dead stop. I was trapped. I waited twenty minutes and called Debra Ann. The call rolled right over to voicemail. Before hanging up, I told her about the freeway jam and hoped she'd get the message and forgive me.

I was driving a plain colored detective car with concealed emergency equipment and was tempted to pull out and drive on the shoulder. I could easily get away with it, but it wasn't the right thing to do. In twenty minutes more the freeway parking lot started to inch forward. I took the first off-ramp and threaded my way through side streets over to Haven Avenue. I drove into the back of Le Chemine and was again rewarded with guilt. I didn't see Debra Ann's car anywhere. The night was ruined. Had I not been on the investigation, hunting for Peggy Kellogg I would've been home to drive Debra Ann. Now she'd gotten tired of waiting and left.

Dusk had started to settle. Long shadows from the eucalyptus trees reached across the parking lot, mingling with the orange and yellow from the fading sun. Maybe she'd parked out on the street and I'd somehow missed her car. I walked down the alley beside the restaurant. If I'd taken my car, driven instead of walking, I know I could've intervened. The simple choices we make have the ability to infinitely impact our lives.

On the sidewalk out front I looked up and down the street. Haven Avenue was busy, fast, and wide, with two lanes going in each direction and a lane in the center for left turns. Haven was steeper than a normal street, so steep that when it rained Haven turned into a whitewater river. To the south about a hundred yards, Haven transected the 210 cross-town freeway with a high overpass.

Right off, honking drew my attention. At the next intersection north, cars flowed southbound naturally through a green light. A huge, sun-faded red cement truck honked as it barreled through the green signal, drivers jerking on their steering wheels to get out of the way.

Another horn honked closer. I looked. Out in front of the restaurant was Debra Ann's silver Honda in the left turn lane, waiting for northbound traffic to clear to make the turn. She smiled and waved. My heart glowed. I smiled and waved back.

Then tires screeched. A loud crash again drew my attention north. The huge cement truck, with its pachyderm-gray barrel on the back churning wet cement, rear-ended a blue mini-pick-up, crumpled the truck bed, and tossed the vehicle aside without losing speed.

Words came out of my mouth in a whisper. *"Debra Ann."*

She saw my expression, her smile disappearing, changing to fear. Instinctively, she looked up in the rearview and saw the threat. She couldn't move forward with another car in the left-turn pocket ahead of her. She hit her horn.

I swung my arm in a wide sweeping motion. "Move, Debra Ann. Move. Get out of the way."

Her head spun from side to side as she looked for an out. The cement truck continued to pick up speed coming down the steep avenue. Debra Ann slammed the Honda into reverse, smoked the back tires, and then slammed it into drive, maneuvering around the car in front of her. She should've violated the law and gone to the left, into opposing traffic. Simple choices we make.

She went right and entered into the path of the beast.

I ran after her, first out into the street, into the two northbound lanes. Cars swerved to avoid me. More horns. The Honda was fast and gained speed. The huge cement truck whisked past me, the drafting wind all but taking me off my feet. For a long moment I thought she would make it, that the car had enough acceleration.

Then in a blink, the heavy front end of the runaway truck struck the back of Debra Ann's Honda with force enough to instantly obliterate the trunk and blow out both back tires. The truck didn't slow and rode on top of the Honda's severely crushed trunk deck. The truck shoved Debra Ann along in front, the Honda's steel rims grinding the asphalt, sending brilliant sparks in every direction.

The scene stunned me. I poured on more speed, yelled and waved my arms. "Get out. Jump!"

She heard me, tried the door, shoved and shoved with her shoulder, but it wouldn't open. The impact had tweaked the chassis.

The rolling wreck drew farther ahead. I ran as fast as my legs could carry me. "Climb out the window. Jump! You have to jump."

The entire event unfolded in mere seconds.

She stuck her arms out and was moving her torso through the window; got her bottom up on the window's edge.

"Good girl. Jump, you have to jump."

The weight of the cement truck continued to bear down on her small Honda, grinding the metal as if on a belt sander. The gas tank ignited. The entire car and the front of the cement truck burst into an immense fireball.

A fraction of a second before, Debra Ann, as if acknowledging her fate, twisted one last time, caught my eyes, and mouthed my name before the fire took her, ate her like a famished beast with a mammoth maw. She shrieked. And shrieked until the burning, rolling wreck reached the 210

Freeway, veered to the right, and went over the edge, dropping on top of the throng of westbound traffic.

26

BACK IN THE hospital Toots stood by my bed holding my hand. Reliving the *event* itself had worked. Electric blue sparked; my heart fluttered. Reality snapped. The machines wired to my body beeped. Debra Ann appeared dressed in what she'd been wearing the day the cement truck consumed her: black slacks, a beige blouse, and a large off-white bead necklace. Reliving the *event* just now had been the first time I had since it happened. The shrink would've called it a breakthrough. But something niggled at my brain. Something wasn't right; something didn't seem to fit.

Debra Ann put her finger to her lips. "Ssssh." She gently pulled down the sheet covering my naked body and moved my handcuffed wrist so the handcuff looked empty, lying on the hospital bed. Her hand was warm and soft. Tears wet my face. I said, "I love you." I would have said to her I was sorry that I had not run fast enough, that I had not saved her, but now I thought she knew. The knowledge gave me a sort of quiet peace. She moved a finger to my cheek and caught a tear. She said, "You really shouldn't use that incident the way you just did. It takes too much out of you. Will, you have little enough to spare. Your heart is a muscle, a tired, over-taxed muscle."

Maybe I was tired and overly emotional, but she had not said that she loved me back. I did need that much from her.

A nurse rushed in with Buck right behind her. They both

FIRE AT WILL

froze when they saw the empty bed. Seeing the look on Buck's face, I felt sorry for him. But this was something that had to be done for Donny Martin's sake. They both spun and fled the room, Buck to chase after his escaped prisoner and the nurse to report the MIA patient.

Debra Ann produced a handcuff key on a ring that looked surprisingly like mine and unlocked the cuff. I was free to go. I got out of bed, short of breath, took her hand, and we walked out of the hospital together. We didn't talk. There were no words, not after what we had just relived together. And maybe I was afraid she didn't love me anymore. I couldn't risk it. I gripped her warm hand too tightly.

THIRTY MINUTES LATER I wore hospital scrubs and drove a stolen Ford Ranger pickup east on the San Bernardino Freeway heading toward Highway 62. Obtaining clothes and the truck—already running at a gas station—was easy in my current state. The electric blue snapped and crackled. My breath came without difficulty. Debra Ann no longer sat in the passenger seat, replaced with Toots in her red diaphanous dress.

I whispered, "Good-bye, Debra Ann, see you soon."

Toots smoked a Virginia Slim, her eyes squinting from the smoke. "You know, I don't mind that you love her."

The owner of the Ford Ranger must have been a smoker.

I didn't answer and wiped the tears from my cheeks. Debra Ann had been right: reliving the *event* hurt me deeply. Hurt me to the core.

Toots said, "Do you know why I don't mind?"

I took my eyes from the road and looked at her, checked her for definition, any fading of the hallucination, seeking some evidence no matter how small that my grief was healing after having accepted the horrific images of the *event*.

She smiled, puffed, and took the cigarette from her painted red lips. "Because you and I both know she's nothing but a figment of your imagination. And that what we have together, you and I, right here, is real."

The absurdity of her statement, the serious tone in which she said it, struck me as funny. I laughed and then froze, afraid I'd crossed the line men tend to accidentally cross in the emotional give and take with women. Toots didn't move for a long second and then threw her head back and laughed. We laughed together. Laughed and laughed. When the frivolity naturally faded, I realized I had not laughed in two years. It felt better; then great. It felt sensational. We drove on into the night.

Before we left the hospital, Debra Ann had somehow lifted the clear plastic property bag that contained all my personal belongings. Of course *I'd* done it without realizing it during that time expansion thing, and my mind now hid it from me. I took out my cell phone and sent a text to Wolford asking him to meet me behind Xavier's Tacos on Highway 62. He didn't answer; I hadn't expected him to.

We rode in silence. The midnight moon's absence made the night dark and the highway difficult to see at any distance. In my head I practiced moving around the outside edge of the *event* to see how far I could go without experiencing the electric blue flash. I stopped short of Debra Ann's shriek and had to immediately think of something else. I'm ashamed to say I went right to the incident in the shower with Toots. Sweat broke out on my forehead. My heartbeat elevated and my hands shook. *Bad move, Will.* I thought of when Debra Ann and I first met, that wonderful night at the Tick Tock. *Aaah, there; back under control.*

When I looked over at Toots she sat with her legs crossed at the knee, still smoking a cigarette, her eyes directed out the passenger window, watching the fleeting darkness. She had somehow read my thoughts and said, "I don't understand this obsession you have for that wench Debra Ann. I thought after our *thing* in the shower we were...we were somehow closer."

"We are. And please don't call her that."

"What does she have that I don't?"

"I do love you, just in a different way."

She took her eyes from the window and looked at me. "Oh, stop your lying. Next you'll throw in that old saw that you love me like a sister. I don't get it, she has a caboose my mama would've called two ax-handles wide."

I shook my head in disagreement, not wanting the verbal duel, and watched the road.

She pointed her finger at me, the one with the cigarette, the smoke curling around the cherry glowing tip. "You're not seeing it because you're love-struck. And you know it hurts me to say love-struck when I'm not referring to me and you."

She finally looked away, an action that by itself took measurable emotional pressure off me. She said, "Seriously, I don't understand it. You tell that woman to haul ass and she'd have to make two trips."

Not true. Toots was Debra Ann in every physical attribute and Toots knew it.

I said, "This jealousy you're displaying is not becoming."

We topped the summit out of the Morongo Valley and dropped into Yucca Valley. Twenty-four-hour self-serve car washes, gas stations, and mini marts littered Highway 62 and were populated with raggedly people, mostly meth freaks who'd been up days on end from using the stimulant. All the good citizens were in bed.

Toots again watched the passing landscape, her mood having gone back to melancholy. I wished she didn't feel that way. I liked it better when she was manic, happy, spouting her snide remarks. I liked it even when she was getting me in trouble. Was this a sign that I was healing emotionally? What would happen then? Would Toots disappear? No, no, that wasn't an option. I had to have my Toots.

"Hey," I said, "I want you to understand, I do love you, and I love you very dearly."

Her head whipped around; her smile lit up the night.

"Really, you really do? Say it again, please say it again just like that—like you really mean it."

"Babe, I don't know how you can think anything else. Of

course I love you." I stopped short of telling the truth, that I loved Debra Ann far more, and hated myself for not telling her that part of it. But I had to spare her.

She leaned over and kissed my cheek. I checked the rear view to see if the lipstick appeared on my skin. Another safety check to confirm everything was still the same and that I hadn't edged that much closer to insanity. She cuddled up, her arm under mine, her cheek resting on my shoulder as she went back to watching the businesses flash by. Her gaze locked on a woman at a phone booth out in front of a mini-mart, nothing more than a glimpse.

Toots said, "The women in this town are like parking spots. The good ones are taken and the handicap ones are free."

She was back.

We drove a little further in silence. I said, "What's going to happen to us as I get older and you stay young and vibrant? You going to kick me to the curb and go in search of some young stud?"

"Of course not, Bub." She snuggled in closer. "I will always love you no matter what. I like it that you're thinking that way, though. Got to admit, Bub. Sometimes jealousy *is* becoming."

In another block I turned into Xavier's and drove around back.

Captain Wolford's Crown Victoria was parked cock-eyed, the passenger door open. Wolford lay half in his car. His torso lay on the ground, his head cocked at an unnatural angle. A widening pool of blood oozed around his head, black ooze on the asphalt in the moonless night.

My cell phone buzzed, indicating a text message.

27

I KEPT DRIVING. There wasn't anything I could do for Wolford; a chunk of his head was missing. A sheriff's captain killed. All hell was going to break loose.

In a daze, my thoughts muddled, I tried to sort it out: who would kill a sheriff's captain?

I drove down the street to the Walmart. I stopped at the far side of the parking lot, under some trees that gave off shades of purple.

Toots said, "Boy, I saw that coming a mile off."

"Oh, you did?"

"Come on, Sherlock, you're telling me you didn't?"

Some of the shock wore off and my brain started working again. "I guess you're right. Blackmailing murderers would tend to shorten your life expectancy. We don't even know who or how many people he's blackmailed. The list could be a long one."

"You're in some deep shit here, Bub."

"No, I'm not. I didn't do anything."

"Think about it," she said. "Why was Wol-pig in back of that taco dive?"

Then I understood what she was getting at. I was the one who texted Wolford to meet me there. The first thing an investigator was going to do was dump Wolford's phone records.

I took the cell from my pocket and saw the incoming message that had buzzed just as we had driven around the back of Xavier's where we'd found Wolford. The text came from Wolford's cell number and read:

"What the hell did you do? Henry Sanchez is here."

Henry Sanchez? Wolford's cell phone? My vision swam. How could this be?

"Bub, Henry Sanchez is dead. I saw him. You used that fireplace poker and parted his forehead right down the center, a furrow deep enough to plant corn. And on top of that bizarro tidbit, throw in the fact that Wolford's dead. How did you get that text when the dude was already laid out decomposing on the asphalt like a machaca burrito?"

I didn't answer. My mind had leapt far ahead. "How did Sanchez find out that Wolford was the blackmailer?" I had given up on the reliability of my memory when it came to reality. Whenever I was in that in-between place where time expanded and contracted I couldn't trust anything I'd seen. I could easily buy into the idea that I had not done-in Henry, but how had he found Wolford? That was the question.

Right now though, it didn't matter. In a murder investigation every minute counts. I dialed 9-1-1. A female operator responded with a voice that was both sweet and calm. "Nine-one-one emergency. What is the emergency you're reporting?"

For a brief moment I thought of poor Sara Lang, the dispatcher who had died exposed to hazardous waste, the same stuff that should've finished me off and instead left me living out on the edge of reality with a blown-out heart. "Yes," I said and shifted back from the edge of the emotional abyss where a dead brother cop had taken me and returned to business. "Shots fired, officer down, code nine, nine, nine. Repeat, officer down Highway 62 behind Xavier's restaurant."

The woman sucked in a long breath; the moment hung in the air, and then she sprung into action. She'd clearly shifted over to the dispatcher's console, taken the mic, and broadcasted it directly. "All Morongo units: shots fired, officer down. Officer down. Highway 62 behind Xavier's restaurant. Med aides en route." Her voice returned back to the phone. "Sir, what is your name and your location?"

I hung up just as sirens sounded to the east. I drove around to the front of the Walmart parking lot, and stopped right at the intersection at Highway 62 where the signal allowed traffic to enter the lot. In seconds two Sheriff patrol units and a highway patrol car zipped through against the red light, their door emblems a metallic blur. As the sirens passed, more took up from the east. Joshua Tree Station was twelve miles away where they manned the command post in the hunt for Donny Martin. Every cop on duty was now rolling code three in a conga line, the cars opened up to their max speed. Some would reach a buck-twenty.

Toots spoke in a somber tone, "Hey you, big guy, this is your chance while all the cops are busy."

Of course she was right. I was beginning to dislike her playing the role of little miss devil on my shoulder, her spurs kicking me into action. I drove toward 45387 Val Verde in search of Abel Jenks.

I didn't have a GPS, but I had Toots. I didn't know how she knew the streets, but she did and called the turns. Humans only use a small portion of their brains. Maybe I had seen the maps sometime in the past, and my mind had photographed them, stored the information subliminally, and now brought it to the surface when I needed it. I guess the mind had to have its governors, or all the data taken in over a lifetime, or even in one day, if not discarded would drive a person mad.

Val Verde was up in the rock-strewn hills that looked down on Yucca Valley proper. As we wove our way along the edge looking for the right house number, all the red lights down below in Xavier's rear parking lot were easy to see. Twenty or thirty cop cars were now on scene at the murder. The sight brought a sickening pang in my stomach.

My cell phone rang again. I pulled over, stopped, and checked the display. I reacted the same as if someone had just opened a deep-freezer door.

Wolford's phone again.

Toots leaned over and peeked, then shook herself like a wet dog. "That's out there, Bub, way out there. Eerie like a Hitchcock movie." She craned her head to see out the windshield. "What next? The psychotic birds are going to attack?"

I hit the send button and listened.

A male voice: "Hello, Will, are you there? Will?"

"Who's this?"

"Will, it's Novak. Where are you?"

"Why?"

Silence.

Novak said, "I guess that answers my question."

"What are you talking about?"

"You know damn well what I'm talking about. Why did you run? You made Buck look like a buffoon. I'm seriously thinking about demoting him from detective back to deputy and tossing his sorry ass in jail for a couple of years. What's worse is now we have to hang an escape on you. Why'd you do it, Will?"

I couldn't answer.

Novak said, "I heard the 911 tape. I recognized your voice and when we dump the records I bet it's going to be your phone number. You need to come in, come in right now."

My heart rate went crazy; I was right on the edge of slipping over. I hung up, put my head back, and breathed in long and slowly. The burnt acrid odor of an unfiltered Camel cigarette wafted up. I opened my eyes. Toots was smoking again. I needed to change cars; get one where the owner wasn't a smoker. The phone rang.

She took a long drag and let it out, "You know you'd better toss that phone. The very next thing they're going to do is ping it. You'll bring them right down on us like blue bottle flies on a fresh pile of dog shit."

"Please, I wish you wouldn't use such vulgar language. It's getting worse, you know."

She was right, but I needed to know something first. I hit

send. "Jim, how did you come in possession of Wolford's phone?"

"You need to come in and we'll talk about it."

"Yeah, like I'm going to do that. Give me a little credit. Just answer the question. Where did you get Wolford's phone?" I looked out the passenger window, down into the valley to all the stationary tiny red flashing lights where Novak had to be standing to the rear of Xavier's.

Novak asked, "Did you kill Wolford?"

"Do you think I'd be talking on the phone to you if I killed him? Do you think I'd have called it in if I killed him?"

Novak said nothing. He didn't have to. I hadn't done anything normal since...

Since Debra Ann died two years before.

I said, "Tell me, where did you get the phone?"

"I don't think it matters now. And to tell you the truth I don't know you anymore, Will. I used to know and like Will Donnelly, but not this guy I'm talking to here on the phone."

"I'm sorry you feel that way. Nothing's changed. And it does matter. Do you want to know who killed him?"

"I think that's evident, don't you?"

I said, "Henry Sanchez."

"What?"

"Yeah, exactly. And if you come after me you'll only waste precious time. You need to go after Sanchez."

Novak lowered his voice, "You mean the guy you met with in Texas? That guy?"

Toots slapped her leg, cried out, "Give that brain trust a kewpie doll."

I ignored her and said into the phone, "Yes, he had motive and opportunity. And I don't need to go into details over the phone about how much motive he had." I couldn't believe Novak still did not want to let out that part of the investigation: the fact that two of his captains were dirty. A captain had been killed. Nothing else should matter.

He asked, "How did Sanchez know who Wolford was?"

"I don't know, but I'd be worried about the safety of that

other captain if I were you. We have to find out who the captain is so we'll be able to warn him."

Toots said, "Or her. Tell him about Ordinary Mary, Bub. Go on, tell him."

Novak was silent. Then came muffled talk. He must've put the phone up against his hand or shoulder so I wouldn't hear.

A moment later he came back on. "Will, I still need you to come in. I've just been told that you have plenty of motive. Something I was unaware of. This is really shocking to me, Will, and I find it hard to believe what I was just told, but we need to look into it and get it all straightened out."

I closed my eyes tight. "What possible motive could I have? Wolford and I were not good friends, but we didn't hate each other. What did you just find out?"

Toots said, "It's nothing but a ruse. He's trying to keep you on the line so they can triangulate on your phone. Bub, I don't look good in jail-house reds. Hang up and toss that phone."

"Jim, I'm hanging up now. I wish you'd tell me where you got that phone."

His voice turned even more somber. "It was in his hand, Will. It was in Wolford's hand."

28

I CLOSED THE phone and tossed it out the window.

Toots said, "That fat-ass down there was flopped out of that car like a gutted fish. We saw both of his hands. He didn't have anything in his hands, did he, Bub? Did he?"

"Don't talk about him like that. Have some respect for the dead." I was livid. "I shouldn't have fled the scene. I should've stayed right there and called it in."

"Don't talk to me like that, Bub, please. I'm saying please."

"Damn. Oh, all right, just don't talk about Wolford that way."

"Okay, Bub, sorry. Don't beat yourself up. You couldn't have done anything for him. Half his head was gone. You saw it."

I looked at her. "You're right. There wasn't anything in his hands, which means someone put the phone there after we left. Which means Sanchez was hiding in the dark close by while we were there."

"Holy shit, Bub, he could've snuck up on us and aced us out." She shivered again. "He's got to be mad over you whacking him over the head with that poker. Whacked him like he was some kinda catfish or something.

"If that's true, how come he let us go down there? You think he thinks we'll lead him to that second captain?" She spun around wildly in her seat, checking the back and side windows.

I hadn't thought of that. "Yeah, that makes sense. He texted us that thing about himself to spook us, to get us to rabbit to who he believes is that second person in the Skype conversation before he blasted the laptop."

The big Buick Jenks drove up in the day we'd seen him out in front of Xavier's, the day Mannerly shot him with the taser, was parked in the widow's driveway. The house was dark and the curtains pulled. I was still mad about Sanchez killing Wolford. Wolford was a crook, but he didn't deserve to be assassinated. I had to continually focus or my anger would rise up and spark my invisibility. There, I said it. I was accepting that unrealistic part of my life as well.

Two years ago Jenks had been professionally beaten into a slab of raw meat by Mannerly, and he had not given up Peggy Kellogg's location or even admitted he'd taken her. Tonight was different. Tonight I would not be deterred.

I drove past the house and parked up the street, and we walked back. Dewitt had said Jenks lived in the garage and the widow kept the inside door to the house secure with a deadbolt. I crept around to the outer, side door to the garage and tried the knob. The door opened to complete darkness.

I wished I had a gun.

I whispered to Toots, who I sensed stood right behind me. "Is he in there?"

She said, "No. He's not in the garage."

I stepped back, quietly pulled the door shut, turned, and whispered, "How do you know?"

"I don't know, but why did you ask a stupid question like that?"

This wasn't the time or the place to get into it with her. I entered and waited just inside the door for my eyes to adjust. Dim outlines materialized. The garage was laid out like a master bedroom with a king-sized sleigh bed, nightstands, and chest of drawers. The place was a disaster. Clothes were strewn everywhere, fast-food cartons moldered and reeked, stacked on the nightstands and in the corners where they'd been tossed. Lots of empty 40-ounce beer bottles, too, a violation of the alcohol stipulation to his parole. Parole hadn't been there to check on him, either. My fault.

The light was too dim to see for sure, but I sensed Toots had been right; Jenks was not in there hiding. I was discouraged and relieved at the same time, until I saw the inside door leading into the house. Jenks had taken a sledgehammer to it. The door hung in the frame cockeyed, the deadbolt smashed. I didn't want to see what lay on the other side.

I eased in and listened. Somewhere deep in the large house music thrummed, the vibration barely discernible through the walls. I had not felt the gunshot wound in my side for a while but now it made itself known, throbbing in time with the thrum of the music. The painkiller must've worn off, which meant the beta-blocker probably had too, making my heart vulnerable.

We moved through the kitchen toward the sound. I outweighed Jenks by thirty pounds, but I knew my limitations. Old age, a broken-down heart, emotionally and physically, gave the younger, mentally crazed Jenks the upper hand. Hell, it gave him the entire game. I stopped, retraced my steps back to the kitchen, and eased the drawers open until I found what I needed. A butcher knife was too dangerous; I couldn't use it without risking a mortal wound. I wasn't sure I could slash or stab someone anyway. Truth was, I knew I couldn't. Instead, I chose a meat tenderizer, a small, but heavy metal hammer with a bumpy head on both sides. Toots said, "Nice."

The handle went slick in my hand from the sweat. The wall reverberated with a loud thump. I startled and jumped. Toots behind me said, "Take it easy, cowboy. Breathe through your nose."

Difficult to do when it felt like the house was coming down around my head.

I had suddenly realized I was sneaking up on a serial killer, a sociopath who could kill without compunction. I shouldn't have been scared. I'd been trained for situations like these. I had made my peace, or thought I had, and was ready to go be with Debra Ann. But now, when it came right down to it, I wanted to stay on the planet a bit longer.

Another thump. This one shook the house even more. My fear level rose in time with the thrumming of the music down the hall and in the next room. I moved closer to the edge, to the electric blue spark. I stopped in the wide hall, set the little meat-tenderizing hammer down, and pulled my shirt off over my head. I undid the string holding up my medical scrub pants and let them fall to the floor. I stood there naked and vulnerable except for the bandage on my side.

As I bent over to pick up the hammer Toots said, "Bub, don't be a scaredey-cat."

I turned to tell her it was all right, that there was nothing to worry about, when the door at the end of the long hall burst open and a madman ran out. Electric blue sparked and lit up my world like a wildfire. Everything snapped to black.

When everything snapped back, I found Abel Jenks wearing nothing but soiled boxers. His chest and arms were slick with sweat and spattered with blood. His eyes were wild pie plates. He stopped and jumped back when he saw me, but then when he looked again I had disappeared.

He shook his head and then smacked his forehead with the flat of his hand. In his other hand he carried a nine-pound sledge. Satisfied he wasn't losing his mind, he moved on past us.

My eyes locked on his hammer, which was conspicuously more lethal than mine. Debra Ann stood where Toots had been, wearing her beige silk blouse and black slacks. Even with what was going on, her presence caused that thought to again niggle at my brain. Debra Ann placed a warm hand on my shoulder and said, "Aah, Will, you have a 'little' hammer envy, don't you?"

I missed her so, and yet I still had this desire to pull up the thought that was bothering me. I was missing something. She was purposely distracting me using sexual language like Toots would. Debra Ann had never talked to me like that in all her life. Something wasn't right.

My heart pittered and pattered, threatening to shut down entirely. I closed my eyes. Focus. *Focus.* I opened them, ignored Debra Ann, and moved down the hall to the room Jenks had exited.

Inside, the room was an absolute shambles. It had been a cozy den at one time with a big screen television, sofa, loveseat, and easy chair. The music played on a portable ghetto blaster. With the door open the music was now nothing more than noise, loud enough to obliterate all else, banging the eardrums to the point of pain. Jenks had bashed gaping holes in all the walls. The 2x6 wood supports were exposed in the craters and in some places the wiring as well. If left to continue, he'd eventually take down the entire house.

Blood spatters littered the walls as if shot with paintballs. Debra Ann again put her warm hand on my back and moved me in. She said, "You have to help her, Will."

That's when I saw the widow strapped down to the couch with gray duct tape. She was naked and covered in blood.

No one was going to help her ever again.

29

I COULDN'T HELP but stare at the naked, mauled widow and wonder if I hadn't caused it. Had I not interjected myself out in front of Xavier's the day Mannerly tasered Jenks, the day I whispered in his ear, this might not have happened. The incident had given Jenks the probable cause he needed to get the restraining order against the Sheriff's Department ordering us to stay away from him. He otherwise wouldn't have felt empowered to go off on society, snatching Donny Martin and doing this to the widow. A small part of me wanted the time transition slippage to be marring what was real and to have this scene placed firmly in another dimension.

Debra Ann stood close and took up my hand.

I asked, "Did Jenks really do this? Am I seeing this for real?" I don't know how she heard me over the noise.

She said, "This isn't your fault. You need to sit down, Will. Your heart; you have to take care not to overstress your heart when you're in this place."

"Tell me."

She nodded in the affirmative.

This carnage *was* real.

I gripped the meat tenderizer handle until my knuckles hurt. "Oh, I'm going to take care of my heart." I didn't like this new emotion, this uncontrolled violent urge.

Jenks, his face streaked with blood, had heard, music me

talking and ran into the room, the sledgehammer held over his shoulder at the ready looking for a target, to strike, to crush and kill everything breathing. Of course he couldn't have heard us talking not with the loud music. He was just simply crazy.

I raised my little hammer and moved toward him.

Debra Ann put a warm hand on my shoulder. "Don't get too close. Stay out of his range. He might get lucky. Play it smart, Will."

She was right, of course. I had let my emotions rule the day and wanted nothing more than to cave in his tiny animal skull. I hoped the exposure to the hazardous waste spill had made me this way and that it was temporary. In all my years in the department I had never tasted this bitterness called revenge. I took a breath, tried to relax a little and then got right down to it, yelled above the din. "Abel, you asshole, *tell me where Donny Martin is.*"

He wasn't scared this time. In fact he seemed ready for the voice emanating without visible source. He lowered his center of gravity and swung the hammer over his head in a wide circle, moving toward my voice, the hammer coming around faster and faster each time as he continued to approach. He must've thought he was Thor. His swings went high.

Instead of backing up, I knelt on both knees and ducked. He came within striking range. I swung the meat tenderizer upward and caught him in the groin with a solid, mushy thunk, the bumpy hammerhead mashing soft organ to pelvis bone.

First he dropped his sledge. His eyes bulged. His hand went to his mutilated genitals. He crouched and then slowly eased over in slow motion until his head connected to the tile floor and bounced once before settling.

I couldn't handle the music any longer. I picked up Thor's weapon and smashed the stereo system. The lack of noise was so loud it hurt.

The violence tasted metallic in my mouth, coppery and tin-like. I leaned against the Lazyboy chair, focusing on my heartbeat.

Debra Ann started to fade.

"Wait," I said, "I need to--."

She came back as my heart beat faster at the thought of what I wanted to ask.

"What?"

I still didn't know what had been bothering me about her, couldn't put words to it yet. Knew it would bubble up soon enough. Then something else popped into my head. "Babe, can you tell me why I didn't pull my gun and shoot the cement truck tires?"

Her expression of fear shifted to a forced half-smile as she moved toward me, her eyes soft, never leaving mine. She slowly reached out and put a soothing hand on my cheek. "Come on, honey, you know that answer. You just have to think about it."

"I can't bring up every detail of that...that *event*. Please tell me. It might ease my guilt a little."

She leaned up and kissed me lightly on the lips. I loved her so. She moved her mouth close to my ear, her breath hot, "The truck tires are designed to support tons and tons of weight; thick, thick rubber. Your handgun bullets would've bounced off; and worse they might have ricocheted and hurt an innocent bystander. You did think of it that day and you rightly ruled it out. You have nothing to feel guilty about, my love. Trust me on this."

"Debra Ann, tell me what I'm not seeing about that day. Tell me what's bothering me."

"Shhh, now close your eyes and breathe slowly." She hugged me, her breasts pressing softly against my shoulder and half my chest. When I opened my eyes she was gone.

"You gonna help me with this piece of shit?" Toots was bent over in her red diaphanous dress and black spiked heels, using the pachyderm gray duct tape to bind up Jenks' legs. Her beautiful legs and heart-shaped bottom were incongruous with the semi-naked waste of humanity she labored to tie up.

The disappearance of Debra Ann as always brought on a thick depression. "It's not going to do any good. He's not going to tell us anything."

FIRE AT WILL

"Oh, stop pissing in your Wheaties and get his hands."

"No, you don't understand. It's not that I'm feeling sorry for myself. Two years ago, before you came on the scene, a deputy named Mannerly put the boot to this guy until he was a pile of raw meat and he said nothing. And I mean nothing."

"Just bind up his hands, cowboy. Let me do the thinking tonight. All the thinking you're doing is with your little head. That wench befuddles you every time. And for the life of me I don't understand it when you have this." She stood upright and opened her arms. She went back to work with the tape. She said, "You won't turn back into your regular self for a couple of hours, until that metaphoric erection recedes. Trust me, I've been taking notes on your reactions."

That sounded about right. She knew me well. I nodded and did as I was told: stood over Jenks and held my hand out for her to give me the duct tape. She gave it to me. I squatted over him, pulled his hands together, and was taping them when he came to.

He screamed, "Okay, okay, I'll tell you. I'll tell you! Just don't rape me. Please, I don't wanna be raped."

I stood. "What?"

Toots put a hand over her mouth to stifle a smile. Then I caught up with what she'd already figured out. I had been squatting over his face while taping. When he came to all he saw was Mr. Johnson dangling close to his nose. I hadn't meant to; I'd just forgotten I was naked.

Toots recovered first. "That's right, you piece of shit. Tell us where Donny Martin is or my husband here will give it to you right up the tailpipe, you get me?"

"No, no, I'll tell you. Oh, my God, you're that asshole cop, Donnelly. I know you. Don't rape me. I'll tell you anything you want."

I turned angry again at the thought that he'd used me to get the restraining order that put all of this in motion. I pulled back and kicked him. It felt good; better than I wanted it to. I was headed down the wrong road, one I'd seen other cops take and in the end turn morally bankrupt. Toots got down on one knee and started to turn him over, yanking hard in an attempt to pull down his boxers.

Jenks squealed like a pig. The sight of a beautiful woman in high heels yanking down his boxers, torturing him, made me smile.

I recovered and said, "Tell us right now, where is she?"

"Out in the desert."

"Where?"

"Off Old Woman Springs Road, out by Giant rock. I don't know the address. It's all unmarked dirt roads and shit. A bunch of nothing out there."

Something Toots had just said sank in. She'd referred to me as her husband. She'd never done that before, and strangely I had never thought of her as my wife. Odd, after two years of being with her, things were changing.

I said to Jenks, "You'll have to do much better than that." I moved as though I was getting behind him. Toots stood and put her spiked heel across the back of his neck to hold him down. "Do him anyway, Bub. This punk deserves it. Do it. I want to watch him squirm and squeal like a little piggy." She even had me convinced she was serious.

Was she serious?

His voice went up several octaves. "Noooo. Wait, wait. Please wait. It's a brown wood shack, a homestead. I'll take you to it. I promise I'll take you to it."

A lump rose in my throat over the thought of that little girl out there all alone and scared. I kicked him again. "Is she alive?"

"What?"

I kicked him again, in the face this time. "Is she alive?"

He shook his head, spit some blood, licked his lips, and spit again. "Don't kick me again, man. I tolt ya I'd take you to her."

"Answer the question."

"Yeah, yeah. At least she was when I saw her last."

30

As always the trip to the other side had zapped every last bit of strength. I had trouble lifting my feet to walk into the hall for my clothes. How was I going to get Jenks outside and into the truck? No way could I do it.

Toots followed me, helping me get into the scrubs and tie the string. She turned and headed down the hall to the living room. "Where are you going?"

She stopped. "Just keep an eye on that waste of skin in there. Make sure he doesn't weasel out of those bindings. He's not as hurt as he lets on. I'll be right back."

I was too exhausted to argue. I needed to sit down and rest, to get some strength back. I went into the den and sat on the arm of the recliner. With the lack of energy the task ahead stretched out far beyond the impossible. From the floor Jenks stared up at me. His one eye, the one not swollen, hardened as he regained some of his bravado. This wasn't good.

I said, "Describe the route we take." I wanted as much information as possible before he flipped back to Thor.

He slowly shook his head. His tongue whipped out lizard-like to wet his lips.

Too late.

My hearing had returned somewhat. The sound of screeching tires penetrated the walls. Seconds later an earthquake hit, magnitude eight point five. The house shook on its foundation. Dust blasted in as the wall came down. The tailgate to the stolen Ford Ranger appeared as the dust parted. The back tires stopped inches from running over Jenks's head. White exhaust blasted out on his face. He coughed. "Okay, okay, I'll take you there. You fucker, you're crazy. Absolutely fucking batshit crazy."

Toots appeared, bent down. "Come on honey, give me a hand with this piece of shit. With all the noise the cops are gonna be swarming here like stink on shit."

I smiled. "Sure, babe. Nice move."

She stopped and looked at me. "Babe? You called me babe."

"That's right. Now let's get moving."

We used the duct tape to strap him down, his back to the tailgate, so he faced the front; taped him up like a mummy, all but his face. Some inward intrusion caused by the tailgate crashing through the stucco wall thrust him forward, his back against a sharp sheet metal point. He would feel any and all bumps in the road. It couldn't be helped. We opened the cargo window at the back of cab to hear his directions. I don't know how, but Toots drove. Well, I did know—it was really me, but my mind liked it better this way. Toots knew the way out to Old Woman Springs Road and turned north.

Jenks, the wind blowing his hair, the dry air making his eyes tear and leave streaks in the plaster dust on his cheeks, nodded his head, and yelled, "Right, right, good. Keep going until you get into Landers but before you get to Johnson Valley. Slow down though, this hurts like hell. Slow down, God damn you."

Toots put her foot on the accelerator and smiled. We drove on into the night.

Toots lit another cigarette.

I reached over and tried to hold her hand. She was still a hallucination. She smiled at the attempt. I liked her more and more; loved her more and more, really. I said, "Something's been bothering me about what happened. With...the cement truck, I mean something that happened that day, that I can't put my finger on."

"I know. I heard you talking to the wench."

"What is it? Please tell me."

"Can't, Bub."

"Why not?"

She watched the road for a long time, thinking about it. I gave her some space. Then I said, "So you do know, then?"

"Yes."

"Tell me, please?"

Tears appeared and wet her cheeks. "I can't."

"Why?"

"Don't misunderstand. I want to, I really do, but I don't think you can take it. Remember I heard what the doctor said about your condition. And I know, believe me when I say you can't take it. Trust me on this one, Bub."

"My heart is stronger than you think."

She shook her head. More tears. "It's not your heart I'm worried about."

Jenks kicked the truck bed, raising his bound feet and bringing them down. "Here, turn right here."

Toots turned back to all business and yanked the wheel. The truck slewed sideways and almost whipped out of control before she corrected. We bounced from the asphalt highway onto a rutted dirt road. Had Jenks not been taped to the tailgate he would have bounced out. He yelped and said, "Sheeeeit. Ouch, come on. This hurts like hell."

The back tires kicked up a dusty rooster tail. We would've never found this place without Jenks along. Toots had to slow or the road would eat the truck.

Jenks yelled again, "Mark it, three point two miles exactly, then turn left. It'll look like a wash but it's passable. Come on, slow down. You're crazy as a coot, old man, talking to yourself like that."

The wind grabbed at his words, making him hard to understand.

Toots flicked the lit camel out the window, blew out a lungful of smoke, and said, "After we get Donny back, I intend to take a pair of pliers to that animal and do some evil-ass things to him."

I wanted to say, "I'll hold him for you," but I didn't want to encourage her. Or was it really *me* I was worried about as I continued to devolve toward moral bankruptcy?

Toots drove on, her tongue stuck out of the corner of her mouth as she watched the odometer and then the road and then the odometer. The desert bounced up and down in the headlights.

Jenks yelled as the sharp metal shredded his back. On both sides the moonless night kept the desert shrouded from view. At three point two, Toots blindly yanked on the wheel. I held my breath. We could have easily been going off a cliff. The truck bogged down, then caught. Jenks yelled, "Slow down. Are you crazy, Donnelly? Slow down or we're both gonna die."

I looked at Toots, "Babe, slow down a little, would you? We won't do Donny any good if we don't get there."

"Sorry, I just want to get there as soon as we can."

"I know. Me too. Slow down."

She eased off. Jenks yelled, "Two miles and some change. You can't miss it. It's on the right, the only shack for miles. A brown POS."

Toots said, "We can't miss it now. I say we pull over, take him out, put his head under the tire, and drive real slow over that pea-brain cranium."

"We're not going to do that. We're going to take him in and let the system deal with him. Keep him locked up for the rest of his life."

"Really? You're kidding, right?"

I didn't answer and looked out the window. I wanted to do exactly what she described but needed to follow the law and do what was right. Not just to follow the law, but to maintain some semblance of my sanity.

Off in the distance, at the edge of the headlights, a brown wood shack flickered in and out as we bounced up and down. My pulse increased at the thought of what we were going to find. As we drew closer the urge to take Jenks out and beat him grew as well.

Toots pulled around so the headlights covered the front of the small, desiccated wood shack. The door was the sturdiest part of the structure, with dried and cracked leather hinges. She turned off the engine and left the lights on.

"I'm scared as hell, Bub. You go in. I can't."

That was the first time she'd ever said she was scared. It scared *me*.

I didn't want to go in, either. I got out on shaky legs, using the truck door for support. I took a couple of deep cleansing breaths to give me strength. I stepped toward the front of the shack, my feet sinking in deep sand. The door didn't have a knob, just a hole with wire hooked to a nail on the outside.

"Peggy? Are you in there?"

Peggy? What was I saying?

"Donny, it's the Sheriff's Department, we're here to help you."

Nothing. Just the sound of the blue Ford Ranger ticking as it cooled. I undid the wire and slowly pushed the door open. The headlights lit up the small interior.

Toots, beside me now, whispered, "Oh, shit."

31

FROM BEHIND US Jenks let out a deranged cackle. Toots ran several steps before she had to stop and pull off her spiked heels, the sand too deep to maneuver. When I caught up to her she was beating Jenks with the spiked heel, Jenks screaming bloody murder as she did a tap dance on his noggin.

I grabbed her but grabbed at nothing. "Stop it. Stop it right now."

Toots was out of breath anyway.

I said to Jenks, "Tell me where Donny Martin is or I'll turn her loose on you."

"You're batshit crazy. There's no one here but you."

"*Where is she?*"

He panted. "Let's make a deal. You cut me loose. Gimme me a two-hour head start and I'll tell you what you wanna know."

Toots said, "No deal, douche bag." She went at him, denting his skull with the spiked heel.

"Okay, okay! Stop!"

Toots stood back, breathing hard. I said to Jenks, "Tell her you're sorry for pretending she's not here."

"You're one crazy fucker, you know it?"

"I suggest you apologize and do it quickly or else…."

He gulped, "Okay, I'm sorry."

"Don't tell me. Tell her."

"Who, God damn you? Tell who?"

Toots said, "Where's the girl?"

Jenks didn't answer, pretending he didn't hear her.

I said, "She asked you where the girl is?"

"Behind the shack there, about fifty feet, there're two mine shafts. The second one. She's in the second one. Now cut me loose and let me go."

Toots said, "No chance buttlicker." She pulled back to go at him again.

"Babe," I said, "we need him. What if he's lying? Cut him loose. Take him with us."

She scowled but produced a knife, from who knows where, and sliced through his bindings. I let the tailgate down with a bang. Jenks fell to the sandy ground, his arms still taped to his sides. Sand stuck to the bloody dents in his head. In the moonless night he could have been a sick, demented sugar cookie.

He spit sand. "Well, help me up, son of a bitch."

I took him under the arm and lifted him to his feet. My heart thumped hard from that little dab of exertion. Toots stiff-armed him to get him going. He lost his balance and fell face first. He screamed before he hit the ground, his mouth filling with sand. He sputtered and spit, coughed and choked.

The odds weren't good for finding Donny Martin alive, not if he'd thrown her down a mine shaft. Still, I told Toots, "Ease off."

He spit more sand and said, "Hands down you're the craziest fucker I've ever seen. And I've seen some crazy bastards in the joint."

"Shut up." I jerked his arm. Toots followed along, hitting him in the back with her high heel.

"Ouch! Come on, man, stop that shit."

I didn't say anything to her. This time, with all the duct tape, she wasn't penetrating down to the flesh. Once behind the shack, the headlights out front deflected to either side, casting a long shadow where we most needed to see. With one hand I held up Jenks until my eyes had a chance to adjust.

Twenty yards from the back of the shack were two holes, just like he'd said, only they weren't mine shafts at all. Jenks was ignorant. The owner, the homesteader, not knowing any better had tried to dig a well. The first one came up dry, so the fool had then shifted over ten feet and tried again. In the back of the shack the ground was sandy and gave way to decomposed granite. The homesteader had to have some tenacity to dig any depth in that stuff.

I said to Jenks, "How deep are they?" I didn't need to ask, not really. We were too late. Toots ran over to the first hole and looked down. We caught up with her.

Jenks said, "Be careful, that one's full of rattlesnakes." He cackled and kicked some rock and sand into the hole. The snakes rattled and hissed.

And Jenks thought I was the crazy one.

When I looked up Toots had already moved to the other dry well. "Bub, Bub, you better get over here."

That's when I heard it, a weak plea. "Help me. Please help me."

A lump the size of Rhode Island rose in my throat. I let go of Jenks and ran to the hole, got down on my stomach, and eased up to the edge. I couldn't see anything but darkness. "Donny, are you down there?"

"Yes, help me. Please help me. It's dark and I'm scared. I'm real scared. I'm so thirsty."

This wasn't happening. No way was this happening. Not a miracle of this magnitude. She couldn't still be alive.

I looked up at Toots. "Is this real?"

Tears filled her eyes for the second time that night. She could only nod at first, then said, "You did it, Bub. You saved her."

I turned back to the hole. "You're safe now, Donny. I'm with the Sheriff's Department. I'll get you out. Help is on the way."

She cried, "Thank you, mister. Hurry, please hurry."

When I looked up Jenks was backing away from a semi-crouched Toots, who was barefoot, spiked heel in hand, stalking him like a big cat. She caught up to him when he stopped. He said, "Tell her to stop. Tell this crazy bitch to stop right there."

I said, "So you do see--."

Toots brought her leg up, her red diaphanous dress fluttering in the warm desert breeze. She kicked him in the chest. Jenks flew back. He bounced on one side but fell down the first hole. He shrieked in terror as the rattlesnakes had at him. In no time his shrieks tapered off to mewing, then to nothing at all.

I said to Toots, "I wish you hadn't done that."

"No you don't. You can kiss my white ass, Bub. You wish you'd had the satisfaction of doing it yourself."

I didn't have time to join her. "How are we going to get her out of that hole? We don't have any rope. I can't leave her here all alone while I go for help."

Donny's meek voice rose up out of the hole. "Mister, are you still there? I'm scared. Hurry, Mister."

I got down on my stomach at the edge of the hole and peered into the darkness. "I'm here, Donny. I'll get you out." I came back away and said to Toots, "There any rope in the truck?"

She appeared beside me. "Nope."

"Maybe I could climb down there, get her, and climb up with her on my back?"

"Come on, Bub, get real. With that ticker you got, no chance."

"How, then? Tell me how."

"There's only one way, but it's not good for you."

"That doesn't matter. Tell me how?"

She handed me a cell phone. "It's the widow's. I thought we might need it. You make that call, you're going to go to jail for a long, long time, Bub."

"That's not even a consideration." I took the phone from her. "Besides, like you said, they haven't made a jail that could hold the invisible man."

"You've been lucky so far. Now you're labeled an escape

risk and you're going into high security lockdown. And you're not really--."

I didn't want to hear the rest. I opened the phone and dialed Novak.

32

"WILL, WHERE ARE you?" His voice was more desperate and angry than the last time we spoke. He'd called me by name. He already knew the number belonged to the widow and figured out I'd been at the house. He continued, "You need to come in. I'm on Val Verde. What a mess, Will. I guess I'm following around a trail of your destruction tonight."

"I didn't kill Captain Wolford."

He'd already made up his mind about me. He said, "The house—Jesus, Will, did you do all of this? Never mind, we need Jenks. Where do you have Jenks? You have to bring him in. He has a hearing in four hours. It's our best shot, our only shot, to get the girl. Will, you haven't...You haven't abused him in any way, have you?"

I looked back over my shoulder, saw nothing but darkness where Jenks now resided in the hole. I ignored Novak's question. "I have the girl."

"*What? Say again?*" The anger left his voice, exchanged for pure excitement. "Where? Where are you? What's her condition? Jesus, Will, why didn't you say so? Where are you?"

"Jenks threw her down a hole. I can't get to her, but she's alive and in pretty good shape considering what's happened. You need to get here fast. Get search and rescue rolling and call in an airship for an immediate medical evac."

"You got it, Will. No problem. Where? Tell me where and

we'll be there."

I hadn't been paying attention on the drive, not exactly. I looked at Toots for help. She said, "Seventeen point eight miles north on Old Woman Springs Road, then turn east."

I repeated it into the phone.

"Okay," Novak said, "but who's out there with you? Who're you talking to?"

"Toots." I said it like it was the most obvious answer.

"Toots?"

I ignored him.

Toots smiled, "You know you've never acknowledged me before except to that dumb-assed shrink two years ago."

Things were definitely changing.

She said, "Go east for three point two then north for two point six."

I told him.

Novak said, "Okay, Will, we have the whole world responding. You sit tight. We'll be there in no time."

"Will?" This time a siren in the background washed out the timbre of his voice. He'd gotten into a patrol car and someone was driving him hell bent to get to us first while he handled things by phone and radio.

"Yeah?"

"How's Jenks?"

"He's close by."

"Okay, I'll accept that for now. But we have to talk, okay?" He paused a long moment then, "I got a lot of folks rolling hot your way. I need to know."

"Yeah?"

"Is this for real? I mean you're not--?"

"I guess you'll have to get here before you find out."

Novak said, "Okay, okay, I gotcha. I'm now being told the closest unit to you is at least thirty minutes away. You going to be good with that?"

"Why wouldn't I--."

Toots had disappeared and now returned driving the Ford Ranger across the sandy desert right toward me the headlights dancing, spearing the night. She stopped, the tires a mere two feet from the edge of the dry well. I ended the call. "What are you doing?"

She got out, still barefoot. "I heard him say thirty minutes. That's not good enough. We have to move now. We have to get her to the hospital, Honey, or she's not going to make it."

"What are you talking about?" I edged over and peered down. The headlights beamed over the hole, but there was sufficient reflection to see now. Ten feet down, Donny lay on a narrow ledge composed of dirt and one large, flat-topped rock. The hole went on down below her another thirty feet. She'd been lucky. Only she hadn't been. She lay there crumpled, unmoving. "Donny? Talk to me, Donny." My heart rate went up. What happened? She'd been fine a minute ago.

Toots was tying a cheap piece of yellow nylon rope to the front bumper. The rope wasn't long enough. She said, "I found it behind the seat."

I slid around, took the rope around my waist, and started easing my feet over the edge.

Toots came over. "No, don't, Bub. You're too big and the rope isn't going to hold you, let alone the both of you. It has to be me. Here, let me do it."

"I can't let you do that." What I should've said was, don't be ridiculous; a hallucination can't conduct a rescue.

At the same time the rope felt narrow and flimsy in my hands. "Okay, but once you get down there, tie a loop under her shoulders and I'll pull her up first, then put it back down for you."

She nodded, fear all over her expression.

I said, "Babe, be careful." Her feet were over the edge as she'd started to walk down the side of the well wall, her head just barely visible.

She said, "I love the crap out of you, Will Donnelly."

"I know you do, kid. Believe me, I know you do."

I watched her progress, holding my breath. She got down to the ledge. There wasn't room for both of them. I don't know how she did it. Somehow she edged her bare foot under Donny and moved her enough to get a foothold. Toots had been right; I could never have done this. She eased Donny up and got the loop around under her arms and tied her off. I started to pull and couldn't. I panicked. I didn't have the strength. My heart. I didn't have enough strength to crawl, let alone pull up this little girl's dead weight. "Toots, I can't do it. We're just going to have to wait until help gets here."

"Bub, look at me." She stared up. She said, "You have to trust me when I say this girl doesn't have that much time left. We have to get her to the hospital now. Get in the truck and back it up real slow. I'll hold her away from the wall as best I can. Do it, Bub. Do it right now. Don't think about it, just do it."

I didn't know how it could possibly work, but I did it. As I backed up, out front in the headlights the top of Donny's head appeared first, brown hair all dusty. Then her closed eyes; they scared me. She was pale, too pale, with dark half-moons under her eyes. She was in a bad way. Now I saw it. Toots had been right; we couldn't wait. We had to move fast. Once Donny was out of the hole I stopped, put the brake on, got out, untied her, and gently picked her up. She was as frail as a broken bird.

Toots appeared beside me. "Come on, shag that ass, Bub. We gotta move."

How had Toots gotten out of the hole without the rope? I didn't stop to ask; I got into the passenger side of the truck with Donny as Toots got in to drive. She backed up, spinning sand and dust into the night. She got it turned around and hit the gas. She never let off.

33

DONNY'S BREATH WAS shallow against my neck as I gently held her. We both bounced in the seat as Toots gunned then let off the accelerator to get around natural obstacles in the road: dips, boulders, downed Joshua trees. I whispered over the noise of the revving engine: "It's okay, little girl, you're going to make it. I promise. We'll be there soon."

In no time at all we climbed out of the desert and were back on the asphalt of Old Woman Springs. The rubber grabbed and chirped. Now Toots really opened it up and we screamed along, the desert wind blasting in the two open windows. The truck rattled all over, pushed beyond its mechanical capabilities, threatening to self-destruct.

Up ahead we could see red-and-blue rotating lights; Novak and his crew headed our way. I said, "Here they are. Pull over. We made it. Pull over, Toots."

She slowed down and brought the speed from eighty, down to fifty, then to forty. Forty, after going a hundred for so long, felt like going ten. The Sheriff vehicles whipped past us in a blur.

"Hey, stop," I said. "What are you doing?"

"I told you, there isn't time. We stop and there's going to be a lot of arguing about which is the best plan: stay and wait for paramedics or an airship or just roll her to the hospital like we're doing now. I told you. There isn't time for that kind of crap. You have to trust me on this."

The Sheriff patrol cars continued to whip past. I had seconds to think about it, to go with it or protest. The last patrol car went by. I watched it grow smaller in the rear view. I looked forward at the road ahead. A straggler was coming, but slower than the rest; one last Sheriff's unit.

I said to Toots, "Tell me it's not that you're afraid they're going to arrest me, because if it is, then we need to stop right now and wait for them. My incarceration is not going to be a consideration, not under these circumstances."

The last Sheriff's car came up fast. Toots didn't look at me or answer. I stuck my hand out the passenger window and waved. The sheriff's unit braked hard but was going too fast and skidded on by.

In the rear view mirror he turned around, fish-tailed in the dirt, and headed back our way. Toots started to speed up. I reached over and put my hand on hers, on the steering wheel. I felt nothing, but she accepted the gesture for what it was, looking at me with sorrow in her eyes. She eased off the accelerator and we rolled over to the dirt shoulder.

Toots said, "Donny has fifteen minutes, no more. This is the wrong move, Bub, and it hurts me to think how much you're going to regret this decision for the rest of your life."

Her words tore at my heart. How did she know there were only fifteen minutes? How did she know anything, though? Too late. We couldn't start up again, not with the Sheriff walking up on us.

The cab filled with the bright spotlight from the Sheriff's unit. A shadow appeared as the deputy walked up on a truck he thought was in distress, just a citizen flagging him down for help. The deputy came up on the passenger side. I saw him in the mirror; recognized him. Before he got all the way to the window—I didn't want him to spook—I said, "Sergeant Dewitt, it's Will Donnelly. We need a code three escort to Desert Valley Hospital, and we need it right now."

He appeared in the window, his mouth hanging open. "Son of a bitch." He reached for his lapel mic to advise Novak what he had.

"Wait," I said, "don't do that. This little girl isn't going to make it unless we get her to the hospital, right now. Give us an escort."

He opened the truck door. "Get out."

"Phil, did you hear what I said, we need to—"

"Don't be a horse's ass, Donnelly, get her in my car. It's faster."

I carried Donny back to the Sheriff's unit. Phil opened the passenger door. I hopped in. He closed the door. He ran around the front, the headlights bright against his tan and green uniform.

Toots jumped in the back seat. Phil got in, put it in gear, and floored it before his door was closed. He'd been right. The Sheriff's unit's quick acceleration stuck me to the seat as the speedometer approached a hundred. He picked up the radio and keyed the mic. "Seven Sam Two, advise Desert Valley Hospital I'm responding code three with Donny Martin. Have them standing by at the ER door. Subject is extremely critical. ETA four and a half minutes."

"Seven Sam Two, ten-four, they're being advised. One hundred. Did you copy that, traffic?"

Novak came up on the radio. "Affirmative. Seven-Sam-Two. Hold your position; we're turning around."

Phil did not even hesitate. "Negative, there isn't time."

I said to Phil, "That's not going to help you get transferred out of the Mongo anytime soon."

"Kiss my ass, Donnelly. Tell me what happened with Captain Wolford?"

"It's a long story."

"You have three and a half minutes until we get to the hospital to convince me."

"I didn't kill him."

Novak wouldn't be put off. His voice roared over the radio. "Sergeant Dewitt, do you have Sergeant Donnelly with you?"

Phil ignored Novak and said to me, "The only reason

you're not handcuffed and in the back seat is because I find it hard to believe someone could commit murder and an hour later rescue a little girl."

"Sergeant Dewitt, acknowledge. If you have Donnelly with you, you are to detain him. Do you understand?"

Old Woman Springs was a two-lane highway divided with a double yellow line. The road rolled with the contours of the desert. Dewitt had the Sheriff's unit barely under control. In some of the dips the suspension came up high enough that the car was all but airborne. It took both hands and all of his concentration.

I said, "A man named Henry Sanchez killed Wolford."

Dewitt didn't look at me; he couldn't afford to and continue to maintain control of the car. "Tell me why?"

Novak would be livid if I let it slip now. "I was assigned here for a specific reason. Wolford was dirty. Novak wanted me to investigate him."

Dewitt's mouth gaped. He turned and looked at me for a second, then back at the road, as we came up on Highway 62. He made the turn against a red signal to go eastbound. Now we were two minutes from Desert Valley Hospital.

He said, "Novak assigned you here under cover, is that what you are telling me?"

"Yes."

We rode in silence.

Two minutes later he made the last turn, drove past the Sheriff's station, and on up to the hospital. Three nurses and a doctor stood by a gurney. They opened the door and gently took Donny Martin from me and laid her down. They ran into the hospital with her, the doctor spouting directions to his staff.

Dewitt slammed the gearshift back into drive and burned rubber. My door closed. With Donny Martin taken care of, every last bit of energy seeped out of me. I'd only been held together by the need to get her help. The long night tangling with Jenks and pulling Donny from the hole was too much for my weak heart.

Dewitt was driving me down the hill to the Sheriff's Station where I'd be booked for murder, and I didn't care. All I wanted to do was to curl up and go to sleep. I closed my eyes for a long while.

When I opened them again we weren't at the jail. We were parked to the side of the Safari Motel. Dewitt was helping me out of the car.

I said, "What's going on?"

"I'm hiding you here until I find out exactly what's going on."

"I don't understand."

He walked me with his arm around my waist holding me up. He juggled me and the motel key until he got the door open. He eased me down on the battered mattress. He said, "Rest. I'll come back in a few hours and we'll talk."

"Tell me now. Why?"

He stopped, his hand on the door, and half-turned. "I wasn't promoted and transferred out here. I was promoted and transferred to Internal Affairs. Captain Rymes, now it seems without the sanction of the department, assigned me to Joshua Tree Station to find out what the hell Wolford was up to."

34

WHAT DEWITT SAID before I fell into an exhausted, mindless sleep swirled around in my brain as I rose up from a black hole, back to the living. Toots lay next to me on her stomach, naked, facing the end of the bed, watching television and smoking a cheap, generic cigarette. Water beaded on her back and down to the cleave of her bottom. Her hair was damp as well from a recent shower. She smelled wonderfully of lilac. I don't know how I detected the essence of sweet lilac with the smoke cloud hanging over her like that. I still wore the now filthy hospital scubs. My voice cracked from the lack of fluids. I'd been in the desert too long without water.

I said, "What's going on?" as I staggered into the bathroom, turned on the tap, and stuck my head under the lukewarm water.

She kept watching television. "Sssh, your buddy Novak's giving a briefing on what happened yesterday."

"Yesterday?" I came out of the bathroom with water running down my front.

"Ssssh."

I looked at the window. Dull yellows and oranges peeked through the edges of the drab curtains. Sunset. I'd slept all day. In a semi-daze I walked to the bed and plopped down.

Novak stood behind a podium in the Sheriff's conference room, his face lined and haggard. Above his head on the wall was a large plaster cast of the five point Sheriff's star, painted in gold and blue and red. He said: "First, I'd like to update everyone on Donny Martin's condition. She is critical but stable, with a positive prognosis. She is improving with every hour. My department will, of course, keep you updated as we receive more information.

"As far as the suspect: we have discovered Abel Jenks' body out at the crime scene, the one located off Old Woman Springs Road. He apparently took the victim to this remote old homestead and held her there." Novak pointed to an enlarged map of the area with a red arrow indicating the exact spot. "It appears suspect Jenks may have accidentally fallen into a deep hole and succumbed to his injuries from the fall."

Toots lightly kicked her legs, the heels of her feet coming back alternately and touching her naked bottom. She smiled. "Right, fell in. That's rich. Ain't that rich, Bub? That's really rich."

Back on the television, off screen, a reporter yelled, "We have information Abel Jenks was wrapped up like a mummy with duct tape. How exactly did he get all taped up like that where he could fall into the hole?"

Novak had a media leak big enough to sink a ship. Someone had talked and now the media had the scent. They wouldn't up give easily.

Toots giggled. "Novak doesn't have the balls to tell them about the rattlesnakes. Ain't that right, Bub? The press would mutilate him if he did. Tear him to shreds just like the snakes did to Jenks. Ain't that right, Bub?" She threw her head back, "Hah."

"Sssh, listen."

Judging by Novak's expression, anger took him; he tried to suppress it. "The entire matter is still under investigation. I will give you the facts as we get them. Moving on." He held out his arm, his expression changed to a forced smile. Sergeant Phil Dewitt came into view, Novak ushering him.

Novak said, "You have asked how we found Donny Martin. Donny Martin was found by Sergeant Dewitt here, after one great piece of police work."

Toots sat up on her elbows. "Buuuuullshit, Bub, that's bullshit. That sawed-off little asswipe is taking all the credit for what you and I did."

"Take it easy," I said. "It doesn't matter who gets the credit as long as Donny Martin's okay." I didn't want to tell her how bad I felt about what she'd done to Abel Jenks. Truly, I could not wish what had happened to Jenks on anyone: Thrown down a hole with his arms and hands taped, face exposed to vipers. Even for the likes of Abel Jenks, that was simply too horrific.

She swung around and sat on the edge of the bed. "No, that's wrong." She said, "If the public knew you were involved and how you saved her, it would go a long way in court and even with probation. They might even give you a suspended sentence. This isn't fair. I'm going to call that horse's ass and tell him what I think."

She'd already forgotten about the felonious assault on Henry Sanchez in Texas. Something else I'd have to answer for.

Reporters yelled: "Sergeant Dewitt, how did you do it?"

Dewitt remained silent and didn't look happy about being up behind the podium with the Sheriff. From what I knew of Dewitt, Novak had to have strong-armed him into doing it.

Novak held up his hands to silence the crowd. "I have some new information. Please settle down."

The questions abated. Novak let the silence hang a long moment then said, "Out at the crime scene on Old Woman Springs Road we have located the remains of a second victim."

I rolled off the bed and stood; the room spun a little from the dizziness. I'd stood up too fast. Or was it this new information? I watched Novak's lips, waiting for him to continue.

He said, "As you know, two years ago we suspected Abel Jenks of being involved in the kidnapping of Peggy Kellogg. This is not confirmed, but we believe there is a strong possibility, and let me emphasize a possibility only, that the remains belong to Peggy Kellogg."

I whispered, "He can't say something like that, not without justification. What if he's wrong? Peggy's family would be unjustly hurt and shoved onto an emotional roller coaster."

Novak held up a clear plastic evidence bag. Cameras zoomed in, brought the contents in bright and large and distinct.

A pink iPhone.

Just like the one in the picture, the one with Jenks lurking in the flea market where Peggy disappeared. Novak was right. They had found Peggy Kellogg.

Like everyone else I had held out a small kernel of hope that Peggy was alive, living with a family somewhere with new brothers and sisters in a good home. What a crock. I was an adult and shouldn't give in to fairy tales. It can only lead to heartbreak and depression. And I'd had my fill of both. I sat back down on the bed and watched the television change and move, not hearing anything said.

TWO YEARS AGO when I had worked the Peggy Kellogg kidnapping and stayed at the Safari, open desert spanned both sides of the motel for several blocks. Now when I looked out the window the sunset colored everything gold, including the new Walmart across the road. I asked Toots, "Do we have any money?" Obviously I was tired and depressed, asking a hallucination if she had any cash.

Toots stood and padded naked over to where her clothes lay, deflated, at the entrance to the bathroom. Unabashed, she bent over, everything on display, and rummaged through her red diaphanous dress. She hesitated in what she was doing and peeked back at me. "Like what you see, Bub? You want a little of this?" She wiggled her naked bottom.

Sweat broke out on my forehead. I didn't answer. She went back to her search.

The dress didn't have any pockets and yet her hand came

away with some folded currency. She stood, came over, and kissed me. I felt nothing physically, but emotionally the kiss sparkled and warmed me all the way down to my toes. She put the wad in my shirt pocket and said, "Daddy going to take baby shopping for some new clothes?"

"Yes, get dressed. And please don't refer to us as Daddy and Baby." I wanted to kiss her again but was a fool for having the urge, the desire, the absolute need.

What I needed even more was a shower, but I didn't want to take one just to put on dirty clothes. We went across the street to the Walmart. The parking lot sparked a memory. This had been the spot where, right after finding Wolford dead, we'd parked and watched the Sheriff's units scream by. Ironic: we were less than two blocks from Xavier's, where Wolford had met his untimely demise. Maybe Dewitt was correct with his vortex theory; this desert was a swirling vortex of the weird and strange.

In the past I had received the emails like everyone else, photos of eccentric folks who shopped at Walmart in their bizarre outfits, hairstyles, and make-up. Now I fit right in and kept a lookout for the shoppers snapping pics with their cell phones.

I bought some casual pants and a dress shirt, underwear, socks, and a pair of their most expensive shoes, Rockline hiking boots with steel toes. The line for checkout was long. While we waited Toots picked up a tabloid magazine and thumbed through it, then said, "Hey, Bub, lookie here." She held up the magazine to add credibility to her jest, "Says someone's spotted the invisible man in Texas. Ain't that a hoot? Hey, how would they know they saw him if he was invisible, huh?"

Of course she was pulling my leg. I didn't think it funny in the least.

On an end cap display I also took two pay-as-you-go cell phones. I hadn't thought to count the money and pulled it from my shirt pocket. The top bill was a twenty, the rest—fifteen of them—were all hundreds. I turned to Toots and held up the wad. "Where did you get this money?" She kept reading the tabloid story, shrugged, and said, "The widow. She wasn't going to need it anymore."

"My God, Toots, that's theft." I'd raised my voice. Toots lowered the magazine and looked back over her shoulder to the aisle, as I did the same. Two people in the aisle had their cell phones out, snapping pictures of me.

I couldn't get back to the room fast enough. I was angry with Toots for taking the money. She knew it and lay on the bed, pouting. I went in the bathroom, stripped down, started the water, and took a shower. The bathroom door opened. "Bub, you mind if I join you?"

I couldn't stay mad at her. She'd only taken the money because she thought it was correct under the circumstances. "All right, come on." The warm water immediately turned her tan skin darker and slick. Her nipples stood erect and pink. She opened her arms and said, "Come to mama."

"I *really* wish you wouldn't—"

"Sssh."

I remembered how much I'd enjoyed the last shower with her. Then I remembered what had happened afterward, the man with the ski mask and the knife. We stayed in the shower too long and wasted a lot of water. I came out of the bathroom with my head down, sexually depleted, one towel around my waist another atop my wet hair.

When I lifted my eyes, I found Dewitt sitting in the only chair in the room.

35

UNLIKE IN HIS recent television appearance, Dewitt was out of uniform, wearing Levi's and a plaid, long-sleeved shirt untucked to hide his weapon.

I said, "Oh, sorry. I didn't hear you knock. Come on in and have a seat."

Toots came out behind me dripping without a towel, lighting up a cigarette. She saw Dewitt and slumped over, her hands trying to cover herself as she backed into the steam-filled bathroom. "Pervert. The guy's not only a liar, he's a pervert, too. A Peeping Tom."

I sympathized with her but I couldn't do anything about it. I went and sat on the edge of the bed. Dewitt didn't say anything for a long time. We stared at one another. Toots came out in her red diaphanous dress and tried to sit on my lap with her arm around my shoulder. I moved her to the side.

Dewitt looked at me funny and said, "You feeling all right?"

"Fine, why?"

He shook his head. " The place on Val Verde looked like a slaughter house. One of the worst I've ever seen."

Toots said, "I guess he hasn't seen too many, huh, Bub? Rookie. Remember that one in Chino Hills, the hatchet job with the entire family diced up for dog food. Ouuuh." She shuddered, trying to shake off the images. She hadn't been there; that was years before she came on scene. Now she was tapping into my memories.

Dewitt said, "I'd like to believe you found Abel on Val Verde and he'd already killed the widow before you kidnapped him, taped him up, and tossed him down a hole."

I held his eyes and nodded.

"You throw him down that hole with the snakes?"

Toots said, "Nope, Bub didn't. That little butt-licker tripped and fell in all on his own. Real shame, though. Bub, here, wanted him to stand trial. Not me, no sir. I thought he got just what he deserved." She laughed.

I didn't like her right then, not with that laugh.

I said, "I didn't push him, if that's what you're asking."

Dewitt nodded.

I said, "Tell me about Captain Rymes sending you out here to investigate Wolford."

"I can't. I was ordered not to tell anyone, and it makes sense not to until I find out exactly what's going on and who all is involved. This whole thing is getting complicated."

"So you're worried about losing your job?"

"Damn straight. Why wouldn't I be?"

"What about aiding and abetting a fugitive and setting said fugitive up in a motel?"

He broke eye contact and looked away. After a moment he said, "I hate this. I drove around for an hour making sure no one was following me. I was checking to see if members of my own department were following *me*. I didn't sign up for this shit."

Toots said, "What a wuss."

I said, "The only way you…you and I are going to figure this thing out is if you trust me. That's what you're really struggling with, isn't it? You know in your gut I didn't kill Wolford, and they're out there trying real hard to hang it on me."

"I guess you're right. I still need to ask, though. Straight up: did you do it?"

"I told you, no. Let's move on. I guess I'm the one most

at risk here, so I'll show you my hand first."

He nodded and asked, "What do you know that I don't already know?"

Toots said, "What a buffoon. What kind of question is that? How can you know what he doesn't know?"

I said, "There's a big coincidence here. Does Novak know that Captain Rymes sent you out here to investigate Wolford?"

"I thought you were going to tell me something I didn't know. You just asked me a question, the same question in a roundabout way as the last, which I didn't answer then and I'm not going to answer now."

"You're right. Okay, I'm sorry. Old habits die hard." I hesitated, thinking it through, and said, "The rumor is true. I did steal that three hundred thousand dollars."

He hadn't been ready for that. His mouth sagged open. He had to be thinking he'd made a mistake trusting me, that if I'd stolen that much money maybe I *had* killed Wolford.

He recovered quickly. "How is that relevant?"

"From the beginning. How all of this started. I went into Novak's office to resign. I told him about the theft. He stalled my admin investigation and the criminal and asked me to come out to Joshua Tree to investigate Wolford."

Dewitt stood up. "What?"

Toots said, "Yeah, exactly. Now do you believe him?"

I said, "Let me ask you again. Does Novak know you are out here doing the same thing I am? Did Captain Rymes brief Novak or is she doing this on her own?"

Dewitt's eyes glazed over as he thought it through. He slowly sat back down.

After a moment he returned to earth and said, "I'm calling bullshit on this one. No way. Novak would not send someone with pending discipline out to do an independent, sub-rosa investigation, especially on a Captain. No way. If you found anything, you wouldn't have any credibility in court."

Toots said, "He didn't keep the money, dipshit. He gave it to MADD, Mothers Against Drunk Driving."

I said, "Not that it matters, but I didn't keep the money. I donated it to a good cause."

"You're right. That doesn't matter and you know it."

"Okay, I guess I have to trust you with this. The reason I was sent out here was because Novak received an anonymous tip on the tip line that he had two dirty captains. He did an investigation and found that Wolford had a suspicious financial background. Novak wanted me to find out from Wolford the name of the second captain. Then I assume Novak would restart the investigation through normal channels to go after them. But first he had to find the second captain. His hands are tied until he does. Novak thought I was his only chance."

Toots said, "Yeah, and tell him about how the little whore Captain Rymes showed up at the Tick Tock when you met Wolpig. Tell him that, huh, Bub. Tell him."

I held up my hand to let her know I wanted her to be quiet.

Dewitt said, "That's way out there, man. No way am I going to believe that."

I said, "All right then, what motive could I possibly have for killing Wolford?"

Dewitt glared at me, his eyes searing a hole. He said, "That's easy. One of the oldest reasons in the book. You found out Wolford was having an affair with your wife."

36

I CLUTCHED MY chest and lay back, fighting off the blue spark that now crept dangerously close. I couldn't afford to turn invisible in front of Dewitt, yet the information had been too emotionally charged to control. I told myself over and over, "No, no, its not true," trying to not make it true. But in the far recesses of my mind I sensed something there, a small niggling I couldn't bring up, and it scared the hell out of me, the thought of the unknown.

Toots lay right next to me and whispered, "It's okay, Bub. Breathe; breathe."

I gasped for breath, whispered, "Is it true?"

I watched her eyes for the lie. She looked away and shook her head no. But I didn't know if she meant no, it wasn't true, or no, she wasn't going to tell me.

I had no idea so few words could rock my world so completely, could change everything I had believed in for too many years. So I couldn't accept it as true. I knew my Debra Ann. She wouldn't do something like that. Especially with Wolford.

Of course it wasn't true, not with Wolford.

Dewitt got up and came over. "Are you okay? You want me to get you some water or something? Sorry, I thought you knew."

My voice cracked, "It's not true. You can take my word

on this."

Dewitt disappeared and returned with a glass of water, foggy water from the rusty tap. I took it and drank hungrily, more thirsty than I thought. I handed the empty glass back to him. He automatically went back to get more. From the bathroom he said, "So now you're saying that the second captain involved in this mess is the suspect in the killing?"

He came back and handed me the water. I took it and drank while I thought of my reply. Henry Sanchez was the one who'd killed Wolford. There had been no doubt in my mind until Dewitt brought up the other captain just now. Of course. Wolford's partner in crime would be a logical suspect. I don't know why I had not thought of it before. Blame it on fatigue. Blame it on the lack of oxygen, the oxygen my lungs and heart were not converting. I hadn't told Dewitt about the blackmail scheme Wolford was involved in. I didn't know just how much Dewitt knew. I still owed an allegiance to Novak and wouldn't tell Dewitt. But more important, someone was trying to pin the tail on the donkey—me—with that crap about Debra Ann sleeping with Wolford.

I said, "Who came up with that information, about my wife?"

Dewitt thought about it for a minute and then said, "Chief Rymes."

"*Chief* Rymes?"

"That's right. Novak announced it this afternoon. He promoted her today.

"Rymes told me when I briefed her at the monthly update on my investigative progress. This was about the time when you'd been assigned out here. She told me Wolford came to her and put her on notice. Wolford told her about the thing he had with your wife two years ago. He told her because he was afraid of what you might say or do. Wolford thought you might try and set him up in some way. He thought you'd asked to be transferred to Morongo just to come gunning for him. Rymes thought I should know about it to keep my eyes open in case you did have some sort of vendetta. And apparently Chief

Rymes doesn't know about Novak sending you out here to track Wolford on the hazardous waste graft. Classic example of one hand doesn't know what the other is doing."

I was still reeling from Rymes making Deputy Chief and the smear campaign on Debra Ann, and the last part almost slipped past me. "What? Say that again about the hazardous waste graft?"

Dewitt sat back in the chair and looked at me. "You don't know, do you? You haven't had enough time out here to find anything out. Of course you haven't. Your second day here you ran right into that hazardous waste dump, scooped up Sara Lang, and ran that death sprint. You've been off the books ever since. Okay, here's what I've been able to find out so far."

I nodded for him to go on, still too stunned to answer.

Dewitt said, "The way I make it, Deputy Mannerly and Wolford were real tight; they did everything together."

I remembered what had happened two years earlier with Peggy Kellogg and how Mannerly and Wolford had conspired to beat the truth out of Abel Jenks. It didn't work; Jenks held strong. Mannerly still owned Wolford over it and always would have, had Wolford not conveniently taken a large caliber bullet to the head.

Dewitt continued, "Mannerly retired from the Marine Corps, from the Twentynine Palms Marine Base, and came to work for the Sheriff's Department as a second career—a double-dipper. Did his last eight years assigned at Twentynine Palms as an adjunct to the commandant or something like that. Anyway he had an in to a contract to dispose of the base hazardous waste. He and Wolford set up a shell corporation to bid on it, and with Mannerly's connections won the contract. I've been in contact with NCIS and they're now working the other end of this thing on the base. Wolford and Mannerly didn't want to dispose of the waste the proper way. It was too costly and would severely cut into their profit margin. They started right off dumping it in remote desert areas. But this thing about a second captain's got me scratching my head. It's the first I've heard of it."

I interrupted him. "So with the death of Sara Lang and Deputy John Randle, the felony murder rule applies. Someone died during the commission of a felony. Wolford and Mannerly are now culpable for those murders."

"You're right, I hadn't thought of that."

Toots stood across the room facing me. She made two fists, brought them up by her face and moved them down, mimicking pulling on a mask.

I let out an unintended yelp.

Dewitt said, "What? What's the matter?"

"That day you and I were driving to the call of the waste dump I saw a truck pull off onto the highway, but it was too far away to make it out. I met Mannerly when I came back to work a couple of weeks later and told him that I did see it and that it was a viable lead."

"So?"

"Mannerly came to my house and tried to kill me."

"You're kidding me, right? And you didn't report it?"

"He was wearing a ski mask. I didn't put it together until just now. I'm sure it was him."

"If that's true, then he missed taking you out. And if you follow that line of reasoning, his only other option would be to take out his partner Wolford, so Wolford couldn't cut a deal and hang out Mannerly."

My mind spun far ahead working the angles. I asked, "How much have you found out in your investigation so far?"

"As in what?"

Dewitt was playing it cagey again. "How much were those contracts worth to dump the waste?"

He looked at me, leery. "One hundred and fifty-six thousand. Divide that by two, for Wolford's share, and it's seventy-eight and some changes. You know more than you're telling me, right? You're playing me, right?"

He didn't wait for an answer. He went on, "I did a financial on Wolford. He's got a lot more unexplained income than the seventy-eight K. That's the part you're not telling me, right?"

Toots said, "Hang tough, Bub. Don't cave and tell him about Texas and Wolford's involvement. That's a whole 'nother horse of a different color."

I let his accusation go. "Do you have enough evidence on Mannerly to take him to a jury?"

"Nothing. I got less than nothing. I got zip. The man has covered his tracks like a leopard. Now that Wolford's gone, Mannerly might even skate."

Toots said, "The man's a real tool and has loose wires upstairs," she pointed to her head. "How does a leopard cover his tracks? He doesn't. Ask him, Bub. I wanna see him squirm when he tries to explain it. Go on, ask him, Bub."

I ignored her and said to Dewitt. "No, there's another way."

"How?"

"I go at Mannerly while wearing a wire."

37

DEWITT DIDN'T SAY, "no way" like I thought he might. I knew why he hesitated, though. He didn't like that I was a confessed felon conducting criminal investigations.

I said, "Look at it this way: you can consider me an informant and not a member of the Sheriff's Department. Informants wear wires all the time."

He waved his hand, his eyes in a far-off place. "That would work except for one thing. If Mannerly did take Wolford out like we suspect and he thinks you're a witness against him, there isn't going to be any conversation for the wire. He'll come in low and slow, check out the surroundings, and if he feels safe he'll simply take you out. So no, I don't think the wire is a viable option. Too dangerous."

"He's right, Bub. You're not going to do that. Mannerly scares the hell outta me."

I said, "I can get conversation while he's checking the area out. He might do that. If we can control the area then we can control the meet."

"We can't control the meet. If he decides to whack you it'd take two seconds to pull the trigger."

"Okay, then what other option do we have?"

"We could bring him in and sweat him."

"He's a cop and an ex-marine. He'll laugh at that one. You know I'm right."

Dewitt pondered it for a bit then said, "On one condition."

"Name it."

"We bring in Chief Rymes."

Dewitt wanted to be able to pass off the liability if the trap for Mannerly ended up with someone dead: me.

I said, "You know what she's going to say. She's an administrator and will go with the safest option or not at all. In this case she's now a Chief, an at-will employee who can be fired without cause. No way will she go along with it."

"That's the only way I'll do it."

"Or else what? What's your Plan B? You don't have one. Or you'll have to arrest me; take me in. That's it, isn't it?"

He said nothing. Didn't move.

I said, "Okay, call her. But think about this: what if she's the second captain who's involved?"

"That doesn't play, either. She's the one who sent me out here in the first place."

I almost told him the rest of it. About the DNA Cold Case blackmail scheme that was muddying the water around this hazardous waste conspiracy, making it difficult to decipher how they fit together.

Dewitt hesitated a moment longer, deciding, I was sure, whether he even wanted to broach this crazy plan to his boss. He got up. "I'll be back. This is something that should be said face to face."

"So you're sure Rymes isn't the second captain."

"Novak sent you out here. He knows about two captains being involved. Do you think he would promote someone who wasn't vetted? He'd look like a country rube if he did it without knowing for sure. Novak's no dummy. No, I'm confident Rymes is okay."

What he said made a lot of sense. He left. When the door closed the room was strangely quiet. By leaving this time, he put a lot of trust in me.

Toots said, "Don't, Bub. Don't do this. I'm asking you, please. I have a real bad feeling about this."

I did too but wouldn't tell her. She'd only worry more. "I'll wear body armor."

"I'm not a fool, Bub. Wolford was shot in the head. Marines are trained killers, trained marksmen."

I didn't want to think about the operation anymore. All that dominated my thoughts were Debra Ann—her last days, her last hours. Debra Ann had been late to La Chemine the night of our anniversary. She should've been there before me by a good long stretch. My mind mulled it over and over, then happened on something else amiss. Something small, but those small things, when added together, could make a big thing. That night when I left the Peggy Kellogg investigation and drove home, I called Debra Ann from our street and never made it into the house before turning around. Had she been there all along? Had Wolford been there with her?

Then my mind, all on its own, tracked Wolford that day. He'd been out at Morongo Station; he'd come out back and defended his man Mannerly when Mannerly brought in "the piece of raw meat," as my boss Coleman put it. If Wolford and Debra Ann had been seeing each other, it wasn't that evening. Unless Wolford could have raced ahead of me? He could've driven like a wild man, exceeding the speed limit, and gotten there ahead of me, but not by much. He wouldn't have had much time at the house. Had he parked around the corner? Had he been in the house?

No chance, and I hated myself for even thinking of it.

Then I thought of something that made my head swim. That day, two years ago, out in back of the station, Wolford had said something. What was it? What were his exact words? Wolford had asked about Debra Ann. That's right, and I couldn't ever remember an event where Debra Ann had met him. Wolford of course knew Joan but had never met Debra Ann. I was sure of it; we traveled in different circles. Debra Ann and I kept mostly to ourselves. But Debra Ann had worked as a manager at The Tick Tock and would've met a lot of the cops who frequented the place. Wolford went there on a regular basis.

This was driving me crazy. There was a simple explanation for every little bit of damning information. I still loved Debra Ann dearly, and without concrete evidence I would not tarnish her memory. I would not believe she had anything to do with Wolford.

Toots said, "Bub, don't do this, please."

"Don't worry about it. Nothing's in stone right now. You heard what I said, in all likelihood Rymes isn't going to go for it. My best guess is that when Dewitt lays out to her what's going on, she'll roll out the SWAT team to come take us down."

Toots smiled. "I like it that you said us. We're like Bonnie and Clyde, aren't we, Bub? Can I have a gun, a big one like a machine gun?" She brought her hands up like she held a Tommy gun and made the noise like kids do. "Brrrrrat, brrrrat, brrrrat." It made me smile.

I'd talked myself into believing what was going to happen, that Dewitt would be overruled. I wasn't ready to lie down and let the justice system bulldoze me right into prison. Not before I finished what I had to do. I said, "Come on, get your things. We're leaving."

We went across the street to the Sands Motel. I registered and insisted on a room that faced Highway 62. The nice Indian woman said those rooms were too noisy and tried to talk me into one further to the rear, away from the highway. We took the room out front, furthest on the end, with just enough of an angle to see the Safari Motel and our old room, the one we'd just left.

I opened the curtain a smidgen and watched The Safari, hoping I wasn't right. Toots sat next to me. We waited in silence for an hour, then two. I was tired of waiting. I opened one of the cell phones from Walmart and dialed Sheriff Novak.

38

"THIS IS SHERIFF Novak."

"Hey, it's me."

Novak hesitated, trying to place my voice. When he did he said in a somber tone, "Will, where are you?"

"You of all people know where I am."

"What are you talking about? How would I know?"

He shouldn't know. I was just testing him, an old interrogation trick. The problem with cop tricks was that Novak knew them all. When I didn't answer he said, "Will, I want you to come in. Don't jack me around on this now. This time it's an order, you understand? I'm ordering you in. No more messing around. Drive to headquarters right now. I'll personally debrief you."

"Do you have a suspect on the Wolford killing? Did you look into Henry Sanchez?"

"There's a big problem with that. I'd rather not discuss it over the phone. That's why I said I would personally debrief you."

"What's going on?"

"Not over the phone."

"Did you promote Captain Rymes to Deputy Chief?"

"Yes. And I know what you're going to ask next. She is not the second Captain."

"How do you know?"

"Will, this game of cat and mouse you're playing here is bullshit. It's me, Novak; I'm not going to screw you over. You know that."

"I have to tell you, Sheriff, I'm a little mixed up here. I don't know who's playing on what team."

At that moment I decided not to tell him about Rymes sending Dewitt out to the desert to investigate Wolford. He may or may not have known, but he wasn't going to get it from me.

Toots sat close, her ear right up by the phone. She said, "He's running scared. He's not going to get re-elected if this mess all comes out at once and he doesn't have a good handle on it. He's looking for a scapegoat, Bub, and he's looking to hang this whole mess on you. I can tell by the tone in his voice. Right now he's pissin' in his boxer shorts."

I hadn't heard anything in Novak's tone that would indicate anything close to what she was describing.

"Come on," Toots said. "Let's go get Henry's money and jam on down to Costa Rica. We could really live the life down there. White sand beaches, palm trees and monkeys. You know they have monkeys down there, Bub?"

I'd forgotten about the go-bag, the grip we'd taken from Henry Sanchez's house and shipped to our house on Kadota in Montclair. Half a million dollars cash now sat on our porch, put there by FedEx with no one to take it inside.

Novak said, "What are you talking about, who's on what team? There's only one team here and you're on it with me. Tell me where you are and I will personally drive there and pick you up."

Maybe he was right. If you couldn't trust the Sheriff, who could you trust?

"You're not going to book me then, for the money, like you wanted to the other night?"

"No. Not the way you helped out with Donny Martin. Don't be ridiculous."

"You're not going to book me for killing Wolford?"

"Will, would you quit with the bullshit. I'd tell you if I was going to do that. You know me."

Toots said, "Yeah, right. He had Buck take you in to book you. We had to escape. We were lucky that time. What's changed?" She got up and moved to the curtains and peeked out at the cars rushing by on Highway 62. She said, "Ask him what's changed?"

I said, "If I'm not wanted for anything, why can't I stay out in the field and work this investigation? I have some great leads."

Toots, still watching the traffic, said over her shoulder, "Good one, Bub. I'd like to hear how he answers that one."

Novak said, "I'll be honest with you, Will, there are some things about what happened in Texas that we need cleared up. Once we do that, I'll let you investigate this whole mess, I promise. I need you on it."

"You mean you finally believe me about Henry Sanchez being the number one suspect in the Wolford murder?"

"I didn't want to get into this on the phone. I looked into what you told me. I called the Texas Rangers. All of it jives and you're not in any trouble with what happened."

When he paused I said it for him, "But?"

"As I said, everything matches: the house address, the description of the crime scene, all of it but the name. The guy's name isn't Henry Sanchez. Which kind of throws a big wrench in the works."

"What are you talking about? Of course it's Henry Sanchez. I talked to him. Did the cops in Texas contact him? I saw the cop cars pulling up to the house when I was leaving."

"No, no one has seen him. He got away clean, though there was lots of blood. Your blood as well. You didn't tell me about getting shot. Buck had to tell me. That's one of those other things we need to talk about. I need a deposition from you to send to Texas. They are going to send out a Ranger to interview you.

"I had the DA issue a warrant for that guy's arrest on those Cold Case hits you told me about, once I confirmed them. Coleman is one pissed-off mother about what's going on, because I hadn't told him and he supervises Cold Case. I only just found out when you told me out at the airport. That's the only reason he promised to keep it quiet until we find out what's going on with the other captain."

Toots still had not looked back from the window and said, "He's a captain. How does Novak know Coleman's not involved?"

I had picked up on it too but was more interested in the other thing. "If you issued a warrant for someone who lived at that residence, then what name did you get the warrant for?

"Robert Campbell."

"What?"

"That's right, Will, Robert Campbell. I checked it out. He's the guy who killed those women all those years ago. The DNA matches the hit. You just got the name confused, that's all. You've had a lot going on lately. Dewitt told me about how you saved Donny Martin. Come on in and let's talk about all of it."

This wasn't good. Novak thought I was some kind of mental case. If I came in now he was going to hang everything he could on me, just like Toots said. He didn't need to find that second captain. He had *me* already fitted for a straightjacket.

Toots said, "Bub, you better come over here and take a look at this." Her tone sucked all the air out of me. The wound on my side started to throb. I went to the window with Novak still talking, trying to convince me, his voice small, tinny. Across the street a black suburban with a stick of SWAT members dressed in black utilities with Kevlar helmets, the men hanging off the sides, drove up to The Safari and deployed on the room we'd been in. They broke out the windows, threw in flash-bang grenades, and rammed the door down. The muffled explosions from the flash-bangs blew the curtains out the broken windows. Smoke billowed. Seconds later the men in black came out shaking their heads. Their fugitive had fled.

39

I CAREFULLY CLOSED the phone on Novak the Sheriff.

Novak the liar.

If he lied about wanting me to come in and said there wasn't a problem, then he might've lied about the Robert Campbell name as well. The Campbell name difference wouldn't have been such a big deal, but if the name *was* Campbell and not Henry Sanchez then I no longer had any business on the street. It would mean, without question, that I belonged in the land of the mentally disenfranchised, doomed to roam the sterile halls of a state-run booby hatch. Henry Sanchez remained too real in my memory and unlike the...the hallucinations that I understood and accepted.

Toots read my thoughts, leaned over, and said, "You saw your phone, the one you threw away on Val Verde. The text from Wolpig used the name Henry Sanchez. Right? Least that's what you told me it said. Right?"

"Do you think you can find that place on Val Verde where I threw the phone?"

"Not a problem at all, but we don't have any wheels and it's five point three miles from here."

"I'll call a cab."

They might have tracked the phone and recovered it already. I had to try. I went to the phone and picked it up as a knock came at the door.

Toots went to open it.

I said, "Hold it, don't do that." Then I realized, what did it matter? We were trapped like a couple of rats. Resigned to our fate, I put the phone down and went to the window. The SWAT team was loading up and not paying attention to what was happening across the highway here at The Sands. I pivoted and peeked at who was at the door: Chief Mary Rymes and Sergeant Phil Dewitt, looking nervous. I opened the door. They both slid in and closed the door, not wanting to be seen by their cohorts across the street.

Ordinary Mary looked the part, with stone-washed denim pants and a light blue, long-sleeved shirt with embroidered flowers. She wore cowboy boots and a narrow leather belt with a small silver western-style buckle. A ball cap with *Upland Feed and Grain* pulled her thick hair in and made her head a little pointy. On her hip she wore a hand-tooled custom leather holster with a compact Glock .45. She wanted so badly to be a street cop.

I asked, "How did you know I moved from the Safari over to here?"

Dewitt said, "I had Buck Dobbs watching you."

Toots said, "So much for trust, huh, Bub? The little twit."

I asked, "How come Buck isn't calling Coleman and telling him where I am? If I'm not mistaken, Buck still works for Coleman."

Mary Rymes hadn't said a thing and only stared. She said, "Tell me, right now: you didn't take out Wolford?"

"You know I didn't or you wouldn't be here, but if you insist on hearing it from me, then no, I had nothing to do with the murder of Captain Wolford."

She accepted my statement and I felt a small pang of guilt. Had it been Henry Sanchez who took out Wolford I might have set all of this in motion. But Wolford was the one who'd sent me on that mission, so it evened out. A little. She said, "Okay, Sergeant Dewitt briefed you on the hazmat corruption case. I believe Mannerly's good for this, which makes him a prime suspect for the Wolford killing. And I agree with you, the best way to go at him is to wire you up."

I said, "Congratulations on making Chief."

Her stern, all-business expression broke into a weak half-smile. "Thank you. We can talk about that later. Let's get this thing rolling."

Dewitt opened his phone, dialed and said, "Come on in."

I said to Mary, "You're taking quite a chance." I nodded toward the window. "It looks like they want me pretty badly."

She said, "It's that bastard Coleman. He's the one pushing so hard. He thinks you're good for the Wolford killing. Can't really blame him, the way things look, anyway."

Dewitt said, "Coleman had his eye on that Deputy Chief slot you just got. So if you ask me, I think he wants to wrap up the largest dirty cop case in the history of the county to rub your nose in it."

When he said it he was looking at Mary with an expression I'd seen before. Sergeant Phil Dewitt was enamored with Deputy Chief Rymes. Probably, though, nothing more than an infatuation. A good old schoolyard crush. Puppy love.

Rymes didn't deny Dewitt's accusation about Coleman, which gave it that much more credibility.

I said, "What does Novak say about it? Didn't he sanction the SWAT op?"

"Novak's a politician," she said. "He's standing back and watching, seeing how it's all going to play out. If you think he's your friend, think again. He'll use anyone to maintain his position. He's going to run for county supervisor in November and this whole mess can really screw him up."

Toots said, "Yeah, and guess who has her eye on the top spot, the Sheriff of San Bernardino County." She hooked her thumb in Mary's direction.

How the hell did she know that?

I said, "He promoted you to chief and—."

"You think I owe him some allegiance, some loyalty for it, right? Let's just say it didn't happen the way it looks. He had little choice in the matter." She wanted to say more but glanced over at Dewitt, who was watching out the window.

I made a mental note to ask her to elaborate later.

I had one more pressing question to ask, but not in front of Dewitt. I said, "Who told you I was flying into Ontario on that flight?"

"What are you talking about? What flight? Where did you go? Wait a minute; you were supposed to be on a short leash with that case hanging over your head. You flew someplace? Well, hell, no wonder Coleman's so pissed off. I guess I didn't have all the information." She looked at Dewitt who, concerned, heard and stepped away from the window. She'd played it pretty well. I couldn't tell if she was lying or telling the truth. She said to Dewitt, "You know anything about this?"

"No, Buck told me Will walked away from a hospital check. I didn't ask Buck where he picked him up. I assumed it was at headquarters after the Sheriff talked to Will. Buck said the sheriff told him personally to book Will."

She pointed a finger at me. "Don't get me wrong. Once this is over you're going to be booked for that theft. I'll do what I can with the District Attorney. If this works out I'm sure we can get you a suspended sentence with only probation and a little public service time."

She'd changed her tune since we'd talked when I drove her home from the Tick Tock.

Another knock at the door. Dewitt checked the peek hole and opened it. Buck sauntered in like it wasn't a big deal, carrying a brushed aluminum case, a dumb smile on his mug. When he saw me the smile changed to a scowl.

I said, "Sorry about stepping out on you." I turned to Rymes. "Mary, you asked me if I shot Wolford, and I gave you an honest answer. Now I need to know why you're doing this knowing full well that Novak wants me in custody?"

She took a step closer. Her perfume wafted up, light, airy. She said, "Maybe *I am* off base here. What were you doing at the airport and what does it have to do with all of this?"

I stepped back and sat on the edge of the bed. "You first. Answer my question. Why?"

She turned angry. "Look, mister, I can call this off in one

hot second. You have nothing to negotiate with." I held up my wrists. "Fine, take me in and I'll take my chances."

She hesitated a long time, wanting it her way. She said, "Okay, here it is: I'm the Commander of Internal Affairs and Novak didn't come to me about this little operation out in the desert that he put you onto. Which I could live with; it's his department. But when Dewitt told me there was another captain involved besides Wolford, that smacked of cover-up, and I will not have a cover-up on my watch."

Her explanation made a lot of sense. But she'd done the same thing as Novak by sending Dewitt to Morongo Station to sniff out Wolford without telling the Sheriff. I wanted to tell her about Texas, but something wasn't quite right and I couldn't put my finger on it.

I said, "I was in Texas, conducting an investigation for Novak. I didn't tell Novak about it because it would've compromised his ability to have plausible deniability. The key here, though, is I didn't tell Novak where I was going or when I was coming back. And when I asked him how he knew what flight, he said you told him."

Her mouth dropped open. "I most certainly did not."

"Yeah, I think I believe you."

"You had damn well better believe me, Will Donnelly."

Dewitt had the brushed aluminum case open and was tinkering with a cell phone similar to the one I'd purchased at WalMart. He'd attached a recorder to it with long wires.

He said, "We're ready when you are."

40

MARY NODDED AND said, "We'll most certainly continue this conversation later."

Dewitt checked his notebook and dialed a number. He brought the phone over to me.

Toots said, "Don't do this, Bub. This guy's a freak show. Remember his eyes when he came for us at our house? Remember, Bub? They were dead eyes. The marines train these guys to kill, and this guy enjoys it."

I had to admit, I was afraid of this man. But if it came to letting him walk or putting myself on the line to get him, it was no choice at all.

My side throbbed more.

Neither Dewitt nor Rymes coached me in what to say. They assumed I knew. They both listened in with ear jacks.

On the other end the phone rang twice, stopped ringing and went quiet. I pictured Mannerly sitting in a Lazyboy chair, reclined, wearing only his BVD's, white and stark against overly tanned skin, with his dark green aviator sunglasses masking all other emotions as he listened, waiting for his caller to say something.

I wouldn't relent. I wanted him to say something first.

He hung up.

I handed the phone to Dewitt. "Dial again. I think we're going to have a problem with this guy. He didn't say anything.

Either he's being overly cautious or he knows something's up."

Mary got excited. "No, that's good. If he did shoot Wolford then he would play it just like that."

I didn't agree with her but didn't feel like going into all the details of the case at that moment.

Dewitt dialed and handed the phone back. Two rings. Then nothing.

Finally, a *click*. As soon as he picked up I said, "Hey, Dickwad, it's me. Say something."

"Who's me?"

"Donnelly."

He said nothing.

"I know what you and Wolford were up to, and I want a piece of it. I want to meet and talk."

"I don't know what you're talking about, but I'll be happy to meet with you. You're a wanted man and it'll be a pleasure to put the cuffs on and drag your sorry ass to jail."

"Like you did to Abel Jenks two years ago?"

He scoffed and said, "You have a lot of room to talk. I was out at Old Woman Springs and saw Jenks down that hole. No way did he fall. The Sheriff's giving you a pass on that one and I don't understand why. I catch up to you, you won't be getting no pass from me."

"I saw you at my house. You were wearing a ski mask."

An intake of air came over the phone and nothing else. I'd hit him with a good one.

I said, "Meet me in the rear parking lot of Xavier's." I didn't know the area that well and was at a loss where to choose. Xavier's was as good a place as any.

"No, out at Giant Rock in one hour."

Rymes adamantly shook her head "no."

"No chance. You could take me out with a rifle and I'd never see you."

"You're smarter than you look."

"I'm flattered."

"Don't be. You're still a dumbass. Make it Café Nervosa on Highway 62 in Twenty-Nine Palms, one hour."

He hung up so there could be no renegotiations.

Rymes said to Dewitt, "You know this café?"

"Sure."

"Take Dobbs and haul ass over there and get set up. He's going to scout the location looking for us, so you have to get there first. Set up where he's not going to see you."

"You sure you want me to take Buck with me?"

He didn't think Mary should be left alone with a confessed thief and a mentally disenfranchised booby-hatch escapee. I didn't blame him.

She put a hand on his chest, a little too familiarly, and pushed lightly. "Go, I got this. Go, Go."

Dewitt pointed to the open case on the bed. "There are two types of body wires there--."

Mary shook her head, "I said go."

When the door finally closed and we were alone in the motel room the silence turned uncomfortable.

Toots said, "Don't get any ideas. I'm not doing a threesome."

If she truly knew me she'd know that was not even a consideration. She must be as uncomfortable as I was, though that would be out of character for her as well. We were all changing: Toots, Debra Ann, me.

I said, "We have a little time. Do you want to take a short drive? I need to pick something up."

"No. Let's get the wire set and test it."

"This is important."

"What?"

"I need to find a cell phone I dropped."

She went to the case, closed it, snapped the latches, picked it up, and headed for the door.

On the road, Toots fed me the directions and I told them to Mary, who drove. I watched her closely to see if she'd lie. I said, "I'm sorry, I have one more question."

She kept her eyes on the road, silent, but her hands tightened on the wheel.

I said, "I think you know what it is. I need you to tell me

FIRE AT WILL

what Wolford said about Debra Ann. I need it word for word."

She took her eyes from the road for just a moment. The streetlights flash-lit the interior compartment as we passed each one. I caught a brightened glimpse of her expression that read sorrow, not for her, but for me.

It hurt to see it. Now I didn't want to know more. It would be better if she said nothing and left it at that. But she didn't stay quiet. "Trust me on this: it's better that you don't know."

From the back seat Toots reached up and put her hand on my shoulder, "I'm here, Bub."

A knot rose in my throat. What the hell, both of these women knew and I didn't. All right, I did. But I was suppressing it.

Mary went quiet, her eyes on the road, her face alternately flashing bright, then dark. I couldn't stand the silence and couldn't make her talk. I said, "I find it hard to believe, and I mean damn hard to believe that Debra Ann would have anything to do with—"

The words hurt too deeply to finish. My heart thumped too hard. I had to lay my head back against the seat, close my eyes, and focus or risk turning invisible.

"Are you all right? Will, are you okay? Do you need me to drive to Desert Valley?"

"No, just tell me, please."

"I would, I really would, but it's a personnel issue and it would—"

"Stop it. Wolford's dead, remember, so who's going to sue? Tell me."

Toots said, "This is it, Bub. Have her pull over." Toots didn't want it out either.

I said to Mary, "Pull over right here." This was something she could easily comply with and did as instructed. Toots opened the door and got out. I thought it odd Mary didn't comment on the door opening by itself. Toots came back in a half-second and handed the cell through the window.

Mary said, "What's so important about that cell?"

"Wolford texted me before he was killed. When we found

the body…I mean when I found the body…"

The emotional stress over Debra Ann was muddling my thoughts. Nothing was linear anymore; thoughts moved in a zigzag design.

"…Wolford didn't have his cell phone. When Novak got to the body he said the cell was in Wolford's hand."

"If that's true then Mannerly was still out at the crime scene and watching you."

Toots said, "Hey, this bitch isn't as dumb as you thought."

"I never thought anything of the kind."

"What?"

"Nothing. Could you open the phone and tell me what the last text message says?"

I put my hand on the door handle, opening it a crack, ready to bail out. Only the door was already partially open.

Toots moved in close, looking over Mary's shoulder. Mary opened the cell. The light lit up her face with a strange blueness. "Who's this? Who's Rober—"

I opened the door and rolled out of the car as the blue spark struck and shut off every other light in the real world, shifting my reality to a thick, ebony silence.

41

THE LIGHTS CAME on again; the ones down in the valley below, only they were strangely subdued in this place. Debra Ann knelt on one knee beside me in her expensive black slacks. She was going to ruin them with the dirt and rocks. Her elegant beauty was out of place in this harsh environment.

"Will, are you okay?"

I tried to sit up. "Oh, no. Mary's in the car. She'll get out to see what happened to me. Help me stand up and run. She can't see me invisible. It'll ruin everything."

She went down on both knees and bent over me. "Hush, you aren't going to be here but a second or two. I took care of the time thing." She laid her head against my chest, her tears warm and wet against my skin. Tears meant doom. A lump large enough to choke rose in my throat. I couldn't say the words. But I had to. I had to know. "Have you been listening?"

She moved her head up and down, not enough to look me in the eye.

"Debra Ann, did you and Wolford--?"

She shook her head no. Then a "no" squeaked out. But there was something else wrong. I sensed it.

I couldn't believe the relief. I let out a huge lungful of air I'd been holding. I closed my eyes and held her, warm and real against my chest. I wouldn't let go this time. Not this time.

After a long pause she choked on the words, "Will, you

know I love you dearly."

"And I love you. You know that."

"I have something to tell you that's going to hurt very badly. I haven't told you because I didn't think you could take it physically or emotionally."

Once the Wolford thing was off the table, I didn't care. I thought I could take anything. "It's okay, I'll love you no matter what. You understand that, don't you?"

I tried to sit up, to pull her away from my chest. "It's okay; you can tell me. Go on, tell me."

She struggled, holding on tighter, not wanting to look me in the eye, her face buried deeper in my chest, muffling her words. "You know already. You've figured it out, most of it anyway and you're hiding it from yourself. That's why...That's why you're this way now, all screwed up emotionally, talking to hallucinations that aren't really there. Once you know, I mean once you bring it out to the light of day and accept it, this world you've created will disappear. It's your only safety net. Will, I don't think you can survive anymore in the real world. It's too harsh out there all by yourself."

Anger rose in my throat. How could she possibly know what I could handle emotionally? I tried again this time with more fervor to pull her away from my chest. The blue light sparked and I found my hand empty physically but filled with Toots visibly.

"She's a grade-A bitch, Bub, and I don't know why you put up with her crap." She too had tears in her eyes. I felt empty. Debra Ann still had not told me. But I knew a bit more, something I guess I always knew, that I did know what she was talking about and was suppressing it. Having this knowledge I could probably sit in a quiet place and ponder it out. Force it to the surface. I wasn't at all sure I wanted to. No, I knew I didn't want to.

Mary came scrambling around the car. "Are you okay? Did you fall out? I'm calling this whole thing off." She sounded genuinely concerned. Did she truly care? Moreover I had a friend in Ordinary Mary, and Toots.

Why wouldn't Debra tell me? Was my weak emotional state the real reason?

I said to Mary, "I'm okay, really. I just got out and stood up too fast."

My mind immediately went back to what had caused the flash. The name Robert Campbell.

MARY INSISTED I wear body armor, a threat level four, wraparound vest with a chest trauma plate. No one drove by on Val Verde; the street was dark without streetlights. We stood behind the car with the trunk open. She helped me strap on the vest. Toots said, her tone not overly concerned, "Watch those hands, you two-bit hussy. Bub, don't let her touch you, okay. Who knows what kind of disease this carpet muncher might have." That was ridiculous; Ordinary Mary was not a lesbian. Toots was being vicious, transferring her fear of what could happen between me and Mary. Then, what really bothered Toots came out. "Bub, this piece of shit Mannerly is a cop. You don't think he's going to account for a vest? You don't think he's going to check? He'll see it. Look how bulking that monstrosity is. It's big enough for three men and a boy. Remember at our house Mannerly had that huge hunting knife. And if I'm not mistaken a knife slices right through a ballistic vest. Slices through it like butter. Am I right? Tell me I'm wrong, Bub."

"Yes, you're right."

Mary stopped what she was doing, "What?"

"I said, Kevlar won't stop a sharp object. It's not designed to."

"I know that. What are you trying to say?"

Toots said, "Tell her you're not going to do it. Tell her all Mannerly has to do is plug you in the brain-housing group. One shot to the forehead and it's good night, Irene."

I said, "I'd like a small gun."

Mary didn't respond right away. She put on an undercover

model, threat-level three, thin, that molded to her figure and was far more difficult to distinguish.

I hooked the body wire under my armpit and ran the mic up to my collar. I put the backup, a small digital recorder with a three-hour duration, loose in my pants pocket. Mannerly had been a cop too long. He'd find them both if he looked, and Toots was right: he'd find the vest. Mary and I watched each other as we suited up. We both knew the real score. I was nothing more than a staked goat. An attempted murder Mannerly committed on my person was better than not having any case at all. That was worst case. Well, not really. There was murder.

He'd find both recording devices, this I was sure. The plan would be for me to engage him in conversation and find out some evidence, physical or otherwise, that could be collected later after the fact: how he and Wolford pulled it off, where the truck was hidden, paperwork, that sort of thing. Otherwise, any conversation against his penal interest without a recording would not be admissible, not with his word against mine, and me an admitted thief with a pending prison sentence.

We finished and were ready to go. Mary said, "Will, I can't in clear conscience let you carry a gun into this thing. With your situation, it's against policy. Of course had the circumstances been different we wouldn't even be doing this. But I think it is the only way to clear you of the Wolford killing. You understand, don't you?"

No, I didn't understand. Had our places been reversed I would have given her a gun. But I had never been in her place – a freshly minted Deputy Chief.

"I understand."

She closed up the undercover case, snapped the latches, put it back in the trunk and closed it. Toots stood close by in the dark. She said, "Here, take this." She handed me a folding knife. I could not for the life of me figure out where she came up with a top of-the-line Gerber carbon-steel folding knife.

She said, "Put it down your pants and let Mr. Johnson keep it warm. Mannerly's one of those macho types. When he frisks you he's not going to grab onto your package. Trust me on this, Bub. I know the type."

Mary moved around to the front of the car and got in. I unbuckled my belt and stuck the knife down there with Mr. —, well in my crotch. It was a good suggestion. The steel was cold and made…my package…contract.

Mary leaned over into the passenger seat, trying to see what I was doing. "Everything okay? What are you doing?"

"Just tucking my shirt in." I finished and got in the car. The vest lay against my chest, almost too heavy for my compromised lungs and heart to handle. I had to focus to breathe.

Toots got in, leaned up, and whispered, "Cold, huh? Bet Mr. Johnson's no more than a button on a mink coat right now."

Mary said, "Tell me where to go? I don't know the way."

Toots immediately shifted emotions, "I'll tell you where you can go, bitch."

"That's enough. Give me directions."

Mary said, "What? Are you all right? I just asked you which way to go?"

Toots waited a long moment, letting me hang. Then she said, "Turn around, go one point one miles, and make a left on Desert Path."

I said, "Turn around, go one mile and take a left."

42

CAFÉ NERVOSA SAT in the middle of the small, downtown section of Twentynine Palms. On the south side, the front opened onto Highway 62 with sparse parking at the curb. The majority of the customers parked in the dirt area to the rear. On the corner was Gabriel's Harp mortuary with an apartment up above. Sandwiched between Nervosa and Gabriel's was a bar called The Rogue Warrior that catered to the base personnel. With most of the Marines from the base deployed in Afghanistan, the town hardly had a pulse. Mary made the first pass of the café; one light illuminated the counter. The rest of the place was dark with a 'closed' sign in the window. Mary keyed her hands-free radio with her foot; the mike was located in the sun visor overhead. "Ten-David-One, are you in position?"

Dewitt came back with, "Ten David One, affirmative, I'm in the apartment over the mortuary with an unobstructed visual from the balcony of the back parking area."

Mary said, "Zebra-Three?"

Buck said, "I'm set up in the backyard of a house to the rear of the primary location. Though, be advised, I have a fence and a dog to get through when it goes down. About a twenty-second delay."

A twenty-second delay is an eternity when someone has a gun held on you.

Buck and Dewitt had seen Nervosa closed and rightly assumed the deal would go down to the rear.

Mary drove to Adobe Road, made a right into the Denny's parking lot, and turned around. Two Elvises stood out front and waved as we passed. With the sharp turn I fought the urge to adjust the Gerber knife that poked and pinched delicate skin.

Back west on 62 headed for Nervosa, Mary again keyed her mike. "We made our first pass. We're going in. Stand by. I'll drop him in front of Gabriel's and let him walk to the rear."

Both Dewitt and Buck clicked their radios in response. This new angle of approach, east to west, exposed the roofs of the Mortuary, the bar, and the café. The same person must have owned all of them, along with two or three other businesses beyond. All the roofs were stripped down to black paper, in the process of being re-roofed.

The brushed aluminum case sat open between us. All she had left to do was turn on the 'record' switch and she'd hear conversation and relay information to Buck and Dewitt via department radio, hopefully in a timely manner. I pressed the record button to the digital in my pocket. Now we had three hours on the digital, plenty of time.

She pulled up, reached a hand out, and placed it on mine. Her skin was cold and clammy against my hot and sweaty. She said, "Will, be careful."

Toots said, "Yeah, right, like she cares. If she really cared she wouldn't be sending you into the tiger's cage with nothing but Mr. Johnson in your hand."

Toots got out and slammed the door.

I said to Mary, "Don't worry about me."

"Wait." Mary leaned to the side, pulled her Compact Glock .45, and handed it to me.

"That's out of policy."

"Don't be a horse's ass. Take it."

I took the heavy little gun, stuck it in my waistband, opened the door, and got out. I leaned in and said, "Take it easy, okay? This should all be over in ten or fifteen minutes."

Mary took her foot off the brake. The car rolled forward as she spoke, the passenger door slowly easing closed. I wasn't at all sure if I heard it correctly. She said, *"That's what I'm afraid of."*

I moved south along the sidewalk until I passed the width of Gabriel's. The back opened into a huge dirt parking area littered with cars, some derelict for awhile with dust thick on the windows, not all parked in a uniform manner. In the middle, close to the Café, sat pallet after pallet of gray concrete tiles for the roof, with a huge canary-yellow forklift to take them up. Something about the color of the tiles caused a niggling at the back of my brain. I wanted to sit and coax it out. Somehow I knew it was important.

I felt vulnerable. I didn't want to stand out in the open, but at the same time I didn't want to go over by the pallets or the cars, where an ambush would be too easy. I went to the center of the dirt parking lot and stood. Toots lit up a Benson and Hedges cigarette and puffed and puffed, like a freight train going up a steep grade. We waited.

I tried to see Dewitt over the apartment, but it was too dark. The houses to the back of the parking lot had tall palm and shade trees, making it darker and impossible to see Buck. A big dog woofed.

We waited.

Toots said, "Over in that baby-shit yellow Plymouth."

"What?"

"Watch the passenger window, the back one."

The Plymouth had too much desert covering the windows to see inside. I couldn't see what she was talking about.

"There," she said. "Right there."

A hint of white smoke seeped out of the car. I didn't need to guess the brand: a Benson and Hedges, the same cigarette Mannerly smoked when he came into our house on Kadota in Montclair, the same one Toots now smoked.

I spoke loudly, my voice cracking from the dry desert air – or maybe it was from the bone-racking fear. "Come out, I can see you in there."

Nothing in the Plymouth moved. "Come on, Mannerly, quit dickin' around and let's get this over with."

I bent over—got dizzy—picked up a rock and tossed it. The rock bounced off the Plymouth's windshield with a loud crack and a puff of dust. The back door opened with a creak. Out stepped Mannerly, smoking. His hair was cut in a military flattop. He wore a plain black tee shirt and khaki work utility pants, the kind with all the pockets, and black jump boots with his pants bloused at the top. He had a black pistol in a holster on his hip and one in a shoulder holster. He'd come prepared. I only hoped that we were.

He slowly ambled over. I knew that something was wrong, only I wasn't sure what it was. Then I spotted the problem. He wasn't looking around for the trap. He was too confident and didn't care.

Why doesn't he care?

He should care. He stopped three feet away. "So, you wanted to talk – *talk*."

"I want a piece of the hazmat contract. I want half, past and future."

"I have no idea what you're talking about. I came here for one reason and that's to make an arrest of the suspect who killed my captain. Turn around and put your hands behind your back. I won't ask you a second time."

I didn't move.

He didn't move, not so much as one little muscle. He suddenly raised his voice, just short of a yell, only moving his lips. "Wait. Wait, put that gun down. Drop it. Drop it."

I hadn't pulled a gun and mine was barely visible in my waistband.

Now he moved, leaned slightly, pulled a small gun from the side pocket of his utility pants and tossed it at my feet. At the same time he drew the gun on his hip.

My heart leapt into my throat. I was a split second away from going invisible. I didn't have time to draw my gun. If I did he'd shoot me before I got it out and aimed. I took two quick giant steps and grabbed his gun as he brought it up.

The gun exploded in our hands when he pulled the trigger. The bullet blasted the dirt, spitting rock shrapnel against my shins. The gun jammed. His hot cigarette breath seared my cheek as he laughed and said, "What a pussy."

He shrugged me off like he would an old sweater.

I fell to the ground at his feet, my heart about to leap out of me through my mouth. He cleared the jam by racking the slide and pointed the gun down, right at my face. He yelled again, "Put the gun down or I'll shoot." Then whispered, "Say good night, you pussy."

From up high Dewitt yelled, "Mannerly, hold it. Freeze."

Mannerly didn't even look that way; he kept his gun aimed at me.

Ordinary Mary was anything but ordinary when she skidded from the street, bouncing her Crown Victoria in the air, into the elevated parking lot, scraping the oil pan off with a loud klang, causing white smoke to billow from beneath.

She distracted Mannerly just enough. I went for the compact .45 in my waistband.

Mannerly saw it and kicked it away. My hand wanted to go with it.

Dewitt fired from the balcony. The rounds skimmed across the hard-packed dirt and thudded into the derelict cars. A vicious dog barked. Another gunshot further away. The dog yelped.

Ordinary Mary drove straight at us as though she were playing a game of chicken. She was going to run us both over. Mannerly pivoted at the waist and fired at her windshield. She swerved and smashed into a VW bug, mashing it with the big Crown Victoria. She rolled out and came up shooting another Glock, the muzzle blasts lighting up the night.

An Afghanistan war veteran, Mannerly didn't move. He aimed and fired three times, striking Mary with all three. Then he swung around and fired three at Dewitt. Dewitt's shadow faltered and fell off the balcony. His body thudded on the ground.

Mannerly laughed and said, "I guess no matter what

happened this thing had to go loud. No problem. I can fix all of this as long as there aren't any witnesses." He pointed the gun right at my face. One curl of smoke rose from the end of the barrel.

The right fork on the forklift caught Mannerly in the stomach and picked him up. He glommed on rather than get run over. Toots gunned the forklift. The little tires spun. She shoved Mannerly right into the side of a Ford F150 truck bed.

Mannerly all but split in half on impact.

Blood spattered.

Too much blood.

His eyes bulged; his mouth opened as large as a train tunnel.

Toots bounced out of the vehicle from the impact, tumbled to the ground in her red diaphanous dress, and rolled a couple of times.

Everything went quiet.

Toots got up, dusting off her hands, and said, "Get forked, asswipe."

43

TOOTS RAN OVER. "Bub, are you okay? Are you hurt? Just lie there, help's on the way."

From the direction of the station far to the west, faint sirens grew louder.

Dewitt and Mary?

I had to check on them. Buck crashed through the cedar plank fence, shotgun at the ready.

"Over there," I yelled. "Check on Dewitt."

I struggled to my feet and shuffle-stepped over to where Mary had gone down.

She lay curled, her knees up by her chest, moaning and moving her feet back and forth as if running a never-ending marathon.

"Mary. Mary, are you okay?"

"Hell, no, what do think? That son-of-a-bitch shot me. That bastard. Jesus, he can shoot." She coughed. "Did you get him? Where's Mannerly? Did he get away?"

"He's dead."

After all the violent action, the night had gone strangely quietly except for the far-off sirens. In the darkness, back from where I'd come, Mannerly's voice, strained and weak, said, "I'm not dead yet, asshole."

Toots said, "I'll fix his little red wagon once and for all." She started to turn to go to him.

I said, "Leave him be." I turned back to Mary. "Here, let me have a look." I tried to move her knees away from her chest. Desert dirt powdered half of her face, got into one side of her mouth, mixed with saliva and speckled her soft, tender lips. Sirens grew louder.

She said, "Go to Mannerly. Get him to talk."

"Any statement will be considered coerced and inadmissible."

"Do it, Will."

I got up as the first Deputy to arrive on scene drove from the side street into the parking lot. The patrol unit's red-and-blue rotating lights bounced off the cars and walls and trees, turning the scene more surreal than it already was. For the deputy in the arriving unit I pointed down at the Deputy Chief and mouthed the words "help her."

I went over to Mannerly. His deadly tableau was too gruesome to view. I looked at his face and not directly at his mangled body below. The flat fork had turned slick with his blood, flickering black, then blue, then red. "Gimme a cigarette, would you?" I moved to get the pack about to fall from his shirt pocket, then I saw the gun still in his hand. He saw what I looked at, thought about it for a long second, then let the gun fall to the ground.

Toots must've felt sorry for him. She took out two cigarettes, lit them both, and put one in his mouth.

I coughed from the smoke. "Did you shoot Wolford?"

Mannerly coughed and sputtered. Some blood ran down his chin. "Why the hell would I kill him?"

"Did you?"

"No."

"Who did?"

"You."

Toots grabbed his hand and twisted it into a wristlock. "Say you're sorry, asswipe."

"Aaah, okay, okay. You're one crazy son of a bitch." Toots let go. Mannerly managed to smile even with all the pain. Or maybe he was in shock and didn't feel too much. He said, "I didn't kill him. Why would I? He was my gravy train."

"Because of the felony murder rule."

Mannerly suddenly turned ghost white. His lips glowed a ruby red. He shook his head and said, "I know, John Randle and his luscious slice of cheesecake—too bad about her. What a waste of nice pussy. Wolford would never have ratted on me. I had too much on him."

Mannerly didn't get it; that was exactly why, if confronted, Wolford would give him up.

I looked around, checking to make sure no one was in hearing range. "Who...what other captain was involved with Wolford?"

His eyes bulged a little. His tongue pushed out, fat and purplish, along with more blood that ran down the corner of his mouth, down the front of his neck. The cigarette came out but stuck to his chin, smoke curling up into his eyes. "You'd like to know that, wouldn't you?" He coughed some more and said, "You move fast for an old man who's supposed to have a bad ticker. Had you on the ground, down and out. Next thing I know you're in this God damn forklift." He tapped the fork with his hand. "Didn't see that coming. Shit no, I didn't. Nice move, slick."

He was turning delirious. How could he have mistaken me for Toots?

I needed to elicit from him a dying declaration, something he'd been trained in as well.

I said, "You know your injuries are grave and it doesn't look like you're going to make it."

"No shit, Sherlock. You want to know who? I'll tell you."

I glanced over to the driveway entrance. The Sheriff must have been out at Morongo station for the search warrant service at the Safari. Novak entered into the headlights of the lead cop car parked in the dirt lot. He'd be over to us in less than a minute.

Mannerly said, "Novak's your other captain. The one you want is Novak."

"You're lying. How do you know? Give me some evidence. Give me a motive."

"Wolford had something on Novak. Novak was going to make him Deputy Chief. Wolford told me so. Something happened, though, and—"

As he closed in, Novak said, "Will, are you okay?"

I looked at Novak, then back at Mannerly. I said, "Quick, tell me—"

Something had happened. Time had again expanded and contracted. This time when I looked at Mannerly the fork wasn't pinning him at the waist to the Ford F150; the fork was higher, impaled in his chest, the middle of his chest. He had to have been killed instantly.

Novak said, "Will, what are you doing? Tough-talking a dead man?"

44

NOVAK REACHED UP and took the Benson and Hedges cigarette from my mouth and tossed it aside. "Jesus, Will, you shouldn't be smoking with your heart."

"Who the hell's heart am I supposed to be smoking with?"

"Wait," Novak said. "What the hell's going on here? What happened? Who shot who? Who ran this poor bastard over with a forklift? Isn't that Mannerly? Isn't he one of ours? Jesus H, what the hell's going on here?"

"Deputy Chief Rymes and I thought we could get some conversation out of Mannerly about how he killed Wolford. Mannerly went for his gun and started shooting. He took out Dewitt and Rymes."

"You think he killed Wolford? What the hell, why didn't someone tell me? Damn it, why'd Rymes do this without more backup? Why didn't she brief me? Why'd you do it? You know better."

"To tell you the truth, I didn't think I had a choice."

His mind had apparently gone off, trying to piece it all together. He nodded as if he was agreeing with me and said, "Who drove this forklift and cut this poor asshole in half?"

"I'm not exactly sure. It happened so fast."

A police car siren distracted us. We turned and watched it take off. Novak turned back and said, "It's Dewitt. He's bad off. I told them to do a *scoop and run*. I think it's his only chance.

I already called ahead. Desert Valley's waiting for him."

I couldn't help thinking it wasn't two nights ago Dewitt had been running code-three with Donny Martin and me. It had been the right call then. Donny Martin made it.

I asked Toots, "Is he going to make it?"

She shrugged, "How the hell would I know? You think I'm some kind of gypsy or some shit."

Novak said, "I told you, I don't know. It's going to be close."

I said, "Dewitt has a kid in Little League baseball."

"I know. What a crying shame."

More cars arrived together in a clot on the side street. Captain Coleman got out of one; he looked over the top of the car at us, a scowl on his face flashing blue and red.

After what Mannerly had said about Novak being the second captain, standing next to Novak made me uncomfortable. I didn't know what to do. I didn't trust Novak anymore. And it hurt because he'd been a good friend. I needed to get Coleman alone to tell him about Novak. I had to tell somebody and Coleman would know what to do. We both watched Coleman move through the dirt lot toward us. He stopped at where Deputy Chief Rymes, lay, said something encouraging as paramedics ran up to treat her. He moved on to us.

Coleman came up, anger plain on his face. "Donnelly, let me have a minute with the Sheriff."

"I need to talk to you too, Captain."

He pointed over to a wide, unoccupied spot in the dirt lot. "Get your ass over there and wait for me."

I nodded and moved to where I'd been told. Toots said, "What's got his panties in a bunch?"

I whispered as I moved. "He's the Commander of Special Investigations. This was a special investigation he knew nothing about. I'd be mad too."

I was too anxious and couldn't stand still. Novak stood close to Coleman, Novak moving his arms as he explained what he knew of what had happened: things I had told him, things he'd seen when he arrived. Paramedics were working on Ordinary Mary. I went over to them. Mary lay on the ground next to the gurney while the paramedics used rapid hands, cutting material, tearing packages, hooking up wires. Her blouse was cut off, her body armor removed. They'd left her bra on, red lace against pale skin. Above her right breast she had a tattoo of a pink-and-blue unicorn partially concealed in the red lace. I would have never guessed her for a tattoo kind of person. Three large angry splotches pocked her lovely body: one high right shoulder, one lower abdomen, and the third in a bad spot right over her solar plexus. Her aorta could be damaged and she could be bleeding internally. She appeared to be having trouble breathing. I knew the feeling. I was worried about her. The vest had stopped the bullets from penetrating her body but blunt trauma was problematic. This was the real world, not like in the movies where after being shot, Mel Gibson stands up, coughs a bit while he takes the vest off, and goes right back to work.

Mary saw me, grew more excited, and waved, "Come here. Come closer."

I did as she asked.

The paramedic, a dark-haired Italian man, stood and put his hand on my chest. "Back off."

I took his arm and twisted him into a wristlock. "The woman wants to talk to me and I'm going to talk to her. You understand?"

He nodded. I let him go, got down on one knee before I released him, and took up her hand.

Her eyes were intense. "Closer, closer."

I moved in, uncomfortable being so near her semi-exposed breasts.

Her voice broken, she said, "I wanted you to know. I think this is important. It wasn't Wolford who came to me. Who told me about your wife and Wolford."

I gulped hard. "Who?"

"Novak. It was Novak who told me."

"What? Are you sure?"

Of course she was sure.

She nodded. Together the paramedics picked her up and laid her gently on the gurney. When they did, her bra slipped and her right breast jiggled. A partial areola peeked out over the edge of red lace. The movement also exposed the rest of the unicorn tattoo that had been hidden. The paramedics covered her up before I saw all of the words. What I glimpsed was "MR" with a red heart in between two other initials. I couldn't make out the other initials. Not that it really mattered. Mary had somehow put it together and knew Novak was the second captain in the conspiracy. He was higher than a captain, but it all made sense. She'd given me the information so I could act on it. But I didn't know what it meant. How could Novak, going to Mary about Wolford having an affair with my wife, have anything to do with what was going on? Why would Novak put me on the investigation if he thought I was involved? I desperately needed to talk with someone about this.

Toots had been quiet too long and said, "Now that trip to Texas makes sense. They wanted Henry Sanchez to take you out. That's why Novak sent you out to the desert to get in with Wolpig. So Wolpig could send you to Texas."

"That doesn't wash. Why would Novak want me out of the way? I wasn't a threat to him."

"Maybe he thought that Wolpig was doing your wife and that he told your wife what was going on. Then she knew and had to be aced-out to keep her quiet."

That last part had a slight air of logic to it.

Coleman and Novak came up from behind.

Novak said, "Will, come sit in my car with me. I have something we need to talk about."

No way was I going to get into a car with him. I needed to get Coleman alone to tell him all I knew.

"I think I should brief my Captain on what happened out here and what led up to it."

Novak turned angry. "*Your* Captain was shot dead behind a taco joint down the road, remember?"

Coleman said, "A little late now, don't you think? I'll get with you later. We're going to be here a long time sorting this mess out; all night and most of tomorrow. Jesus, what a cluster fuck." He held up his cell phone. "Just got word there's another crime scene down the road. This one here's secure. I'm going to head over to that one. When I get back we can talk."

He moved away, went over to a deputy stringing yellow crime scene tape and told him to move it wider to block off the entire side street. Coleman stood there a little longer, making sure it was done right.

Novak grabbed my arm. "Come on, we have to talk."

Toots said, "Don't get into a car with him. He plans to ace you out, Bub. I can see it in his eyes."

I pulled away from him. "I don't care if you are the Sheriff, there are some very important points I think Coleman should know so he can be informed well enough to direct this investigation."

"Damn it, Will." He pointed a finger right up in my face, opened his mouth to say something more, then changed his mind. He calmed down and held up the flat of his hands. "Okay, look...okay. I'll tell you right here and now. What I wanted you to come in for was to tell you that, that name you kept throwing around, it sounded familiar and it finally came to me." He snapped his fingers. "Just like that."

"What are you talking about, what name?"

"I didn't remember it right off because it was two years ago."

The air started to leave the world. Sucked right out as if some giant had punched his fist through the atmosphere. What Novak was about to say was something I already knew, one of those things niggling at the back of my brain, one of those things I had repressed.

Novak continued. "He was that hit-and-run driver. That's why I was so worried about you, why I wanted you to come in so we could talk. So we could get you some help. You putting that name on someone else scared me and it didn't make any sense."

Toots put her hand on my arm. It startled me. I jumped. I felt her touch. That had never happened before. Toots lowered her voice, her expression serious, more so than I had ever seen before. She said, "Get ready, Bub. Here it is, part of it anyway. Make him say it. Make him say the name so you can bring it out to the light of day, turn it over and look at it for what it is. So you can finally start to heal."

My voice cracked. "Who? What are you talking about?"

"That guy, the hit-and-run driver we never caught. The guy driving the cement truck, who hit your wife."

My knees started to shake, to go weak. "*Who?*"

"Henry Sanchez."

45

NOVAK CAUGHT ME, held me in a tight hug, and softly said, "It's okay, it's okay."

I wanted to speak but couldn't; the words clogged in my mouth, backed up, the brain trying to force them all down in a rush.

Over Novak's shoulder, I watched Coleman approach. Coleman talked on his cell phone. He reminded me of what I'd just learned about Novak, that I needed to talk to Coleman, about Novak being dirty. I tried to push away but was way too weak. Coleman came around our front, closing his cell phone. "Hey, Will, I'm told now that you might be needed over at the other crime scene."

Novak stepped away from me. I wavered. Novak said, "What's with this other crime scene? Where is it? I'll tag along."

Coleman said, "Sure, we can take my car. From what I gather it looks like another homestead with a possible Jenks victim, one we didn't know about."

I needed to talk to Coleman alone. I also needed someplace to sit and think this Henry Sanchez thing through. The name now hurt to think about, made my head ache.

Novak made it sound like he didn't want me out of his sight. He was afraid of what I might tell Coleman.

I said to Novak, "Shouldn't you be at the hospital with your injured Deputy Chief and Sergeant?"

We'd been moving toward Coleman's car when Coleman stopped to see what Novak was going to say. "Yeah," Novak said, looking torn. "You're probably right. But I'm concerned about you, too. You sure you're going to be okay?"

Toots said, "Kick the bastard in the nuts for lying to you."

I nodded. "I'm fine, really."

Coleman always gave a half-smile that was a little crooked on one side, when he attempted sarcasm. He said, "If you two really want to be alone I can drop you at the Safari and you can get a room. But one way or another make up your mind, because I'm heading out."

Novak said, "Fine, fine. You're right, of course. I need to be at the hospital; that's a priority. I'll catch up to you guys a little later. Coleman, you keep a close eye on Will. I'm worried about him."

Novak had lagged behind a little. Coleman kept walking. He didn't turn around. "You do that, Boss, you catch up to us. Like I said, we're going to be at this all night."

I followed close at Coleman's heels and couldn't help feeling like a puppy dog, but I did breathe easier now that Novak was out of the way. We were thirty feet away getting into Coleman's gray Crown Victoria when Novak said, "Hey, wait. I changed my mind. I don't think this is a good idea, not in Will's condition. It'd be better if I took him to the hospital with me to get him checked out."

I got in the car and closed the door, pretending I didn't hear. Coleman got in, chuckling, started the car, and chirped the tires when he backed up.

We rode in silence for several miles on the long, dark highway. Toots sat in the back seat. I wanted to ask her about the revelation, the name Henry Sanchez; talk to her about the fact that he was the driver of the cement truck who'd killed Debra Ann. I thought back to the day two years ago as I ran down the street chasing Debra Ann's Honda as the truck shoved it down Haven Avenue in Rancho Cucamonga. I couldn't see the driver's face. All I saw was his arm in the window as he jockeyed the behemoth truck, fighting the

FIRE AT WILL

steering wheel. In the memory, I got too close to the part where Debra Ann shrieked. I backed away. I didn't want to turn invisible in front of Coleman.

Coleman brought me back from the brink. He said, "So what was it that was so important that you wanted to talk to me?"

Toots said, "Bub, how come he's no longer yelling to have you thrown in jail?" My head whipped around to look at her. Coleman looked in his mirror to see what I was looking at. I said, "Because too much went on tonight. Two cops were shot and another one killed."

Toots sat back. "Oh."

Coleman said, "You have really gone off your nut for real this time, haven't you?"

"Yes, I think maybe you're right, and I'll get some help soon, I promise. But right now I need your help."

"As soon as this long-assed night is over, you're going to jail for grand theft, baby."

Toots said, "Yep, you were right."

Coleman continued, "So, if it's help with that case you want, then you're barking up the wrong tree here, pal."

"No, it's not that. I think that Novak is dirty. I think—"

Novak was my friend and it hurt to betray him. All of a sudden I realized the right thing to do was to confront Novak; give him a chance to explain. If he could.

"Dirty how?"

I looked at him. He went back to watching the road and jerked the wheel. We flew off the highway onto a dirt road, the night too dark to see. How did he do it without piling up? He got the car back under control. "What are you talking about? You're accusing the Sheriff himself of malfeasance?"

I shook my head. "No, I'm sorry. I misspoke."

"Damn straight, you misspoke. That man's the only person between you and the gray-bar hotel. I had my way you would've been in there long ago. That man's a pillar in the community. A rock. We've had our differences, but you better watch your mouth, mister."

He made another turn. The headlights lit up a homestead. This one had not been as far off the highway as the one Jenks took Donny Martin to. The structure was low, squat, with broken and cracked stucco painted beige, faded now from the harsh desert. The place was no more than a one-room shack. Parked out front sat a light blue Ford Taurus. Dim yellow lines of light peeked out through shabby curtains in the broken windows.

We got out to pure silence and went up to the desiccated wood door that stood slightly ajar, our feet sinking in the sand. Toots came right along, too. She had trouble in her heels. She slowed, Coleman now in between her and me. She said, "Bub, something stinks in Demark."

I turned to tell her it was okay.

Coleman shoved me through the door.

Inside stood a man. The dim yellow light shadowed his face, turning his eye sockets black, made his nose longer, his mouth a clownish grin.

But I still instantly recognized him.

The man reached out with a stun gun.

Fifty thousand volts of electricity, certain death to someone with a bad heart.

The stun gun's little blue arc slowly came toward me. But it wasn't slow, not in real time. It moved with the speed of a snake. Henry Sanchez touched me with it.

Toots screamed, "*Bub!*"

46

I ROSE UP out of purple-blackness to hear two men arguing, Coleman and Henry Sanchez. Only now I knew the truth. This wasn't Henry Sanchez; it was Robert Campbell. Sanchez no longer looked Hispanic like he had in Texas, with black hair and a stocky build. He was now Caucasian, fat and dumpy, with thin, balding sandy hair. My mind had been playing tricks on me before. Now I saw the truth.

These rat bastards, the both of them.

My hands were bound behind my back with flex ties, my feet bound together with the same. Debra Ann lay right next to me, her lovely eyes smiling, her hand stroking my hair. I whispered, "Am I invisible?"

"Hush, don't say anything. They'll hear you." She faded out, then came back. No, don't leave me. I did as she asked and didn't say it, only wished it with every fiber of my soul.

She said, "You're a smart man, Will Donnelly." She stroked my hair. "I want you to listen to me and not say anything until I'm done. You understand?"

I nodded.

She said, "You never could turn invisible. You only believed you could. You have post-traumatic stress, a severe case. You know this and you're repressing a great deal of very important information. Information that once revealed will allow you to start the healing process."

I opened my mouth to talk. She put her finger to my lips. "Hush. Think back when you were invisible. You *did* take your clothes off; you *were* naked but you were not invisible. Your mind changed the events to fit the scenario. It wasn't Toots who did all those things. It was you. *You* drove the truck through the widow's wall on Val Verde. *You* kicked Jenks into the snake pit. *You* drove the truck while holding Donny Martin. *You* were the one who stuck the fork in Mannerly. I won't go into all of the events, but as you heal emotionally you'll remember how they really happened." She sparkled and faded, the red diaphanous dress fading in then out as Toots tried to come back.

"Wait, don't go. Tell me what happened. Tell me what happened that day. I have to know."

Hearing me, Coleman shoved Robert Campbell and said, "You're lucky he's still alive, asshole."

Debra Ann said, "Toots will tell you. Make her tell you. I can't; it hurts too much." She faded out, replaced with Toots wearing the red diaphanous dress.

The red diaphanous dress.

That was it. I now knew at least a part of it.

Campbell kicked me in the gut. His toe sunk in, tearing the sutures to the gunshot wound, the wound he'd given me in Texas with the lever-action Winchester. The shirt turned sopping wet. All the air went out of me; I couldn't breathe.

"Leave him alone. Leave him alone, you rotten son-of-a-bitch." She shoved on Campbell but he didn't move. Her hands went right through him, because in reality when Toots did something physical, it had always been me, and I was down and out on the dirty floor. I understood that now. More important, though, I understood it and knew why…most of it, anyway. She gave up, fell to the floor, and crawled to me. I felt her touch. "Bub, he's going to kill you. Tell me what to do. I don't know what to do."

Campbell yelled, "Where's my money?" I now remembered the five hundred thousand. I'd put three hundred in the interim evidence locker at headquarters under the narcotic case number, the case from which I'd taken the money. The other two? I'd sent a hundred K each to Peggy Kellogg's family and to Donny Martin. Campbell wasn't going to get his money, no matter what he said or did.

I ignored him, feeling more at peace than I had in the last two years. I said to Toots, "It's the red dress, isn't it?"

She cried and buried her face in my chest. I didn't know why or understand how I felt her touch, her warm, wet tears. But they helped. They helped a lot. She nodded.

Campbell said, "He's crazy as a shithouse mouse. Why's he talking about a red dress?" He pulled back to kick me again.

Coleman stopped him, grabbed his arm, pulled him away, and said, "No, we agreed we find out what he knows—what Novak knows—and then you can have him."

Coleman said to me, "You shouldn't have whacked this guy on the head like a baby seal, left him for dead, and taken off with his money. Now all he wants to do is take you apart piece by piece."

I coughed and coughed until I settled down and said to Toots, "Debra Ann was supposed to pick up her favorite dress at the dry cleaners and wear it that night, the night of our anniversary two years ago. When she was in the Honda, when I saw her in the Honda that night out in front of La Chemine, she was wearing a beige blouse and black slacks. That's it, isn't it?

"I'd known it all along and was repressing it? That's why when I see you, you're always wearing the red dress."

Toots nodded, "I don't want you to die. Tell me what to do. I'll do anything you tell me to."

Campbell said, "Who the fuck's this Debra Ann?"

Coleman said, "His wife. The poor fool can't give her up." Coleman leaned over, jerked me up to a sitting position, and leaned me against the wall. Toots came along, clinging to my chest. Coleman said, "Will, tell me, how much does Novak know?"

I looked from Toots' worried, adoring eyes to Coleman. "He doesn't know anything," I lied. I was worried that if I told him Novak knew, then maybe he'd go after Novak as well. This wasn't logical. I still wasn't thinking straight. Novak was smarter than I was and would never get into a car with a killer like I had.

"I don't believe you." Anger rose in his voice. "You told him. When you got off the plane you ran right to your daddy and told him all of it like a good little boy. I got to the airport too late to stop you. That's what happened, isn't it?"

"Think about it. If I told him, you think Novak would've let me get into the car with you? When I got back from Texas, I wasn't sure who was involved, who was on Skype, which two captains, so I kept it to myself."

I knew now that it was Wolford and Coleman.

Campbell said, "See, you were worried over nothing. Now, asshole, tell me where my money is?" He moved to a different part of the one-room cabin, picked up a sister grip to the one we'd taken from him in Texas—the one with the money and new ID in it, his go-bag—opened it, and took out some tools. All stainless steel, long and curved, some with sharp edges. The light hit him differently. A furrow, not deep enough to kill him apparently, ran down the right side of his head, making his head shape slightly lopsided; an optical illusion.

I said, "But there is something Novak knows that can lead him to you. Once he pieces it together, you're going to take the fall for all of this."

"What is it? Tell me."

"Who killed Wolford?"

Coleman gave me that crooked half-smile, "Okay asshole, I'll play your game. But just for a little while. Then I'll let this demented jerk-off have you."

Campbell, who was pulling on some industrial grade blue rubber gloves, stopped, angry now. "Call me a jerk-off again and we're going to have a problem. I'm a well-respected medical doctor. Remember that."

Coleman ignored his partner. "I didn't kill him, if that's what you're asking."

FIRE AT WILL

"Who did?"

"How should I know? If I had to guess, I'd put my money on Mannerly."

Campbell was ready now. He picked up a small stainless steel hammer and what looked like a wood chisel.

Toots said, "He's going to kill you, Bub. Do something. Tell them that the place is surrounded with two hundred deputies all with Ithaca Deer Slayer 12-gauge shotguns, and they're going to blast this whole place to the ground."

I smiled. "I say that, they're going to think I'm more like Agent 86 on *Get Smart*."

Campbell said, "Let me go to work on him. A little pain might get the truth out of this wing-nut. No guarantees, though."

Coleman said, "Hold it."

I said, "Did this jerk-off here kill Wolford?"

"That's it." Campbell took a long step over to us. Coleman swung his coat back to reveal his Glock in a hip holster. "I said stand down, jerk-off." They looked at one another a long moment, then Campbell lowered his little hammer.

Coleman said, "Okay, you want it all, I'll give it all to you. It's not going to matter anyway, not in another fifteen minutes or so.

"Wolford was a fool. He came up with the scheme. It was brilliant, absolutely brilliant. He came to me with it. You don't get to pick your in-laws and in some cases you don't get to pick your crime partner. I had no choice. I got stuck with him as a partner. We had it made. We were dragging down a hundred grand a month extorting these fools and had three more jerk-offs on the hook. It would have taken us to two hundred grand a month. Can you imagine two and a half million a year, more than enough money for the both of us? But no, Wolford wanted the power, too. He wanted to be Deputy Chief and that wasn't going to happen while Novak was in office. Then Wolford goes and gets dirty with Mannerly. Mannerly had Wolford by the short and curlies.

"Two years ago when Mannerly drove into the back of the

station with Jenks beaten into a piece of raw meat, I called Novak and told him. Novak wanted Wolford relieved of duty on the spot and an investigation opened. I couldn't have that, not with this extortion scheme humming along. So, the only thing I could do was to get something on Novak. I knew what Novak was up to. That's why I sent you home to your wife that day on your anniversary."

Toots put a warm hand on my cheek and nuzzled in closer. "Here it is, Bub. Hold on to me tight."

But I couldn't hold on, my hands were behind my back. If ever I needed someone to hold, it was right then.

I said to Coleman, "What are you talking about?" I was frightened, more frightened than ever. I didn't want him to say it, yet I had to hear the words.

He gave me that crooked little smile. "You poor fool. You don't know, do you? Novak was banging Debra Ann."

47

"Noooo."

The room wobbled and shifted violently, like the deck of ship in high seas. Toots was there, stroking my face faster, whispering, "It's okay, I'm right here for you, Bub."

But when the heavy seas subsided she was gone.

The truth in the light of day had snatched her away from me.

"Toots, Toots, come back, come back."

Campbell said, "The damn fool's delirious."

Coleman continued on without consideration to the ticking clock or how severely he was stomping on my emotions--how he'd just revealed the horrible *thing* with Debra Ann. He had only one thing on his mind, the completion of the mission at hand. Toots had left me forever, never to return. Left me when I needed her most.

Coleman didn't miss a step. He said, "I thought sending you to catch Novak with his hand in the honey pot was a logical plan for what needed to be done. Until I went in the station and told Wolford how he'd screwed everything up by telling Mannerly to beat a confession out Abel Jenks. The horse's ass, Wolford, told me not to worry about it. He told me it would all be taken care of, that he'd had it handled. That his plan was already 'on the move.'

"Wolford was like a god with his little army of assassins at his disposal. He'd called Henry Sanchez, said he'd forgive the monthly extortion money if he would take out Novak. *Novak, the Sheriff of the county.* The dumbass thought Wolford could take out the Sheriff and get away with it. That's how far gone he was. I told you not to call Debra Ann, told you to make it a surprise. But did you listen? *No,* you alerted them, made the call. Debra Ann dropped off Novak. Sanchez was following the Honda and in all the traffic missed the drop-off but was able to pick up the car again. He thought Novak was still in the car."

I'd gone emotionally barren. "Where is Henry Sanchez now?"

"He's in Frisco. He's the largest cement supplier in the Bay Area. It took a lot of paper shuffling to keep the investigators off him. I was lucky you nutted-up so badly. If you'd gone after him I know I couldn't have kept you off him.

So now, as the saying goes, I showed you mine, you show me yours. What is it that Novak knows?"

"He knows all about the extortion conspiracy. As soon as I got off the plane I ran to daddy and told him like a good little boy. He knows but doesn't know who. Once he audits the Cold Case investigations he'll make you for it. Your only chance is to run. But you won't be able to run far enough. I will follow you and take you down. You can count on it."

Coleman's mouth hung open. He had wanted to believe he was safe, that his life of two hundred thousand a month could go on unabated. He took a couple of steps backward, waving his arm at Campbell. "He's all yours. Do your worst on this asshole."

Campbell took two steps. Two more and he'd be on me with his chisel, dismembering me while I screamed.

I said, "You're a fool letting Coleman get behind you like that."

Campbell hesitated, smiled, then came on again, taking another step. I said, "Coleman needs a patsy and you're it, jerk-off."

His jaw muscles knitted, but he stopped and looked back

over his shoulder at Coleman.

Coleman shifted his feet. "Don't listen to that asshole."

I said, "Everyone saw me leave with Coleman. They find me dismembered in a shack, he'll have to have a story. You're his story. He's going to shoot you when you're done with me. Think about it."

Campbell spun and charged Coleman, who tried to draw his gun, getting it out but not up far enough to fire. They went down in a dog pile, the light glinting off the stainless steel utensils in Campbell's capable hands. Coleman yelped like a victim on the elementary school playground. I didn't feel sorry for him. He'd called my Debra Ann a honey pot.

Coleman tried to roll Campbell off him to bring his gun into action. Campbell locked his legs around Coleman's. Campbell's hand with the chisel came up and flashed downward, burying into Coleman's shoulder. Coleman shrieked like a little girl. He shrieked like Debra Ann had when the fire ate her that day out on Haven Avenue. My heart leaped out; beat hard against my chest. I waited for the blue flash, for the invisibility to take me. But I knew the truth now. It wasn't going to happen, not ever again.

A muffled explosion. Coleman had fired his gun between them. Then came another explosion. And another yet. Then more in quick succession.

I didn't wait for the outcome. I fell over to the floor and slipped my flex-cuffed wrists past my butt so they were in front. I shoved my hands down my pants into my crotch and recovered the Gerber folding knife. I cut the flex ties on my wrists and then my feet just as Coleman, with great difficulty, shoved Campbell's body off. I got up fighting dizziness, leaned over, picked up the discarded stun gun Campbell had used on me, and went to Coleman. He saw me coming and pointed his Glock at my belly. The gun's slide had a stove-pipe jam, an expended shell locking the gun open. I leaned over and touched his ankle with the stun gun.

Coleman cleared the jam and was about to point the gun at me when I said what Mannerly had said to me not two hours before, when he was about to shoot me in the face: "Say goodnight, you pussy."

48

THE WORLD WAS colorless and drab without my Toots. I got in the gray Crown Victoria and started it up. All on their own, memories flashed in on me. As I put the car in gear I realized I'd seen this car on Haven that day two years ago. Coleman must've raced to Rancho Cucamonga to stop Sanchez, to keep Novak from being killed. Too bad he was late.

I drove to Desert Valley Hospital and parked in the slot by the ER door marked "For Law Enforcement Only." I got out with Coleman's gun in my hand. I didn't want to see Novak, but if I did and he said one word, I was going to shoot him in the head. I'd come to talk with Ordinary Mary.

Novak had told Mary that Wolford had been having an affair with Debra Ann to throw the scent off of Novak. The bastard.

The twin doors whooshed open. I entered the bright light. Novak jumped up from his seat in the waiting room filled with cops. He took two steps and then froze, his smile melting away to fear. He'd seen my expression and knew I knew. He held out both hands, pleading. "It's not like you think, Will, we were in love with each—"

I ran at him, pointing the gun right at his face. "Don't. Don't you say it. Don't you dare say another thing."

The other cops jumped to their feet, drawing their guns, ready to defend their sheriff to the death. We stood that way for a long couple of seconds while I tried to decide if I had anything worth living for. Toots was gone from me now. I still needed to finish this, to talk with Mary. I let the gun drop to my side.

Novak let out a long breath. He eased down until he sat on the floor. The deputies started yelling. "Freeze! Drop the gun. Drop the gun *now*."

I looked at Novak. His voice cracked; he held up a shaky hand. "It's okay, let it be. Let him go."

I didn't wait for them to lower their guns. I went to the automatic door that opened and let me into the back. The curtain was pulled open where Mary Rymes sat balancing on the edge of the gurney/bed trying to put on her shoe. Someone must've brought her clothes from her car. She smiled when she saw me, but it changed when she saw the gun in my hand. I set it on the bed next to her.

I said, "I'm glad you're okay. Did the doctor say it was okay for you to leave?"

She nodded, "He said I was fine as long as I took it easy."

"You're not a good liar." The memory came back of her lying semi-naked with just the red-lace bra, the tattoo with the initials MR, the heart in between. I had seen the other initials and had suppressed them. They were JN for Jim Novak. Novak had thrown her over for Debra Ann. That was how she'd made Deputy Chief: she'd known part of the drama, had not told me, and exchanged the information to get promoted. No one involved was without at least a little shame.

I helped her with her shoe.

She said, "Thanks."

I pulled out the digital recorder and handed it to her. "You want to be the Sheriff?"

"What are you talking about? What's this?"

"You need to send a unit code three out to Jack Rabbit Road and Tucker Point. There's a dead body there. And you need to hurry. Coleman's tied up and bleeding pretty bad."

"Will, what's this all about?"

"Listen to the recording, all of it, before you release

Coleman." I turned and left.

She said, "Wait, come back, Will. You're bleeding. Come back."

I kept going.

She said, "Where are you going?"

"I don't know," I told her. "I've got nowhere to go."

49

THE DESERT NIGHT had finally cooled when I got back into Coleman's Crown Victoria. I got onto Highway 62 headed west in the general direction of home in Montclair. Not home, not anymore. Just a house, really: a hot and empty and lonely house.

"Toots, come back. I want you to come back."

Nothing happened. The seat next to me remained empty, painfully empty. I missed her sharp tongue, her beautiful eyes, and the way she made me laugh. Without her I'd never laugh again. Tears flowed down my cheeks. I had to know what had happened that day in order to get better. But I didn't like this real world, not anymore. I'd been gone too long, hidden from the harsh light of reality.

All on its own the Crown Victoria gradually increased speed, the speedometer climbing: eighty, ninety, a hundred. I gripped the wheel tighter. Tears blurred my eyes. One-ten, one-twenty. I crested the summit of Yucca Valley and dropped down into Morongo Valley, the downhill grade steep. One-thirty, one-forty. Not long now.

"Toots are you there? Come and stop me. Please come and stop me."

Wait, I made up Toots in my mind when I gave up believing in reality. Yeah, that's it.

"Toots, I don't believe Debra Ann. I know I can turn

invisible. I know I can. Do you hear me? I turned invisible when the doctor in the ER shocked me after being contaminated in the Hazmat spill. When Robert Campbell shocked me again back in that shack he cancelled it out. That's true, isn't it, Toots? Isn't it?"

I leaned forward and took the stun gun from my front pocket as the Crown Victoria quickly ate the miles. I was running out of highway. Soon, at the bottom, the highway would make a sweeping turn. I would be going too fast to stay in it. The curve's terminal velocity would toss me out, hurl me to certain death.

I stuck the stun gun to my leg. "Toots, tell me if this is the right thing. Tell me now or forever hold your peace."

A big CalTrans sign flashed by that read: Runaway Truck Ramp ahead. The runaway truck ramp suddenly appeared. I depressed the trigger to the stun gun while I simultaneously jerked the wheel. The world turned into a giant blue arc that lasted a second and then flashed to pure blackness.

The kind I'd expect to find in hell.

50

I DIDN'T WANT to open my eyes to purgatory, to a red-faced Beelzebub.

At first I couldn't feel my legs or arms. Gradually the feeling came back. So did my hearing. Hissing filled the air. Smoke. I coughed. I tried opening my eyes.

I was on the floorboard in the front seat. The airbags had deployed and were deflating. White powder from the deployment filled the air.

I was alive.

"Sticking that stun gun to your leg while doing a hundred and fifty and runnin' up into this ramp. I gotta tell ya, Bub, that was really bizzaro."

Toots sat in the driver's seat wearing a two-piece bikini, looking absolutely gorgeous as she held onto the steering wheel.

I wept tears of joy. "You're back. You came back to me."

She put the car in reverse and spun the tires. When the Crown Vic wouldn't move she said, "Back from where? I never left. Hey, call the auto club for a tow. We have to get on the road. We got shit to do."

I struggled up onto the seat and leaned over, moving in close to her face. I so very badly wanted her to really be there. I closed my eyes and kissed her warm wet mouth. She kissed me back.

When she finally pulled away she said, "Hey, call the auto club and while we're waiting for them we can break out these puppies for you to play with. She pulled down the front of her bikini top, exposing her lovely breasts.

I pulled out a cell phone and dialed. While I waited for the ring, I asked, "What's the hurry? Where do we have to go?"

"Quit pulling my leg, Bub. You know."

I shook my head that I didn't.

She smiled. "We're going to Frisco to fit a man for some cement galoshes."

ABOUT THE AUTHOR

During his career in law enforcement, David Putnam has done it all: worked in narcotics, violent crimes, criminal intelligence, hostage rescue, SWAT, and internal affairs, to name just a few. He is the recipient of many awards and commendations for heroism. *The Vanquished* is the fourth in the Bruno Johnson series, following the best-selling and critically acclaimed *The Disposables, The Replacements,* and *The Squandered. Fire at Will* is the first book in the Bad Bill series. Putnam lives in Southern California with his wife, Mary.

Connect with David at:

www.Davidputnambooks.com

Twitter.com/daveputnam

Facebook.com/authordavidputnambooks

ALSO BY
DAVID PUTNAM

The Bruno Johnson Series

The Disposables (Oceanview Publishing)
The Replacements (Oceanview Publishing)
The Squandered (Oceanview Publishing)
The Vanquished (Oceanview Publishing)

Made in the USA
Lexington, KY
05 June 2017

ALSO BY
DAVID PUTNAM

The Bruno Johnson Series

The Disposables (Oceanview Publishing)
The Replacements (Oceanview Publishing)
The Squandered (Oceanview Publishing)
The Vanquished (Oceanview Publishing)

Made in the USA
Lexington, KY
05 June 2017